RITUAL DEMISE

SALLY RIGBY

TOP
DRAWER
PRESS

CRIME FICTION BOOKS

GET ANOTHER BOOK FOR FREE!

To instantly receive the free novella, **The Night Shift**, featuring Whitney when she was a Detective Sergeant, ten years ago, sign up for Sally Rigby's free author newsletter at www.sallyrigby.com

Chapter One

Forensic psychologist Dr Georgina Cavendish's stomach rumbled as she pulled up to a traffic light. Her students at Lenchester University had broken up for the summer, and she was busy doing the admin involved in marking late submissions and loading final grades for all of her courses into the system. She also had faculty meetings to attend and needed to do some preparation for a paper she was presenting at a research conference in a couple of weeks' time. All of which meant she had little food in her cupboards, as there'd been no time to go shopping for dinner.

She turned into her street and frowned. A crowd of people were outside her Victorian terraced house.

What on earth was going on?

She leant forward. Beside the gate, holding a camera, was a young woman dressed in jeans and T-shirt. Next to her stood an older woman, with steel-grey hair and more smartly dressed. She had a microphone in her hand. There were at least ten other people milling around, including several more with cameras. She muttered under her breath and kept driving, for once hating that she had such a flash car. Fortunately, no one seemed to notice as she drove past and stopped in the next road, unsure what to do next.

Were they there for her? And if so, why? She wasn't going back to find out. But where should she go?

Ross's place was out of the question as she hadn't spoken to him since their relationship had ended a few months ago. He'd proposed and she'd turned him down. It still weighed heavily on her mind, but she'd done the right thing. He'd wanted them to continue seeing each other, but she'd said no as she believed it would be impossible for things to go back to how they were. She'd had a disastrous experience living with someone before she met Ross and didn't wish to repeat it. Even so, she still missed him. Especially at times like this.

She'd have to contact Whitney, a detective chief inspector in Lenchester CID. They'd worked together on several murder cases and were more than just colleagues. In fact, Whitney was the closest friend she had, which wasn't hard as she'd never been one for having lots of friends. Acquaintances, yes. Friends, no. She much preferred her own company.

She pulled out her phone.

'Hi, George,' Whitney said, answering almost immediately. 'How are you? We haven't spoken in ages.'

'It's chaotic with the end of the academic year and getting grading completed. And, obviously, we haven't had any cases.'

'I hope you're not jinxing it,' Whitney said, laughing.

George shook her head. One day she might be able to convince Whitney there was no such thing.

'I've just driven past my house and there are an inordinate number of people waiting outside. It's the media.'

'How do you know?'

'Cameras. Vans. People with notebooks in their hands.'

'Are you sure it's you they're waiting for?' Whitney asked, sounding puzzled.

'They were by my gate. Who else would it be?' She winced. She hadn't meant to sound so harsh. 'I can't imagine what they want.'

'Do you have anything major coming out in your research? Something to do with serial killers, maybe?' Whitney asked.

'No. Nothing's been published recently and there's no reason for them to be waiting for me at home. All PR is done through the university. It's definitely not that.' Her body tensed. She hated not having control over a situation. 'What shall I do?'

'Come over here. We'll have dinner and a catch-up. Lucky for you, I've recently bought a bottle of your favourite wine. I must have had a premonition. I don't usually splash out.'

George breathed a sigh of relief, ignoring the *premonition* remark. 'Okay. I'll be with you shortly.'

Twenty minutes later she pulled up outside Whitney's small, semi-detached house. Her friend was waiting at the door, her arms folded tightly across her chest and her lips set in a thin line.

'You'd better come in and sit down,' Whitney said, before she'd even made it up the short path to the front door.

'Do you know what's going on?' She followed Whitney into the lounge, worried by the tone of her friend's voice.

There were two full glasses of wine on the coffee table.

'I think you're going to need this,' Whitney said, as she handed one to her.

'Why?'

'I've been online and know why the media was waiting for you. It's to do with your dad.'

Her body stiffened. 'My father? Is he okay? No one's been in touch. Has there been an accident?'

'Don't worry,' Whitney said, leaning forward and resting her hand on George's arm. 'He's fine.'

'What is it, then?'

Something important enough for the press to be tracking her down ought to warrant a phone call from her family. Even with their distant relationship, she didn't deserve a media invasion in order to learn what was going on.

'He's all over the internet. According to what I've read, he's involved in some financial irregularities relating to tax.'

'Irregularities? That's ridiculous.' Her father was many things, including being a world-renowned cardiac surgeon, but a crook he wasn't. He was much too concerned with his reputation and social standing. He revelled in being the go-to person for anyone requiring heart surgery. Anyone, that is, who could afford his services.

'It's not only him. There are many celebrities involved.'

'This makes no sense. I'm going to look.'

'Okay, but you won't like it,' Whitney said.

George took out her laptop and began a search. A headline screamed out at her. 'The Rich Get Richer'. She scrolled down and there was another. 'Celebrity Tax Dodge Exposed'. She swallowed hard as she read the article. It was poorly written, and the three typos made her cringe, but the content was clear. Her father and a group of high-profile people had invested in a scheme devised deliberately for tax avoidance and now HMRC were after them. The scandal had been uncovered by one of the tabloid newspapers and now everyone had jumped on the bandwagon. There wasn't a single media outlet not reporting it. Looking at the list of celebrities and high-profile people involved, including government ministers, she wasn't surprised it was receiving such attention.

She shut her laptop and rubbed her brow.

How the hell could her father be involved in such a scheme?

'I can't believe this. He's got an accountant. Surely he wouldn't allow Father to act in this way,' George muttered.

'And you haven't spoken to him about it?' Whitney asked.

'No. But that's not unusual. We rarely speak or see each other. I'll try to get hold of him now.'

She tried her father's number, but it went straight to voicemail. She then tried her mother. The same. Finally, she called her brother, and he answered.

'Hello, Georgina,' he said.

'What's going on with Father? I have the media camped outside my house.'

'Don't tell them anything.' His infuriating pompous tone sounded remarkably like her father's, and her grip tightened around the phone.

'I'm not going to, and I resent you thinking I would. I need to know what's going on.' She dragged in a breath. Losing her cool wasn't going to help.

'Father's with his lawyer at the moment, and that's all I know. It's a case of marking time and remaining tight-lipped. Can you manage that?'

She didn't believe for one moment that he had no idea what was going on. Knowing more than her gave him a sense of superiority, despite him being younger.

'Do you know anything about these financial irregularities?' she asked, not prepared to let it go.

'I'm not going to elaborate, especially on the phone.

We can't risk it. Also, you have your connection with the police to consider. It's not appropriate.'

So that was it. Her parents hated that she was mixing with Whitney and her team. They saw them as below her station. Now her brother was using it against her.

'How am I meant to find out what's going on? Through the sensationalism in the media?' she challenged.

'You should come here. Mother and Father will need your support. We have to create a united front.'

'I can't drop everything and be there. I have work commitments to consider.'

'You need to think about your priorities, Georgina. Some things are more important than what you're currently undertaking.'

'If that's the case, why didn't you warn me that the shit was about to hit the fan?'

'Not telling you was a mistake. None of us realised it would have this impact.'

That was as near to an apology as she was likely to get from her brother.

'Keep me informed and I'll make a decision.' She ended the call, not wanting to discuss it further.

'Well?' Whitney said, sitting forward in her chair and staring directly at her.

'It seems there is a *situation* and my father is with his lawyer. My brother wants me there, but I'm not going. At least not until I have a fuller picture.'

'You can stop here. Stay the night. There are clean sheets on the bed, and I'll lend you a nightdress. Although I expect it will be more like a T-shirt on you.'

'If you're sure it's not too much bother,' George said as she lifted up her glass and took a large swallow.

'Of course, it's not. I'll be glad to have the company.

Now Tiffany's gone back to Australia, it can get lonely here.'

Whitney's daughter, Tiffany, had been overseas since the beginning of the year, recently returning for the trial of the psychotic twins who'd attempted to murder her. At least now they'd been found guilty and the trial was over, the young woman could put it behind her.

George had assumed her friend was too busy to get lonely. She always had so much on her plate. Her job was demanding, and her mother and brother were both in residential homes as they needed constant care. Whitney liked to visit them as often as she could.

'If you're sure,' George said. 'Thank you very much for your hospitality. It's much appreciated.'

'Yes, I am sure,' Whitney said, laughing. 'I'm not sure about the *being hospitable* bit, though.'

George frowned. 'What you're doing is hospitable.'

'If you say so. Although I do have pizzas in the oven for us, so perhaps you're right. '

'Sounds divine. I'm starving.'

'They'll be ready in fifteen minutes. While we're waiting, tell me what's going on with you,' Whitney said.

'Nothing out of the ordinary. Up until now.'

'What about Ross? Have you heard from him?'

George's insides clenched. 'Can we not talk about him, please?'

Whitney had been against George ending it from the start. Her friend had thought Ross the perfect match. Maybe it was true, but it was pointless dwelling on it. Her time with the sculptor was over.

'Does that mean you're regretting it?'

'I didn't say that. I just don't want to talk about him. It's been three months now and I'm getting along fine.'

Whatever *fine* meant.

'Okay. I won't mention him again,' Whitney said, though somehow George didn't believe her.

'What have you been up to? How's work?' George asked, pleased with herself for remembering to engage in a bit of small talk, despite it not being something she did naturally.

'Work's been good, apart from Jamieson. He's still not come to terms with being passed over for promotion and is being a pain in the arse. But, when isn't he?' She laughed. 'To be fair, he's been keeping out of the way, most of the time. That's all I can ask.'

George admired Whitney's skills in her job, but she had a problem with certain authority figures, and it often got in the way. Not that she'd ever bring it up with her friend. Even she realised that some things were best left to sort themselves out.

'I'm sure he'll be offered a promotion soon. Something's bound to come up. It always does.'

'I'd like to think so, but I'm not holding my breath. I got so excited at the thought of him leaving, and when it didn't happen it took me weeks to get over it. I'd even decided on the leaving present I was going to give him.' Whitney smirked. 'A police manual.'

The ongoing battle between Whitney and her boss, Superintendent Jamieson, was mainly due to him coming through on the fast track scheme and Whitney didn't have a lot of patience for officers who hadn't worked their way up through the ranks, like she had.

'I don't think that would have gone down well,' George said.

'I'm joking,' Whitney said, shaking her head.

'I know that.'

She didn't.

'Let's not talk about work,' Whitney said. 'We'll have

something to eat, a few drinks and then settle down for the night. It makes a change for us to meet and talk without there being a murder, or five demanding our attention.'

'I'll drink to that,' George said as they clinked glasses, determined to put her father's issues to the back of her mind for a short while. It would still be there in the morning and she could deal with it then.

Chapter Two

Whitney woke and glanced at her watch. It was only five-thirty in the morning. She was wide awake and knew she wouldn't get back to sleep, so decided to go downstairs and grab a coffee. As she walked into the kitchen, she glanced at the invite she'd received for the forthcoming school reunion. She'd never been in the past and wasn't sure why she was considering this one. She still had a few days to make a decision.

While waiting for the kettle to boil, she switched on the TV and perched on the edge of the sofa. Crap. The story of the day was still George's dad and the other high-profile people. The media was going to town on what they'd done and how they'd tried to defraud the country. There were calls for knighthoods and OBEs to be rescinded. She doubted this was going to disappear any time soon. Millions of pounds were owed in taxes, and the government was gunning for them.

She made herself a coffee and one for George, which she took upstairs. As she got to the top, George was coming out of the bathroom, wrapped in a towel. Looking so tall and model-like, her sleek short blonde bob, accentuating her cheekbones. Whitney grimaced. Why had she got the short straw where height was concerned?

'Morning,' she said. 'You're up early.'

'I want to go home to collect a couple of bits and pieces for work. I'm banking on them not waiting for me.'

'I made you some coffee.' Whitney handed her the mug. 'You'll need to pick up some clothes as there's no way you can stay at home yet.'

'Why ever not?'

'I've been watching breakfast TV and that's all they're talking about. It's the story of the day. If you go home now, they won't stop hounding you.'

'I can't stay here indefinitely. I've got work to do.'

'It won't be forever, but for now I think it's best for you to remain here until they get fed up with not being able to find you. It's safe. They'll move on to a different story soon. Give me ten minutes to shower and get dressed and we'll go.'

'You don't need to come with me,' George said, running a hand through her hair.

The dark circles under her friend's eyes were evidence she hadn't slept much. George was usually on such an even keel, but this had clearly affected her more than she was going to let on.

'It's best if we go in my car, in case the media's already there, which I wouldn't put past them. They'll most likely know your vehicle.'

'Really?'

'Yes, really. They'll have connections with the police and would have found out overnight. Rest assured they'll know all about you by now.' Whitney gave a wry smile.

'This is ridiculous. It's not like *I've* done anything. Nor do I have any details of my father's exploits.'

'Don't worry, it'll soon blow over,' she said, attempting to comfort her.

'You're right. I'll just have to deal with it.' A determined expression crossed her face.

'There's the George I've come to know and love. You'll be fine, and you're welcome to stay here for as long as you'd like.'

Despite the circumstances, Whitney had enjoyed the company last night. She liked visiting her mum and brother in their respective care homes, but their conversations were limited to basic topics. Understandably, as her mother had dementia and her brother had irreparable brain damage following an assault on him when he was a teenager. Conversations with George were challenging and fun.

'Thank you. I appreciate your kindness.'

Whitney got herself ready and they drove out to George's house. They were early enough for there not to be anyone waiting.

They hurried inside and Whitney waited in the lounge while George collected her belongings. She'd never be able to afford a house like this, even though it was quite small. George had exquisite taste, and everything was expensive. Nothing was out of place, either. Unlike Whitney's house because she never put anything away. She kidded herself it was *lived in*, but really, it was a mess.

George's garden was also beautiful. Lovely flowers and plants. A pang of regret that she wasn't more like George washed over her. But they couldn't both be the same. That was the whole reason for their successful working partnership. They each brought different things to solving their cases.

She walked into the hall and peered out of the glass

pane in the front door. A car had parked over the road and the woman inside was staring at the house.

'Hurry up, it looks like they're beginning to arrive. We'll go back to mine,' Whitney called up the stairs.

'I won't be long. I'll collect my car from your house and go into work early.'

'No. I'll take you,' she said.

'I could walk, it's not very far,' George said, as she headed down the stairs, laden with clothes and papers.

'Except you're staying with me. You certainly can't walk that far carrying everything. Come on, George. Get with it.' She grinned, trying to ease the situation. 'We'll go back to my house, drop off your things, and then I'll take you to work. You call me when you want to be picked up. That's it. End of story.'

She doubted George had any idea how awful being subjected to the ongoing hassle of the press could be, because she'd never been involved in anything newsworthy. The media was renowned for taking intrusion to its extreme. It could well be a nightmare.

George sighed. 'Okay. If that's what you think is best.'

Whitney glanced at her friend. She'd never been so compliant before.

'Yes, I do. You'll thank me in the end. I'll cook us a nice dinner tonight.' She grinned and George cracked a smile.

'Not going to happen,' George said, shaking her head. 'I'll be the one to cook.'

'A wise move,' Whitney agreed.

She was the world's worst cook, and George was an exceptional one, as she was with most other things. It amazed her that they'd become friends. George was talented in so many ways, apart from her lack of social skills in certain situations. But that added to her enigmatic allure.

She smiled to herself. She'd never have used words like that in the past, but that's how she thought of her friend. She was special. More so because it was down to George that Whitney still had her daughter, Tiffany. George had been the one to discover where Tiffany was being held when she'd been kidnapped. For that, Whitney would be eternally grateful.

'We'll need to stop at the supermarket later, as you no doubt won't have the ingredients I require,' George said, cutting across her thoughts.

'That works for me. You can make something good for dinner and I'll make sure you get to work and back,' Whitney said, just as her phone rang.

'Walker.'

'Sorry to bother you so early, guv.' It was Matt, her detective sergeant.

'What is it? I'll be in in half an hour,' she said, glancing at her watch.

'We've got a suspicious death. A woman has been found stabbed in Bluebell Woods.'

'What do we know?' Whitney glanced at George and mouthed. 'A murder.'

'Not a lot more than I've told you. The body was found by someone out running,' Matt said.

'We'll go there now.' Whitney knew exactly where the woods were. When Tiffany was younger, they'd often go there. Especially in spring when it was like walking on a blue carpet. 'I'll meet you at the station later.' She finished the call and scowled at George. 'I've told you before about jinxing and now look what's happened. I don't know why you don't believe me. It happens every time. Every time.'

'Tell me about the death,' George said.

'A woman's body has been found in the woods. Do you want to go to work or come with me to the crime scene?'

'I can rearrange my workload.'

'I knew you'd say that,' Whitney said, not even trying to hide the smug expression on her face. George couldn't resist a murder. 'It's been three months since our last suspicious death. You're missing the excitement.'

'I wouldn't go that far. What else do you know about it?'

'The body was found by a jogger. She'd been stabbed. We'll head out there now. We'll leave here out of your back door and you can wait for me at the end of the alley while I collect my car. That way we won't be spotted.'

It took thirty minutes to get to the crime scene and she was pleased to note that a cordon was in place and several uniformed officers were strategically placed, ensuring no one could enter the fairly small wood. She parked the car and they walked up to the officer by the cordon entrance.

'Good morning, Jade,' Whitney said to the constable who she recognised. 'Who's here at the moment?'

'Just uniform, guv. PC Brooker and I were first responders and the others joined us a short time ago.'

'Is the scene properly contained?' She'd checked out of habit but assumed it would be. Jade was an officer who could always be depended on to stick to protocols.

'Yes, guv. Cordons are in place, and I have the log here.' She held it out and George and Whitney wrote down their details.

'Where's the body?' Whitney asked.

'She's through there.' Jade pointed to a gap in the trees.

'And the person who found her?'

'He's with PC Brooker, by the patrol car.'

'We'll take a look at the scene first, and then I want to interview him.'

They left the officer and walked along the footplates to the clearing. The body was lying on the ground, surrounded by clumps of bluebells. The woman, who looked to be in her thirties, had blood smeared over her jeans and short-sleeved cream broderie anglaise blouse.

'Her clothes look perfectly intact, so it doesn't appear there's been a sexual assault, but we'll have to wait for confirmation from the pathologist,' Whitney said. 'Nor does it look like there was a struggle on the ground, judging by the flowers not being disturbed. Apart from the blood, her face and hands are clean. I suspect she wasn't murdered here, and her body was dumped post-mortem.'

'The scene is certainly staged. Look at the way she's been left,' George said. 'Her head's resting on a small, red cushion, with her hands loosely by her side.'

'What does it mean?'

'My initial interpretation would be the murderer was making the victim comfortable. We don't know the motive yet, but it suggests that either the victim was special to the killer, or it's the actual kill which was important and the victim unfortunate to be chosen.'

'Are you saying it's the killer's way of apologising to her?' Whitney asked.

'It's possible, but—'

'Move out of the way.'

Whitney started at the familiar voice from behind. She turned. Dr Claire Dexter, the pathologist, was striding towards them. She was dressed in white coveralls, but that didn't conceal the gold lurex bow peeping out of the top. Claire's short red hair looked in need of a brush.

'Good morning, Claire,' Whitney said.

'It might be for you. But it isn't for me. I'm getting fed up with murderers who think it's okay to leave a body so it's found early in the morning, and for my sleep to be disturbed.'

'The killer can't be certain about what time a body will be discovered. Also, if you're on duty, surely you should expect it,' George said.

Whitney clamped her jaws shut. George was brave speaking like that to Claire.

'I was up late last night. So hop it.'

They stepped to the side to allow her through. Claire could be officious at the best of times, and first thing in the morning, especially if she was tired, was a recipe for disaster. But Whitney would put up with that any day of the week if it meant Claire was there. Recently, the pathologist had been tempted by the offer of another position. Somewhere she didn't have to constantly fight for resources. Fortunately, she'd turned it down and had decided to stay. Whitney had breathed several sighs of relief when she'd found out.

'We're going to interview the jogger. We'll come and see you later once you've had a chance to take the body to the morgue. Okay?' Whitney said.

'Phone first,' Claire said.

They headed to the man wearing running gear who was standing with PC Brooker.

'I'm Detective Chief Inspector Walker, are you the person who found the body?' Whitney asked to clarify.

'Yes.'

'And your name is?'

'I'm Eddie Kent.'

'Are you usually out at this time of day?'

'Yes, I always go running first thing in the morning before work.' He glanced at his watch. 'When can I go? I'm already late. I have an important meeting today which I need to prepare for.'

He seemed remarkably calm for someone who had just found a dead body.

'What do you do?'

'I'm a conveyancing lawyer.'

'I understand you've already spoken to PC Brooker but, before you go, I have some questions. Can you explain to me exactly what happened?' She took out her notebook and pen from her pocket, poised to jot down his answers.

'I was taking my usual route, which is down Cable Street, through the woods, along Compton Street, and then back home. It's a five-mile run that takes me around forty minutes.' He leant forward and began stretching out his leg.

Was it to impress? Surely stretching now would be a waste of time.

'How did you come across the body?'

'I ran through the clearing and almost tripped over her. She was there for anyone to find.'

She glanced up at him, checking for signs of shock as he recalled what had happened. Nothing. 'Then what did you do?'

'At first I didn't realise she was dead. Until I saw the blood. So I called the emergency services and they told me to wait there until the police arrived.'

'Did they ask you to check the body for signs of life?'

'No. When I explained about the blood, they told me to stand away from her.'

'While you were running, did you see anybody?'

'No. There was no one around. That's why I run at this time.'

'Did you see any cars parked up with someone inside? Or cars that aren't usually in the vicinity?'

'No, I didn't see or hear anything. I wear headphones when running and listen to podcasts.'

Of course he did. He wasn't going to be much use to them.

'What about over the past few days? If you come here every day, have you seen anybody hanging around?'

He shook his head. 'No, there's been nothing out of the ordinary that I can recall.'

'Here's my card. If you do think of something, contact me,' Whitney said, handing it to him.

'May I go now?' he asked.

'Yes, but we might be in touch if we need further clarification.'

'That's fine. I've already given my contact details to the other officer.'

He turned and headed towards the road.

'He seemed remarkably calm, considering what he'd seen,' she said, once he was out of earshot.

'It will most likely hit him later,' George said.

'You're probably right. It was a shame he couldn't be more helpful. We need to identify the victim. Did you notice if there was a handbag or anything close by?'

'No, I didn't.'

'We'll go back to Claire. She's not going to like it, but by now she might have found something to help us discover who she is.'

They returned to where the body was lying, and where Claire was concentrating on her work.

'Why are you back here?' the pathologist asked, looking up from snapping photos.

'Have you found any identification on the body?' Whitney asked.

'There was a phone in the pocket of her jeans. It's on the ground beside the body.'

'Have you photographed it yet?'

'Yes. You can take it.'

Whitney pulled on some disposable gloves and picked it up, putting it into an evidence bag. 'Do you know what killed her?'

'No comment,' Claire said in a flat tone.

'Where did the blood come from?' Whitney asked, knowing she was pushing it.

'All I will tell you is there's a stab wound, but I have no idea whether that was the cause of death.'

Whitney blinked. Claire giving information wasn't usual. 'Thanks. Approximate time of death?'

'Between 9 p.m. and 4 a.m. I'll be more specific in my report.'

'When can we look at the cushion?' George asked.

'Not until the body's been moved. It will be back at the lab, so I can take samples.'

'Thanks, Claire,' Whitney said. 'We'll see you later. Come on, George, we'd better get back to the station and retrieve the victim's details from her phone.'

'Assuming it's hers,' George said.

'That's what we'll find out.'

Chapter Three

George gave a quick call to work informing them she wouldn't be in that day. She normally wouldn't have bothered as she worked fairly autonomously, but several months ago she'd had problems with her departmental managers complaining about her working with the police. That had all changed recently, as the managerial structure had reverted back to how it was previously. Two weeks ago, the assistant professor who'd had a stroke returned to work. This pleased her on many levels. Not least because it meant her vindictive ex-partner was no longer temporarily in charge. He'd tried to land her in trouble, but she'd successfully put him in his place. She didn't trust him not to try to derail her situation again, though.

She followed Whitney into the incident room and was hit by the high level of noise generated by the team. Some were standing in groups talking and others were sitting working, the computer keys clicking as their fingers flew over them. The large room held twenty desks, each with screens on them.

'Listen up, everyone,' Whitney said, calling her team to

attention. 'We've just come back from Bluebell Woods, the murder scene. Our victim, a woman, was left in the open, a cushion placed under her head. She appeared to have been stabbed. No attempt was made to hide the body.'

'Here we go again with the murders,' Frank said.

'We don't have any ID, but we do have her phone,' Whitney said, appearing to ignore the comment. 'Ellie, I want you to use the self-service kiosk and extract as much information as you can. Check for any selfies so we can confirm it's the victim's phone. We need her name and any next of kin. Also, see if there's anything in there about her plans for last night. Dr Dexter has given us an approximate time of death from nine last night until four this morning, so we need to know what she was doing before then. We have to inform her family as soon as possible.'

'Yes, guv,' Ellie said.

She was the department's research guru. If you wanted anything found, she was the one to do it. George admired her skills greatly. She was an incredible researcher and Whitney had fought long and hard to keep her on the team when she'd first been seconded to them a couple of years ago.

'In the meantime, Matt, I want you to oversee door-to-door enquiries. Take Sue, and some uniformed officers. Concentrate on Cable Street, Compton Street, and East Road as they lead directly to the woods. The scene was clean, which indicates she was murdered elsewhere and then dumped. We'll need SOCO to confirm. Before you go, check on whether they're there yet.'

'Yes, guv,' Matt said. 'I do have an appointment later today, if you remember.' A conspiratorial look passed between them. What was that all about?

'No problem. Let me know how you get on. Frank, I want you to examine any CCTV footage from around the area. Look for anything untoward happening. Take note of all the cars going back and forth from there.'

'I don't think there are cameras out that far,' the older detective said.

'Check and see. Then look around the town in particular at the main roads leading to the woods and see if there's anything of note.'

It fascinated George how the team ran like a well-oiled machine. They each had their own set of abilities which were effective in murder investigations. Whitney had mentioned she'd tried them in different roles, but it had made them less efficient. Ellie's strength was research. Frank was an expert in examining CCTV footage, despite him often complaining, and Matt's calming, interpersonal skills were extremely useful when dealing with the public. It was quite different from the competitiveness at the university, especially when it came to funding and research.

'I'd hardly call the body *dumped*, if she was resting on a cushion,' Frank said. 'Why would someone do that?'

Whitney turned to George. 'Have you had any further thoughts?'

None she wanted to share at this point, as it would be conjecture.

'No, as there's only one body. You know my views on making any assumptions based on that.' Her voice sounded harsher than she'd intended.

She really needed to calm down and focus on the death and not be distracted by what was going on with her father. She was about to apologise when she saw Whitney's attention had been diverted.

'What the bloody hell does he want?' Whitney muttered, as Superintendent Jamieson strode towards them.

George braced herself. Whitney wasn't going to be happy.

'Good morning, Dr Cavendish,' he said, giving a sharp nod.

'Good morning,' she replied.

'What are you doing here? Surely, we don't require your services for one body.' He looked from her to Whitney.

George tensed. He wasn't her superior and she resented him speaking to her like he was. 'I happened to be with the chief inspector when the murder was reported and I went to the scene with her to take a look.'

'But this is only one death. I hope you're not expecting it to turn into several because I won't allow it. This has to be solved immediately, or I'll want to know why.'

Did he ever listen to himself? Whitney might occasionally overreact as far as he was concerned, but he often deserved the lack of respect her friend had for him. Comments like that being a case in point.

'The crime will be solved as soon as possible, but we can't predict what's going to happen, sir,' Whitney said, in clipped tones. 'Are you here to see me?'

'Yes. We need to set up a press conference.'

Why? Even George could see it wouldn't be helpful yet.

'It's a bit soon as we've only just returned from viewing the body, which we haven't yet identified.'

There was something different about his behaviour. Yes, he was still being officious, but he appeared uplifted, despite feeling the need to flex his muscles when around them. She'd speak to Whitney about it, perhaps he was already in the running for another position.

'As I've told you, I want this sorted out straightaway and we'll need public help.'

'Which we'll receive from our door-to-door enquiries. I

really advise against the press conference until we have more information,' Whitney said.

'What can you tell me about the murder so far?'

'We believe the victim was stabbed and then taken to the scene. We're waiting for the cause of death from the pathologist. The body was found in Bluebell Woods by a jogger. She was left lying on the ground with her head resting on a cushion.'

'On a cushion? What does that mean?'

The question on everyone's lips and one which George needed to investigate more once they were able to examine it.

'The killer might have been making the victim comfortable,' Whitney said, glancing at George and giving a shrug.

'Why would they do that?' He averted his eyes and focused on George.

'There are a variety of reasons as to why, but with no knowledge of motive or if there will be further bodies, I'm not prepared to speculate. That would be counterproductive.'

George locked eyes with him. They were similar in height, so he couldn't try to undermine her in the same way he tried, albeit unsuccessfully, with Whitney.

'So, you can't tell me why someone would commit a murder and then lay the victim out like that,' he pushed.

'As I've said, there are a number of reasons which I'm not prepared to go into as I don't wish to send the investigation in the wrong direction.'

He turned away from her. Clearly angry, but not going to push it. Wise move. She wouldn't stand for it.

'Walker, we'll have the press conference this afternoon at four.'

'I might not have anything more to tell you by then,' she said.

'You will. It's not up for negotiation. Find something. We require public help to solve this.'

'I think you're being unreasonable,' Whitney said.

'I'm not prepared to discuss it. Be at my office by a quarter to four and you can brief me on where the investigation is.' He turned and walked away.

'See what I have to put up with? He's been nothing but a pain in the arse since being turned down for promotion.'

'He's certainly not acting the same as in the past,' George agreed. 'But he didn't seem down and dejected. If anything, it was the opposite. The way he stood, his chest puffed out and the way he spoke to us.'

'You're the expert. But I still blame his attitude on him not getting the job. It's been three months. You'd have thought he would have got over it by now, but all he does is get on my back the entire time.'

George doubted that was the case, considering only earlier her friend had mentioned that he'd been leaving her alone. It was just Whitney, being Whitney.

'Has he applied for any other positions?'

'How am I meant to know that? I'm not his confidante.'

'I thought you were,' George said.

'That was before. Now he uses me as his metaphorical punching bag. And, quite frankly, I'm fed up with it.'

'You'll have to put it to one side and not let it affect you.'

'Here we go again, you and your compartmentalising.' Whitney's eyes narrowed. 'I'm not like you.' She placed hands on her hips and stared at George. Her face like stone.

'Nothing can be done about him. He'll get over it,' George said.

'Guv,' Ellie called. 'I've got the name of the victim.

Rita Selwyn. She lived at 4 Tanner Street with her husband David. It appears from the photos on her phone that she had two children.'

Whitney's eyes flickered with emotion, but she pressed her lips together, as if fighting it back. George winced. Whitney was obviously thinking about the two kids who no longer had a mother.

'Good work, Ellie. Show me a photo, I want to confirm she's our victim.' Whitney walked over to the officer and peered at her screen. 'Yes. That's her. I want you to do a background search. Anything you can find. Friends, work, social media, finances. The usual.'

'Yes, guv.'

Whitney headed to the board and wrote up the victim's name.

'Doug, find out if our victim has been reported as missing and let me know. If she's been gone a few days, it could mean the killer kept her prisoner somewhere.'

'Yes, guv,' the officer said.

'George and I will inform the family now.' Whitney turned to her. 'Is that okay with you?'

'I'm with you for the whole day,' George said.

'Come on, then. Let's go,' she said in a grim voice. The lines were tight around her mouth in anticipation of the news they were about to deliver.

Chapter Four

Whitney felt guilty for snapping at George earlier. Her friend had enough on her plate with all that was going on with her father, so of course she'd be distracted. If the position was reversed, she'd be the same. She laughed to herself. How likely was it she'd ever be in that situation? She'd come from a working-class background and had lived in Lenchester her entire life. The closest she'd got to celebrities was watching them on the telly. It was probably a good thing George was able to compartmentalise it.

'I hope someone's going to be there,' she said, as they drew up outside the semi-detached 1980s property, which was identical to all of the others in the street.

She rang the bell and within a minute a man answered.

'Are you David Selwyn?' Whitney asked, already hating what was to come.

'Yes. Who are you?' A worried face stared back at her.

'I'm Detective Chief Inspector Walker, and this is Dr Cavendish.' She held out her warrant card for him to see. 'We'd like to come inside to speak with you for a moment.'

'Is this about Rita? I phoned earlier to report her

missing and gave the officer her details. I didn't expect to see you so soon as he said that because she didn't have any health issues, and wasn't high-risk, it wasn't considered an emergency.' He rubbed his brow with his hand.

Who had he spoken to? The front desk knew they had an unidentified body, and even if they didn't know the name of the victim, they'd have known the victim was female. She'd be having a word with someone on her return.

'Please may we talk to you inside?' she asked, keeping her voice gentle.

'Um…okay,' he said ushering them in. 'I was getting the children ready for school. They don't know about their mum as I didn't want to worry them. I told them she had to go out early.' His jaw tightened, accentuating the lines around his eyes.

'Where are they at the moment?' Whitney asked.

'Upstairs cleaning their teeth.'

'How old are they?'

'Charlie's ten and Ava's twelve. We'll talk in the lounge, so they can't hear us.'

She couldn't meet his eyes. Those poor kids, losing their mother at such a crucial time in their lives.

They followed him into a small room, with a sofa and two easy chairs. In the corner was a computer desk, with a pile of books to the side of a closed laptop.

'When was the last time you saw your wife?' Whitney asked after they'd all sat down.

'Last night. She left at six, as usual, and went to work. When I woke up this morning, she wasn't here. Normally, she doesn't arrive home until after we've all gone to bed. She …' His voice broke.

Whitney drew in a breath. She hated doing this so

much. 'I'm very sorry to have to inform you, we've found the body of a woman who we believe to be Rita.'

The colour drained from his face. 'Are you sure?' he said, his voice barely audible.

'Do you have a recent photograph of her?' Although she'd looked at the phone, she wanted to make doubly certain.

'There's one on the windowsill.'

Whitney walked over and stared at the photo of the family together and immediately knew that it was Rita. 'I'm sorry, but from this photograph it does appear to be Rita. We will need you to come down to the morgue to make a formal identification. I'm very sorry for your loss.'

Whitney returned to the sofa and remained quiet while he stayed silent, staring out into space.

'Rita's dead,' he finally said. 'What do I tell the children? What happened?'

'We're still investigating, but at the moment we're treating her death as suspicious.'

'You mean…murder?'

'Yes.'

'How did she die?'

'We're waiting for the pathologist's report. All we can tell you is she was found in Bluebell Woods.'

'But that's miles away from here. How did she get there?' He frowned.

'We don't know at this stage.' She didn't want to discuss it until they'd heard from Claire.

'Was her car there? She drives a silver VW Polo.'

'There were no cars parked close by, so most likely she didn't drive herself.' That was all she was prepared to share. 'Do you have anyone we can contact who can be with you?'

'No. None of our family are local. We've only lived here for a little over a year. We moved for my job.'

'What do you do?'

'I'm a surveyor for a firm in the city.'

'Would you be up to answering a few more questions?'

'Yes, I think so,' he said, swallowing hard, and then sitting upright in what appeared to be an attempt to compose himself.

'You mentioned that Rita was at work last night. What did she do?' She pulled out her notebook and pen from her pocket.

'She's been working at the Bat and Wickets, a local pub, for the last six months. She works nights so she can be home for the children when they finish school.'

Whitney's insides clenched. Those poor kids. Their lives would never be the same again.

'How many nights a week did she work?'

'Three. She's also studying part-time for a degree at the university. She has online lectures and spends time on the forums during the day and sometimes the evenings.'

'What was she studying?' George asked.

'English literature. She's currently working on a module about female Victorian authors. She …' His voice trailed off, and he stared at them, his eyes glazed. 'W-what am I meant to do now?'

'I'm going to arrange for a family liaison officer to come and stay with you and be your contact person with the police. Any questions you have, or anything you want to know about the investigation, they will be the person you go to.'

Did he understand? She suspected a lot of this was going over his head. He was too shocked for it not to. Assuming the shock was genuine. In so many murder cases the culprit was someone known to the victim, in particular someone close. But if it was him, why such an elaborate killing?

'What about the children? What should I do?'

Shelter them from the inevitable shitstorm that was going to hit once people found out their mum was murdered. But, of course, she wasn't going to tell him that.

'You'll need to tell them and keep them off school. It might take a little while for it to sink in. But they'll need your support.'

'Yes,' he said. 'We'll get through this together.'

'We'd like to take a look at your bedroom and Rita's computer desk to see if there's anything that might help us in our enquiries, if you don't mind.'

'Okay.' His voice was automated and his eyes blank.

They walked over to the desk. It was neat and tidy with only textbooks on there. 'Do you mind if we take Rita's laptop?'

'No.'

Whitney put it into an evidence bag, and they followed him up the stairs. As they reached the top, his daughter walked out of her bedroom.

'What's going on, Dad?'

'Go into your room for now, Ava, and I'll speak to you soon.'

'Who are you?' she said looking at Whitney.

She turned her body to shield the laptop in her hand, so the young girl couldn't see it. 'I'm Whitney and this is George.' She didn't want to say she was a police officer.

David shot her a grateful look.

'Finish getting ready and I'll be with you shortly,' he said.

He took them into the bedroom, and they looked around. It was modern with white furniture and a bed in the middle of the back wall. Whitney winced. It was only messy on one side.

After looking around and finding nothing of use, they returned downstairs. Whitney went outside and called Matt.

'I want you to arrange a family liaison officer for David Selwyn and his family.'

'Yes, guv.'

'And don't forget to let me know how your appointment goes.'

Matt and his wife had been trying for a child using IVF. He'd told her in confidence a few days previously that it looked like it had been a success. They were going to the clinic for confirmation, and a scan. He was nervous it could be a multiple birth – the clinic had told them around twelve per cent of IVF pregnancies were twins, as opposed to the one per cent of naturally conceived babies. He didn't think they'd be able to cope with two newborns at once. Whitney didn't agree, she was sure they'd be wonderful parents, however many babies they had. He hadn't told the rest of the team. No doubt there would be huge celebrations when he did.

'Will do, guv.' She could hear the smile in his voice.

She returned to the lounge where George was with David Selwyn. She had yet to ask the one question needing an answer. However awkward it was, she had to do it.

'David, please can you tell me what you were doing between the hours of nine, last night, and four this morning?'

'I was here with the children, of course. They're too young to be left. Why are you asking?' He frowned.

'We need to eliminate you from our enquiries. Is there anyone who can vouch for you being here?'

'Charlie and Ava. But they were in bed by nine.'

'And you didn't go out at all?'

'No. I would never leave the children alone.' He paused for a moment. 'My mother phoned at ten and we spoke for twenty minutes or so. You could ask her. Other than that, there's no one who can confirm I was here the whole time.' A tear slid down his face. 'Rita. My Rita,' he moaned. He leant forward and rested his head on his hands.

'David,' she said gently. He glanced up at her. 'Can you think of anyone who might have wanted to harm your wife?'

'No. Everyone loved her.'

The doorbell rang.

'I'll go,' Whitney said.

When she opened the door Constable Caroline Howe, the FLO, was standing on the doorstep. Caroline was in her early forties and very experienced. She was excellent at her job. Whitney was pleased it was her.

'Hello, guv.'

'How did you get here so quickly?' It had been less than ten minutes since she'd asked Matt to arrange it.

'I was in the vicinity, so it didn't take me long.'

Whitney stepped outside, and pulled the door behind her, not wanting to be heard.

'I'm very happy to see you, Caroline. The victim's husband is in shock. There are two young children, aged ten and twelve, who as yet don't know about their mother. I've had a brief chat with the husband, but we're relying on you to gather, and forward to me, any information you think will be useful.' She didn't really have to spell it out, because the officer knew exactly what was expected of her. But she did so, nonetheless.

'Yes, guv.'

'The husband had actually phoned the station to report his wife missing when he discovered her absence this morning, but whoever spoke to him hadn't connected it with our death. I'll be looking into that when I get back to the station.'

'He only noticed her missing this morning?' Caroline said. 'That's strange.'

'She'd been working at the Bat and Wickets pub last night and he'd gone to bed before she was due home.'

'Okay. That makes sense.'

'Let's go inside and I'll introduce you.' They headed into the lounge. 'David, this is Constable Howe. Caroline. She's your family liaison officer and she'll be staying with you during the investigation.'

'Hello,' Caroline said, sitting beside him.

'We've got to go now. Caroline, if you could please arrange a time for David to make the formal identification, and we'll be in touch later.'

'Will do, guv.'

Whitney and George left and headed back to the car.

'What next?' George asked.

'I'd like to revisit the crime scene.'

'What about the pub where Rita worked?'

'We'll go there later.'

Chapter Five

Whitney phoned the incident room to ask for any updates and informed Frank they wouldn't be back for a while.

'What is it you want to examine?' George asked as they were driving to the crime scene.

'I didn't get a good enough sense of the scene with Claire being there. It won't take long.'

'Won't the scenes of crime officers still be there?' George asked.

'We'll work around them.'

When they arrived, they signed the log and walked in the direction of the scene. In the distance, heading towards them, were Jenny and Colin, two members of SOCO, dressed in their white coveralls.

'Have you found anything?' Whitney asked as they approached the pair.

'It's all fairly clean, apart from evidence of leaves being dragged along the path close to where the body was left,' Jenny said. 'We're not helped by the fact we've had such good weather recently and the ground's dry.'

'We'll be sure to keep clear of it,' Whitney said as they stepped on to the footplates.

The bluebells were smashed on the ground where the body had once been situated. The cushion had also been removed.

The breeze brushed her arm and Whitney glanced up. Although spring had passed, there was still a sea of flowers and the strong, sweet smell of the bluebells invaded her senses. Without the victim, it was beautiful.

'So why here? And why leave her out in the open and not even attempt to hide her?' she mused. 'Clearly the killer wanted her to be found.'

'It would certainly seem so,' George agreed. 'Although, if they wanted the victim found sooner, they could have left her in a different place. Somewhere closer to the city.'

'In which case, do you think there's something symbolic about leaving her here, in the woods?'

'Possibly there's a nature connection, but at the moment that's speculation. There's also the cushion to consider, and why it was used.'

'I agree. It's not like the victim was going to be uncomfortable with her head on the ground.'

'The sooner we can get a look at it the better, as it appears pivotal to our investigation. But, we have to remember, there's only one body and, although I don't wish to go on about it because you'll say that's what I always do… more bodies mean more clues.'

'We can't afford the luxury of additional bodies. You heard Jamieson. He'll blow a gasket if there's another murder.' She scanned the scene again. 'Let's try to find where the killer most likely parked in order to bring the body through to where it was dumped. If it was me, I'd use the isolated side road which runs towards the rear of the woods. Let's check there, first.'

'Do you know these woods?' George asked, as they marched off.

Whitney might have been lacking in height, but she was an extremely fast walker. Her legs doing twice the number of steps as most people, over a given time period.

'Yes. I've been coming here for years.'

She led them through the trees, and followed the windy, bark chippings path until they reached a secluded narrow country road.

'This would be a good spot,' George said. 'There are no houses.'

'Exactly. Hardly any cars come down here as it's a dead end. A perfect place. If the murderer knew about it.'

'It's still a fairly long walk to get to the dump site. How did the murderer move the body?' George asked.

'Carrying the victim would have been difficult. A better way of transporting it would be needed. What about a wheelchair?' She peered down at the ground, looking for tracks. 'Can you see any tyre marks?'

'No. But they wouldn't be easy to find on this surface. Also, the balance of a wheelchair is such that it most likely wouldn't leave a deep imprint,' George said.

'One scenario could be that the killer parked here, put the body into a wheelchair, or even a wheelbarrow, and wheeled it to the dump site. The body was pulled out and dragged over to its resting spot. The cushion was then placed under the head. It appears to be the most logical. What do you think?' she asked George who was also bent over staring at the ground.

'A wheelbarrow would have made a single deep imprint because all of the weight would be pushed down on to the front wheel.'

'And there isn't one here, unless the killer smoothed it over,' she said.

'Claire should have some trace evidence for us, which might help in identifying the exact manner in which the body got to the scene,' George said.

Whitney glanced at her watch. 'We'll go back to the scene and see if there's anything resembling tyre marks, then grab some lunch before going to see Claire.'

'Did she say we can go? You know what she's like.'

'We can't leave it any longer. I've got to see Jamieson this afternoon and have something for the bloody press conference he's insisted on calling.'

They headed back to the scene and spent several minutes scouring the ground.

'It's impossible to see on this dry ground,' George said.

'Also, the killer may have covered over the tracks. Once the body had been dumped, it would be easy to carry the wheelchair back to the vehicle, if it was a light folding one.'

After lunch, Whitney drove them to the morgue. They pushed open the double doors and straightaway the antiseptic smell invaded her nostrils. When they arrived at the lab, they poked their heads into the office area but there was no one there. Then they walked into the main area where Claire was peering at a body on one of the stainless-steel tables situated in the middle of the room.

'Hello,' George said.

'What the hell are you doing here so soon?' Claire asked.

'One day, you might surprise us with a warm welcome,' Whitney said laughing.

'Don't hold your breath,' Claire retaliated, though her eyes twinkled.

'I have a press conference coming up. We've identified

the victim as Rita Selwyn. She went to work at a local pub last night and didn't return. What have you got for us?'

'Actually, this is very interesting, and I was going to call you later but, as you're here now, you can come and look.' She beckoned them over.

The woman's petite body was doll-like on the large table, and her blonde hair hung limply around her shoulders. The red stab wound in the centre of her stomach was in stark contrast to her pale translucent skin.

'What is it?' Whitney asked, swallowing hard. How could this poor woman's life end so tragically?

'Initially, it seemed the victim was killed by a single stab wound to her abdomen. The blade entered the abdominal cavity, penetrating the stomach. See the bruising on the entry point? It was caused by the rim of the handle hitting the skin. The jagged pattern indicates it was a double-edged blade. Judging by the angle of entry the killer was right-handed.'

Whitney frowned. 'But you don't believe that was the cause of death?'

'It's not unambiguous. During the post-mortem I found water in the lungs, consistent with her being drowned.'

'Was the stabbing post-mortem?' George asked.

'Judging by the pressure trauma to the sinuses, the victim was alive when she entered the water. The blood in the airways was a secondary indicator. What it isn't possible to ascertain one hundred per cent is whether the stabbing took place before or after the drowning. If it was after, it would have been almost immediately. If pressed, I'd say most likely the stabbing occurred first, perimortem.'

'*Perimortem*?' Whitney asked.

'At or near the time of death,' Claire said.

'There's a lake in Bluebell Woods. Could it have happened there?' Whitney asked.

'No. Her lungs were full of tap water.'

'Can you tell how she was drowned?' Whitney asked.

'There were pressure marks on the face and some very faint ones on the lower body.' Claire pulled the overhead light across and revealed purple marks shaped like finger-tips. 'The victim was held down with two hands. Probably in a bath, or something of a similar size, where the whole body could be submerged.'

'Can you get any fingerprints from the body?' Whitney asked.

'No. The marks were consistent with the person wearing gloves. Most likely latex as they're thin enough to leave a complete fingermark, without the actual prints.'

'Why are the marks on the lower body so faint compared with the face?' George asked.

'The victim was fully clothed at the time of the drown-ing,' Claire said.

'How do you know?' Whitney asked.

'The clothes were still slightly damp, especially inside the jeans pocket.'

'What's your estimated time of the drowning?'

'Between midnight and two this morning,' Claire said.

'Was there any sexual interference?' Whitney asked.

'No.'

'So, what we've got here is somebody who was stabbed and then almost immediately drowned in a bath, while fully clothed,' Whitney said.

'Were there any signs of struggle?' George asked.

'There was nothing under the nails. Any fibres would most likely have come off in the water.'

'We believe the killer might have used a wheelchair, or something similar, to transport the victim from the road to the dump site, and then dragged the body into place. Could you ascertain whether that had happened? Could it have left soil and bark chippings on the body?' Whitney asked.

'There was debris on the body consistent with it being dragged. I've sent everything off for analysis. From my observation there were different types of soil, one of which wasn't found close to the crime scene.'

'That gives us more questions than answers,' Whitney said. 'What about the cushion? What can you tell us about it?'

'It's over there,' Claire said, pointing to a set of stainless-steel drawers in the corner on which the item was placed. 'Help yourself. It's a heraldic cushion.'

Whitney blinked, but before she could ask what that meant, George marched towards it, her mouth set in a curious line.

'How old?' George asked.

'Not antique,' Claire said. 'It's a mix of wool and man-made fibres. The coat of arms isn't one that's familiar to me.'

'Okay, we'll take it with us and get someone on the team to source it,' Whitney said as she joined George by the drawers. She pulled out an evidence bag and placed the cushion inside. 'Thanks, Claire. We'll get going, now. The press conference beckons.'

They left the lab and made their way down the corridor.

'While you're in the press conference, I'll research the coat of arms,' George said. 'It's the first solid clue the killer has given us.'

Chapter Six

Whitney was a few minutes late when she hurried upstairs to meet Jamieson to prepare for the press conference. His voice was booming out as she reached his office. As usual, he was on the phone. She waited until he'd finished, knocked on the door, and walked in.

He glanced at his watch. 'You're late. Fill me in on what we've got so far.'

'The victim's name was Rita Selwyn and she lived with her husband, David, and two children on Tanner Street, Lenchester. She worked last night at the Bat and Wickets pub, and when her husband woke up this morning, she wasn't there.'

'Have you interviewed him? The most likely offender in these sorts of cases is someone close to the victim.'

'Yes, I know,' she said, trying to hide her frustration. It was as if he was trying to tell her something she wasn't aware of. 'We have interviewed him, and he was at home with the children.'

'Is there anyone who can verify that?'

'Only the children, and for a short while, his mum.

Obviously, we're still going to keep an eye on him. The family liaison officer is with him and she'll find out anything we need to know.'

'Which officer are you using?'

Whitney stared at him. 'Constable Howe.'

Why on earth would he want to know that?

'Okay,' he said, averting his gaze. 'Have you been to the pub where the victim worked?'

'No, not yet. The plan is to go after the press conference.'

'Shouldn't you have already gone?'

Whitney drew in a breath. 'There are only so many things I can do in a day. You wanted to have the press conference this afternoon, otherwise I would have been there now. Once we've finished, I'll speak to the landlord. Going later might be to our advantage, as there are likely to be more customers in the early evening than mid-afternoon. One of their regulars might be able to help.'

'Okay. It's your investigation,' he said.

Exactly, so he should back off.

'Yes, sir.'

'What are we going to tell the press?' he asked.

'We should keep the heraldic cushion confidential, otherwise we'll have a continual stream of people phoning with obscure and totally ridiculous theories as to its presence. Dr Cavendish is researching the coat of arms right now.'

'What has Dr Dexter told you?'

'Not only was the victim stabbed, which would have caused her to die eventually, but she was also drowned. Water in her lungs. It's quite bizarre, as there was no need to do both.'

'What was the *actual* cause of death?'

'Most likely, it was the drowning, but the stabbing took

place very close to it. I suggest we only mention the stabbing.'

'I do know what should be kept quiet and what should be shared,' he said abruptly.

Whitney frowned. What was it with his change of mood all of the time? It drove her crazy.

He put on his uniform jacket and did up the buttons. He was looking in pretty good shape, compared with when he first arrived. He seemed to be taking more care of himself since his wife left him and their three daughters last year. Was he seeing someone? It wasn't something she'd ever consider broaching. Did she care? No. She had no desire to know about his personal life.

They left his office and walked in silence to the conference room. Melissa, their PR officer, was waiting. She opened the door for them to walk in and, as she could have predicted, it was full. There were cameras at the back and reporters filling the chairs. They seated themselves behind the long table at the front.

'Good afternoon,' Melissa said. 'Thank you for coming in. I'm going to pass you over to Superintendent Jamieson for the briefing.'

Jamieson leant over and pulled the mic towards him. 'Thank you, Melissa.' He nodded in her direction. 'Unfortunately, I have to inform you that a woman's body was found in Bluebell Woods, and we are treating it as a suspicious death. We would like members of the public to contact us if they saw anything out of the ordinary in that vicinity last night from around eleven. Anyone hanging around or driving past slowly and acting in an odd manner.'

'What's the victim's name?' a reporter called out.

'We're not releasing her identity at present, out of respect for the family. Next question.'

'How did the victim die?' another reporter called out.

Whitney glanced at Jamieson. What was he going to say? Would he stick to what she'd said? He could be a loose cannon in these situations.

'I'll pass you over to Detective Chief Inspector Walker and she will answer any further questions.' He slid the mic over to her.

She bit down on her bottom lip to stop from giving a grim smile. During their last set of murders, when trying to impress who he thought would be his new employers, he took centre stage and didn't give her a look-in. It appeared they were back to how it used to be, which she was grateful for, as it meant she could control the dissemination of information and there would be no surprises.

'We suspect stabbing, but we're waiting for the pathologist to confirm cause of death and once we have that we'll release further details,' she said, giving her usual *say nothing* comment.

'Do you have any leads?' a female reporter in the front row asked.

'We're following our usual procedures, and that's all I can tell you presently, as we don't wish to jeopardise the investigation. Our main concern is to hear from anyone who saw anything suspicious in and around the crime scene. All calls will be treated confidentially.' She scanned the room, waiting for the inevitable question.

'Are you expecting another serial killer?' another of the reporters quipped.

And there it was. As she'd predicted.

She glanced at Jamieson who was staring at her, his face set hard.

'We are not,' she said, firmly. 'Thank you all for coming in. We'll keep you up to date with the investigation as it progresses.'

They left the room together, and Melissa went on ahead.

'Right, Walker, get this case solved. We are *not* going to be known for attracting serial killers. It's getting out of hand,' he said.

'Yes, sir. I understand. I can assure you we will do what we can. There's no evidence whatsoever that this is going to be a serial killer.'

She'd said it to reassure him, but as far as she was concerned, the whole nature of the death didn't strike her as a crime of passion or a one-off. The fact the murderer felt the need to kill by stabbing *and* drowning, as well as laying the victim out on a symbolic cushion, was most odd.

The one thing she agreed with him on was the need to solve the case as soon as possible.

Chapter Seven

George sat at one of the desks in the incident room, staring at the image on her computer screen of the heraldic cushion found at the murder scene, but she couldn't concentrate. Her parents hadn't returned her calls, and she'd no idea how things were going. She didn't want to call her brother again because he'd try to persuade her to drop everything and go to London to be with them. She wasn't convinced it was the best course of action because she didn't have anything to add.

'Found anything?' Whitney's voice interrupted her thoughts. She hadn't realised the officer had returned to the incident room after the press conference.

'I've been looking at this coat of arms and checking whether it's registered, but so far it seems not. It's very unusual.'

'In what way?' Whitney wheeled the chair from the next-door desk and sat next to George.

'The shield is designed to be the body of a bird which, in itself, is common. We have the head coming out from the top and the wings coming out from the side.' She pointed to the area on the photo.

'Yes, I can see that. What makes this one different?'

'The body part is in the shape of a bell. I don't recall seeing that before. I checked with heraldic terminology and a bell symbolises a warning.'

'A warning about what?' Whitney asked.

'It's not specific in that sense. Another thing of note is that the bird depicted is a vulture. Again, not usual, as it depicts rapacity.'

'Which is?'

'Aggressive greed.'

'Anything else?'

'Yes. On the shield there are foxes.' She pointed to the four animals. 'A fox represents cunning, intelligence, and a refusal to be captured.'

'Put all this together and—'

'I'd say we're looking at a message from the killer,' George interrupted. 'The killer is warning us that they're smart and cunning, and out for themselves. They think they're clever enough not to be caught and they don't care about their victims. In my opinion, it's a game for them.'

'Bloody hell. There's no way this is a one-off then.'

'I tend to agree with you.'

'Is there anything else on there?' Whitney asked.

'The colours are interesting, too. The vulture is purple, a colour which symbolises sovereignty. It's a royal colour. It could depict a belief that the murderer sees themselves as on a higher plane than the rest of us.'

'Or they're an aristocrat.'

'That's possible, but not how I read it.'

'This is excellent.' Whitney stood. 'Listen up, everyone. George has come up with some interesting facts about the cushion our victim was resting on.' She looked down at George. 'You tell them.'

She stood and scanned the room. Everyone was staring back at her. 'We have what's known as a heraldic cushion, because it contains heraldic symbols. They comprise coats of arms and other symbols which identify families, or groups. Some cushions will be plain with a coat of arms on them. Other cushions have a single symbol woven into the fabric which covers the entire cushion. You often see the fleur-de-lis on fabrics. It's the lily flower and is associated with the French crown. It's important to remember these symbols are steeped in tradition and history.'

'Does that mean our murderer is posh?' Frank asked.

'Not as posh as you,' Doug said, smirking.

'Give it a rest, you two,' Whitney said shaking her head. 'How many times do I have to tell you? Show Dr Cavendish some courtesy.'

'We don't know whether the murderer is *posh* or not,' George said. 'Anyone can design their own coat of arms. What's interesting about this one is that we're being sent a message via the symbols on there. A warning.'

'What sort of warning?' Doug asked.

'In a nutshell, they believe they're too clever for us to catch them and, by implication, we should expect more deaths of a similar nature.'

'Not clever enough?' Frank said. 'What a load of crap. We have you working with us, Dr Cavendish. That should outsmart them.'

'Thank you, Frank. I'm just one of many. We're a team. But I agree, there's nothing to suggest the killer will outsmart us.'

'We'll nail the bastard,' Frank said, his fist clenched.

She glanced at Whitney; self-satisfaction written across her face. The officer was proud of her team, and rightly so.

'Absolutely, Frank,' Whitney said. 'Thanks for your input, George. Ellie, we need to find out where this cushion was made. Was it a one-off, or are there several?'

'Yes, guv.'

'Dr Cavendish and I are going to the pub where our victim worked. We'll have a briefing tomorrow morning, first thing.' She turned to George. 'Are you ready?'

'Whenever you are,' she said.

'Let's go.'

As Whitney drove out of the station George could see her lips were set in a thin line. 'Is there anything wrong?'

'I was thinking about Jamieson. He was doing his usual interfering but also he was acting different from usual.'

'In what way?'

'I can't put my finger on it. He looked a little more *spruced up*, for want of a better word. He'd obviously had his hair cut recently and he's still watching his weight. I thought he might let himself go after his wife left. Maybe he's found himself another woman. Not that it's anything to do with us,' Whitney said.

'You're right, it isn't,' George said. She wasn't interested in him. It was a pain in the arse the way he sucked up to her, not to mention how he treated Whitney.

'The pub's on Newton Street. It's fairly close to where the family lived. It's not a place which causes us any problems. I've been there a couple of times, but not for years.'

Whitney found a parking spot right outside. Although it was only six, there were already a number of people in there. They walked up to the bar.

'Is the manager in?' Whitney asked the tall, burly man standing behind it.

'That's me,' he said, smiling. 'Dan Judd.'

Whitney held out her warrant card. 'Detective Chief

Inspector Walker, and Dr Cavendish. We'd like a word with you in private.'

'What have you done now?' one of the men sitting at the bar said.

'I've no idea, John.' Dan shrugged and grinned and then turned to Whitney. 'Come around the back of the bar and we'll go through to the kitchen.'

The kitchen had units around the edge, a large oven and hob, and a stainless-steel commercial table in the centre which appeared to be the place they prepared food, as utensils and trays with condiments were situated in the middle.

Sitting eating was a man wearing a green T-shirt with *Bat and Wickets* written across the front. 'Phil, can you take over in the bar while I talk to the police?'

When they were alone, Whitney turned to Dan. 'We'd like to speak to you about Rita Selwyn.'

'Rita? What about her?'

George kept focused on his face, wanting to assess how he took the news of the death.

'Unfortunately, she was found dead this morning.'

His eyes widened. 'Dead? What happened to her?'

'That's what we're investigating. She was found in the woods.'

He frowned. 'I saw it on the TV a while ago. You're telling me it's Rita? I can't believe it.' He gripped the table, his knuckles turning white.

'Why don't you sit down,' Whitney said gently, as she pulled out one of the wooden stools.

'Thank you.'

'Are you up to answering a few questions?' Whitney asked.

'Yes, of course.' He let out a long sigh. 'It's such a shock.'

'We understand Rita worked last night.'

'Yes. Her shifts were Monday, Wednesday, and Friday evenings, from six to twelve. She was a great worker. The customers liked her. The staff liked her. How can she be dead?'

He seemed genuine enough, nothing alerted her otherwise.

'Can you think of anything that happened last night which might help us with our enquiries?' Whitney asked.

He ran a shaking hand over his mouth. 'No, it was a normal Wednesday night.'

'Was it busy?'

'Not particularly. A few of our regulars were in, and there were a couple of older women here for an hour early on, who I didn't recognise, but that was all.'

'Was anyone paying particular attention to Rita?'

'No more than usual. Wednesday is always one of our quieter nights and often we'll use the time to stock up. There's only me and a cleaner on during the day, and I don't have time to do it myself.'

'Did Rita mention anyone acting strangely towards her recently?' Whitney asked.

'No. And I didn't notice anything, either.'

'Did she talk about her family? Do you know whether there were any problems with her husband or other members?'

'Rita didn't confide in me in that way. She was a quiet, steady worker. She was always pleasant and never rude to the customers. She hadn't been here long, but already she'd proved to be one of my best members of staff.'

'What time did she leave?'

'After we'd cleared up and the pub had emptied. Maybe around twelve-fifteen.' He glanced at the clock on the wall.

'How did she get home?'

'She drove herself.'

'Where did she park her car?'

'In the street, I believe.'

'Was it still here this morning?' George asked.

'I'm not sure which one is hers.'

'Why not?' Whitney asked.

'I'm behind the bar when she arrives and still here when she leaves.' He glanced away.

Was he telling the truth?

'Are any of the customers who were here last night in now?' Whitney asked.

'Yes. There's John. He was sitting at the bar when you arrived. The one who made the comment.'

'Does he come in every night?' Whitney asked.

'He's here four or five nights a week since his wife left him a year ago, and took the children. He …' He paused.

'What is it?' Whitney asked.

'He's always had a thing for Rita. But …'

'When you say *thing*, what do you mean?' Whitney asked.

'He was always here on the nights she was scheduled to work and sometimes I'd notice him staring at her. But he's perfectly harmless. He's been coming in here for years. He's a nice chap. I can't see him doing anything like…you know …'

'It's often those we least suspect,' Whitney said.

'Has he ever given her any presents?' George asked. Obsessions could escalate easily if the offender thought their affections were returned.

'She worked on Valentine's Day and got some flowers. They were delivered here, and she was certain they weren't from her husband. We laughed about it. She didn't seem unduly worried. I did wonder whether they were from

John, but didn't pursue it.' He shook his head. 'Maybe I should have.'

'Why did you choose not to?' George asked.

'It's not unusual for customers to like members of staff. It goes with the territory.'

'Was there anyone else who had a *thing* for Rita?' Whitney asked, making quote marks with her fingers.

'Not that I'm aware of.'

'Did you have any contact with her family?'

'No. Her husband looked after the children while she worked. She was very clever. She was studying for a degree at university.'

'Yes, we know about her studies. We'll go back into the pub and speak to John. May we bring him through here?' Whitney asked.

'Yes, of course.'

They walked out, but the man wasn't there. George and Whitney exchanged a glance.

'Where's John?' Dan asked Phil.

'He suddenly decided to leave and didn't say why. Most unlike him,' Phil said.

'Did he say he'd be coming back?' Whitney asked.

'No. He downed his beer in one and then left.'

'That's very unusual,' Dan said. 'Once John's here, he stays until at least ten or eleven. Or even later. He's often the last to leave.'

Whitney beckoned Dan to one side, out of Phil's earshot.

'Do you know where he lives?' Whitney asked.

'Yes. I've had to take him home a few times when he's had too much to drink. He's at 337 Devon Street.'

'What's his last name?'

'It's Hawkins. John Hawkins.'

'Thank you. We may be back to talk to you again. But

if, in the meantime, there's something you remember, please let me know immediately.' Whitney pulled out a card from her pocket and handed it to him. 'I realise you'll want to tell people about Rita dying, but for the sake of the family, I'd appreciate it if you could refrain from saying her body was found in the woods, as we're not releasing her name yet.'

Chapter Eight

'He left because of us,' Whitney said as they exited the pub, annoyed with herself for not noticing the impact their presence had made on him. 'We'll go to his house. It's only a few streets away.' Before driving off, Whitney pulled out her phone and called Ellie, hoping the officer hadn't left for the day.

'Hello, guv,' the young officer said.

'I'm glad you're still there. I want you to look into a John Hawkins, living on Devon Street. He's a possible suspect. We're on our way there now. Call me when you've got something.'

'Yes, guv. It shouldn't take long.'

When they arrived, they walked up the path to the terraced house and she knocked on the door. There was no answer, so she knocked again. In her peripheral vision, she saw him heading towards them on the other side of the road, limping slightly on his left leg. He was holding a small packet in cream paper. Fish and chips?

'He's over there,' she said to George. 'We're hidden by the trees on this side of the road, so he shouldn't have noticed us. Let's tuck in the porch so he can't see us until he gets closer to his front door.'

They kept out of sight and waited until he had pushed open the gate and begun walking up the path. She stepped out of the shadows and George followed. He stared at them; his jaws open.

Was he about to scarper? He could try but she'd soon catch him.

'Stay where you are,' she shouted, as she moved towards him, closing the gap.

'What do you want?' he asked.

'A word with you, John. Inside,' Whitney replied.

He glanced behind him, and she braced herself to run if he tried to make a dash for it, but he appeared to think better of it.

He unlocked the door and led them into the lounge where they sat down on a faded dark blue sofa. He sat opposite, still holding on to his package. Definitely fish and chips, she could smell it. Her stomach rumbled.

'Why did you leave the pub?' Whitney said.

'I was hungry.' He held out the packet in his hand.

'Nothing to do with us being there?' She locked eyes with him, and he lowered his gaze.

'All right. Yes. I left because you were there,' he said.

'Why?' Whitney pushed.

'I thought you were coming for me.'

'What for?' Surely, he wasn't going to admit to killing Rita.

'Because I'm behind on my child support. I reckoned you'd come to the pub to arrest me, and I didn't trust Dan not to rat me out.'

'That isn't why we were there, or why we're now here. We want to speak to you about Rita Selwyn.'

'Rita?' He frowned. 'Why?'

'Her body was found this morning and we're treating her death as suspicious.'

His face turned ashen. 'Rita's dead?' he said slowly.

'Yes. I want to know more about your relationship with her.' Whitney leant forward and scrutinised his face. Was his distress genuine?

'I didn't have a *relationship* with her.'

'You'd like to have had one, though, wouldn't you?' Whitney said.

'I don't know what you mean,' he muttered.

'We understand you were attracted to her and sent her some flowers on Valentine's Day. Is that correct?'

His head shot up. 'Who told you that?'

'It doesn't matter. Did you, or did you not send Rita flowers?'

'I liked her.' He squeezed the packet resting on his lap. She doubted much of the food would have remained intact.

'Even though she was married, you still thought it was okay to pursue her.'

'I didn't *pursue* her.'

'What did you do, then?' Whitney asked, locking eyes with him.

'She wasn't happy in her marriage,' he replied, sitting up straighter, a defiant look in his eyes.

'What makes you say that?'

This was very different from the picture they'd got so far. Perhaps the husband wasn't as clean as she'd first believed.

'She wouldn't be working in a pub if she was? People work in pubs to meet others. If she was happy at home, she wouldn't have been there.'

Whitney shook her head, dismissing her previous

thoughts. 'I think that's a gross generalisation, and I don't believe it relates to Rita. Do you know where she lived?'

'No comment,' he said, clamming up.

The number of times suspects said *no comment* drove her mad. Too many cop shows on TV was what did it.

'Have you been following her?' she pushed.

'No comment.'

'I think you'd better come down to the station with us,' Whitney said. 'We don't have time for this.' She stood and took a step towards him.

'What's the point? I have nothing to say.'

'It's up to you. You can either come with us voluntarily or I'm going to arrest you and then you'll be leaving here in handcuffs. For all of the neighbours to see.'

Threats like that invariably led to a suspect taking the easiest option. She'd rather no one saw Hawkins being arrested, in case they used their phone to record them and then forwarded it on to the press. Just one more thing to remember these days. Sometimes, she longed for the time before smartphones were invented.

'What choice do I have?' he said, standing. 'What about a solicitor, do I need one?'

'That's your call. You're entitled to have one present if you wish. Do you have one?' Whitney asked.

'Do I look like I'm rich enough to have a solicitor on speed dial?' he asked, his jaw clenched. 'If I had, I'd have used them in my divorce, and not had to agree to all the conditions and demands my ex made.'

'If you'd like one with you during questioning, we can arrange that. We have duty solicitors available.'

He shrugged. 'I'll let you know when we get there.'

'I'd also like to search your house,' Whitney said.

'Why?'

'As part of our enquiries. You can give us permission,

or we'll get a search warrant which would mean no corner of your home would be left untouched. It's up to you.'

She didn't doubt that they'd get one, but she'd rather not have to wait. With his permission they could begin searching straight away.

'I've got nothing to hide,' he said.

'Are you giving your permission?' she checked.

'Do I have a choice?'

'Yes. But you know what will happen if you refuse.'

'I don't care. Do what you like.' He gave an angry sigh.

'Give me the key and then we'll take you to the station.'

'How am I going to get home?' he asked, as they left his house.

'I'll arrange for an officer to escort you back here after we've finished with the questioning.'

'I'm eating my dinner in the car,' he said holding up his somewhat squashed packet.

Whitney's stomach growled all the way back to the station as the smell of his fish and chips circulated. She hoped George didn't mind the aroma. She hadn't said anything, although she'd had her window open the entire journey, despite the chill in the air.

When they reached the station, Whitney left Hawkins with the sergeant on the front desk to be put into one of the interview rooms. They went upstairs where several members of the team were still working.

'Attention, everyone,' Whitney said. 'We have someone in custody. His name is John Hawkins and he was infatuated with our victim.' She walked over to the board and wrote his name. 'We know he sent her flowers on Valentine's Day and suspect he followed her home at some point. He *no commented* when we asked if he knew where she lived. Matt, I want you to take Doug to his house and do a thorough search. He's given his permission and here's the key.'

'Yes, guv,' Matt said, taking it from her and smiling.

She must remember to find out the results of his IVF appointment. He certainly seemed cheerful. Fingers crossed it was positive.

'Ellie, have you found anything on him yet?'

'His full name is John Gavin Hawkins and he's got a record for assault from ten years ago. A pub brawl. He works as a fire extinguisher engineer,' Ellie said.

'He told us he's divorced and owes child support. That's why he did a runner when we went to the pub, believing we were there to arrest him. I want someone to check out the CCTV footage around the Bat and Wickets pub to see if we can see when the victim left and if there was anybody close by at the time.'

'I'll do it,' Sue said.

'What about me? I usually do the CCTV work,' Frank said.

'Let's switch it up for a change,' Whitney said. 'You can come with me to interview him.'

Frank was good, but it wouldn't hurt to give Sue more experience with the CCTV.

His face brightened. 'Okay, guv.'

'Ellie, find out Rita Selwyn's car details and let Sue have them. We want to know the time she left work and where she went. Frank and I will interview him now. George, you can watch from outside.'

She fetched a mic and earpiece from her office and the three of them left for the interview room.

'What role do you want me to take during the interview?' Frank asked as they were on their way.

'You're my backup. I ask the questions, you can watch.' She flashed a grin in George's direction, who arched an eyebrow in response.

When they entered the interview room, Hawkins was sitting upright in the chair, staring straight ahead.

Whitney pressed the recording equipment.

'Interview on June twenty-fifth. Those present: Detective Chief Inspector Walker, Detective Constable Taylor. Please state your full name for the recording,' she said to him.

'Why are you recording this?'

'Standard practice. Please state your name.'

'John Gavin Hawkins.'

'Thank you. We'd like to know more about you. What do you do for a living?' Although she already knew, she still wanted to check, to make sure he was telling them the truth.

'I'm a fire extinguisher engineer and I work for G & S Fire Detection.'

'How long have you worked there?'

'I'm not sure.' He shrugged. 'Maybe, four years.'

'You mentioned earlier that you live alone. Please could you confirm that?'

'Yes. Since my divorce I've rented the house I'm in.'

'You also told us you have outstanding child support payments. Could you explain in more detail?'

'I got behind and couldn't afford to catch-up. In the end I stopped paying. The ex-wife knows my job's not secure, and that I'm struggling, but she still wants money out of me. Even though she's now living with another man.' He clenched his fists and banged them on the table.

'I'd say it was more that the wife is with someone else, than job insecurity,' George said in her ear.

'You say money is tight, yet you can afford to go to the pub most nights,' Whitney narrowed her eyes.

'I've got to do something with my time. Do you know how boring it is to sit on your own, night after night?'

'How do you feel about your wife having found another partner?'

He glared at her. '*Ex*-wife. I don't care what she does.'

'Not true,' George said. 'It's written all over his face, check those tight lines around his mouth.'

'We've been informed that you always went to the pub on the nights Rita Selwyn worked. Is that correct?' He looked away and bowed his head. 'Mr Hawkins, please answer the question.'

'Yes. She was always kind and approachable, and we'd have good conversations. She didn't put me down every time we spoke.'

'Unlike his wife, I expect. Continue with this line of questioning,' George said.

Whitney gave a slight nod. 'Was she different from your ex-wife?'

'No comparison. Rita was a total opposite. And now you're telling me she's dead.' Tears formed in his eyes and he blinked them away.

Were they fake? Was he regretting what he'd done?

'Do you think Rita acted differently towards you than she did to other customers in the pub?'

'I don't know.'

'Did you see her being rude to them?' Whitney pushed.

'No, she wasn't like that. What are you getting at?' He scowled in her direction.

'You're riling him,' George said.

Good. That was when the truth came out.

'What I'm saying is, she didn't single you out for special treatment.'

'I suppose not. But she was still nice to me.'

'Which means, although you had a thing for her, it wasn't reciprocated,' Whitney said.

He bristled 'You don't know that.'

'Do you know where Rita lived?'

'Yes.'

'How do you know?'

'I just do.'

'Answer the DCI's questions, and stop acting like a dick,' Frank snapped.

Hawkins jerked his head back. 'I don't appreciate your rudeness.'

'He wouldn't need to be if you'd answer our questions, instead of skirting around the issue,' Whitney said, taking charge. Although she hadn't wanted Frank to ask questions, he might have moved the interview forward by interrupting.

'One evening we happened to leave the pub at the same time, and I noticed where she drove to. I was on my way home.'

Now they were getting somewhere.

'But she lived in the opposite direction to you,' Whitney said.

The silence hung in the air.

'Okay,' he finally said. 'I followed her home. It's not a crime.'

'I thought you walked to the pub,' Whitney said.

'I was in my car because I'd come straight from work.'

'Had you been drinking?'

'I don't drink much when I'm driving. My job depends on me having my licence.'

'Why did you follow Rita home?' She leant forward and stared directly at him.

'I wanted to make sure she was safe.'

Of course, he did.

'She was in her car,'

'But she still had to go from the car to her front door. There was an opportunity for something bad to happen.'

'Did you notice her car parked outside the pub when you arrived this evening?' Whitney asked, changing the direction of the conversation.

'No. It wasn't there.'

'Were you expecting it to be?'

'No, because she doesn't usually work on a Thursday.'

'Where does she usually park when she's at work?'

'A little way down from the pub.'

'When was the last time you followed her home to *check on* her?'

'Maybe two weeks ago,' he said, his fingers lightly tapping the table.

'That's a lie,' George said.

Whitney gave another slight nod.

'Think again,' Whitney said.

'Last week.' He bowed his head.

'Did she know you'd been following her?'

'I don't think so as I'm careful to keep my distance. All I wanted to do was make sure she got home safely. You can't be too careful, these days. There are a lot of weirdos out there.'

Whitney bit back the temptation to call him out on being one himself.

'What were you doing last night after the pub shut?'

'I drove straight home.'

'Can anyone vouch for you?'

'No.' He shook his head

'And you definitely didn't follow Rita home last night?' she pushed.

'I've already said I went home.'

'Why was that?'

'I didn't do it all of the time in case she got suspicious and thought I was some kind of stalker.'

'Except you had been stalking her, and you sent her flowers on Valentine's Day.'

'I like her. It's not stalking.'

'That's a matter of opinion,' Whitney said. He was hiding something. She knew it. 'What time did you go to work this morning?'

'I didn't go today.'

'Why not?'

'I called in sick.'

'Why?'

'I had quite a bit to drink last night, more than usual.'

'You said you drove home. Were you fit to drive?'

'I wasn't drunk when I left the pub. I had more beer at home.'

'Why was that?'

'I was upset.'

'Over what?' Whitney asked.

'I'd had a phone call from my ex-wife threatening me.'

'How often do you see your children?'

'I haven't seen them for over a year.'

'Why not?'

'My wife was granted full custody and I have no visitation rights. I just have to pay for them.'

'What's the reason for you not being able to see them?'

'No comment,' he said.

Whitney gave a frustrated sigh. 'Don't start that again. You might as well tell us because we're going to find out, eventually.'

'She accused me of assaulting her.'

'Did you?'

'She didn't press charges.'

'That's not what I asked. Did you?'

'I might have got a bit handy with her, but nothing she didn't deserve.'

Whitney glared at him. 'Explain.'

'Ours was a volatile relationship. We fought. It wasn't just me. Have you ever been hit on the head with a saucepan? I'll tell you, it fucking hurts, so if I actually hit back occasionally…that's how it was.' He was the most animated he'd been the whole interview.

Had he tried it on with Rita and when she rebuffed him, took it out on her?

'We're going to need you to stay here until my officers have completed the search of your house.'

'Are you arresting me?'

'No. But we can if you refuse to stay. It's your decision.'

'I've got nothing else to do.' He shrugged.

Whitney's phone rang. It was Matt.

'Interview suspended,' she said, ending the recording. 'Walker.'

'Guv. We're at Hawkins' house. You need to come over, we've got something.'

Her heartbeat quickened. 'Okay. We'll be with you shortly.' She ended the call and looked at Hawkins. 'We've got to go out. You can wait here.'

'Why can't I go home?'

'Because we haven't finished.'

'What if I want to go to the bathroom?'

'There'll be an officer stationed outside of the door. Let him know and he'll take you.'

She left the room with Frank, and George joined them in the corridor.

'What's happening?' George asked.

'Something's turned up at Hawkins' house. Frank, you go back to the incident room and help with the research into his background. George and I will be back later.'

Chapter Nine

Whitney drove them to Hawkins' house and parked behind a patrol car. As they got out, Matt came from the house and headed towards them.

'This had better be good,' Whitney said. 'You interrupted his interview.'

'I think he might be the one. You'll agree when you see what we've found.'

'You think we've caught the murderer already?' George said, frowning.

Whitney looked at her. 'What do you mean *already*? We can solve cases straightaway.'

'That's not what I meant. I'm not convinced he's the killer.'

She'd be as happy as the next person if Hawkins turned out to be their man, but she doubted it was him. The actual murder, the positioning of the body on the heraldic cushion, implied someone with an education and a level of finesse and control. Hawkins hadn't displayed any of those qualities throughout the entire time they'd been with him.

'Let's take a look before we jump to any conclusions,' Whitney said.

They followed Matt upstairs to the bedroom. It was small and bare apart from a wardrobe, chest of drawers, dressing table, and an unmade bed.

'We almost missed it,' Matt said, as he went over to the white dressing table, which had a tall, free-standing mirror on top of it. 'See? The mirror moves.' He flipped it until the rear was on show, revealing photos of the victim taped to the back, together with two pairs of lacy knickers.

'Do they belong to Rita?' Whitney asked.

'I'd bet my pension they do,' Matt said.

'Great find, Matt. Leave everything as it is, and we'll call in SOCO.'

'Did you find anything else of interest?'

'No, guv. Just this.'

'No problem. This is enough for us to arrest him.'

They left Matt waiting for SOCO and returned to the car.

'I'm not convinced it's him,' George said, as they drove off. Whitney might not want to hear it, but she wasn't going to sit back without letting her view be known.

'He's got the motive. He was besotted with her and she didn't return his feelings. How many times have we seen that?'

Whitney was clutching at straws because Jamieson had demanded an early resolution to the case.

'Then why the elaborate death? Did he strike you as clever enough to come up with such a scenario?'

'If he was in love with Rita that could account for him making her comfortable in death and leaving her on the cushion.'

'What about the coat of arms?'

'It could have been a cushion he found or bought without knowing anything about the crest on there.'

'That aside, if it was him, what is the significance of both stabbing *and* drowning?'

'To make sure he'd completed the job. He might have thought she was still alive after he stabbed her.' Whitney sighed. 'Even if you are right, we still have to investigate.'

'Did you notice the bathroom only had a shower? No bath. So where did the actual murder take place?' she asked.

'Again, that's for us to find out.' There was a slight hesitancy in Whitney's voice. Was she beginning to accept George's premise?

'Are you reinterviewing him as soon as we get back to the station?' George asked.

'After we've been to see the team.'

As soon as they entered the incident room, Whitney called the team to attention. 'Listen up, everybody. We may have found our killer. John Hawkins, who we've got downstairs.'

'Nice work, guv,' Frank said. 'What did Matt find at the house?'

'Photos and other items we believe may have belonged to the victim. I'm about to interview him again. Ellie, what else do you have for me?'

'In addition to the assault charge, police were called out to Hawkins' house twice when he lived with his wife, but it wasn't taken further. He doesn't have a social media presence. Financially, there's not a lot of money. Very little in his bank account.'

'Okay. Sue, CCTV?'

They walked over to where the officer was sitting, facing her computer screen.

'I didn't see Hawkins' car following her when she left

the pub last night. There's footage of her leaving, but the cameras stopped shortly after she turned into one of the residential areas. She appeared to be heading in the direction of her home.'

'Did you see Hawkins leave the pub?'

'Yes, about ten minutes after Rita.'

'Did he drive in the same direction?'

'Yes, guv.'

'That's the opposite direction from where he lives. George, you can come with me to speak to him again.'

They left the incident room and headed to the interview room. There was a uniformed officer waiting outside the door.

'Any trouble?' Whitney asked him.

'No, guv. He hasn't made a move.'

'Thanks.'

They walked into the room and Whitney pressed the interview equipment. 'Interview resumed. Dr Cavendish replacing Detective Constable Taylor.'

His demeanour had changed since George had last observed him through the two-way window. There was a tightness around his eyes and his arms were folded tightly across his chest.

'About time, too,' he said, glaring at them. 'I've been waiting for ages and nobody even offered me a cup of tea.'

'This isn't a café,' Whitney said. 'John Hawkins, I'm arresting you on suspicion of the murder of Rita Selwyn. You do not have to say anything, but it may harm your defence if you do not mention something which you later rely on in court. Anything you do say may be given in evidence. Do you understand?' He stared unblinking at them. 'Do you understand?' Whitney repeated, only louder.

'You've got this all wrong. I do understand what you're saying, but it's crazy.'

'You are entitled to legal representation. We can appoint a duty solicitor for you, or you can call a solicitor of your own choice.'

George took a sideways glance at Whitney. The determined expression on the officer's face was enough to show she wanted to be convinced of his guilt. Time would tell.

'I don't have one, as you know. You'll have to call the duty solicitor.'

'I'll arrange that. In the meantime, one of my officers will check you in to the system and escort you to one of the cells.'

'Tell me what's going on? Why did you decide to arrest me?'

'When we went to your house, we found incriminating evidence behind the mirror.'

His face drained of colour. 'J-just because I've got some photos and things belonging to Rita doesn't mean I'm the one who murdered her.'

The whole fight left his body and he slumped in the chair.

'We will discuss this further when your solicitor arrives. Come with us to the custody sergeant.'

'I'm innocent. I didn't do it,' he said, as he followed them out of the interview room.

Chapter Ten

I hum along with the music playing on the radio. This is when I'm at my happiest. When I can survey my handiwork and see my plans coming to fruition. I've made sure everywhere is clean and tidy in anticipation of my next victim.

Another person who deserves exactly what they have coming to them.

Slight me at your peril. That's my message to anyone who comes in contact with me. Because you could regret it, more than you'd ever imagined possible.

If I say so myself, I'm extremely proud of doing such an exceptional job with the first one. I'd like to see anyone else coming up with the idea of murdering in that way.

I'm a fucking genius. And God help anyone who disagrees.

The next murder will be as interesting as the first.

Because now I'm beginning to implement the second part of my plan.

My murders are not simply individual events. Think of them as being like a symphony, where all of the instruments come together to produce a piece of pure magnificence.

They are a work of art. Designed for me to be remembered forever, for my ingenuity and expertise.

I'm going to prove to my family that I'm better than all of them put together.

Chapter Eleven

Whitney glanced up from eating her cereal as George walked into the kitchen and headed for the kettle. Her head ached from the amount of wine they'd consumed the previous evening, but a couple of painkillers would cure it, if she could be bothered to get up and find them. They'd had an Indian takeaway as, by the time they'd left work, they couldn't be bothered to stop at the supermarket and, after discussing the case, had spent the rest of the evening talking about the fix George's dad had got himself into.

'I've got to go into work today,' George said.

'No problem. I'll drop you off.' She finished her last mouthful and took the bowl to the kitchen sink.

'I can drive myself.'

'It's up to you, but remember you could still be under scrutiny by the media, and they'll notice you if you're in your own car. Why don't you let me take you? I can pick you up later when you're ready to come home. Unless you don't want to keep being seen in my car.' Whitney grinned, but she meant it.

'Thank you. That's an excellent idea. Sorry I can't

work on the case today, but I've got a pile of admin to do. What are your plans?'

'First, I'm heading back to Rita Selwyn's house. I want to interview the husband again now he's had time to process the murder. He might be able to provide further insight into Hawkins' obsession with Rita.'

'Yes, she could have shared useful information with him.'

George had some breakfast and, after dropping her off at work, Whitney phoned Matt to let him know where she was going. She knocked on the door of the Selwyns' house and Caroline answered. The FLO was dressed in casual jeans and a T-shirt. As much as her role was to support the family and act as a liaison, she was also there to watch and listen, making sure nothing sinister was going on that the family hadn't admitted to. By not wearing a uniform it made it easier for her to blend in and observe anything out of the ordinary.

'Good morning, guv,' she said.

'How's it going in there?'

'Much as could be expected, the kids seem to be getting on with things and are spending the majority of time in their rooms playing video games.'

'And David?'

'He mainly sits in the lounge, not knowing what to do with himself. It's not like he can be busy with funeral arrangements, as we don't know when Rita's body will be released. He doesn't talk much, although I have tried to engage him in conversation.'

It was a complex situation for her to navigate. Although she was there to aid the investigation, she couldn't force the issue when the family was so grief-stricken.

'Has he mentioned *anything* which might help with the enquiry?'

'Not so far. I've asked him several times if he could think of anyone who might have wanted to harm Rita, but all he says is no. Everyone loved her.'

'What about his wider family? Has he asked any of them to be with him?'

'No, he's adamant he wants to be alone with the children.'

'Has he talked about Rita in a more general sense? What she was like? How their relationship was? How she interacted with the children?'

It was like clutching at straws. If Caroline was unable to get him to open up, it was unlikely she would either.

'Not really. He's been on autopilot. When he's not making meals for the children, he's sitting staring into space. Looking after them is what's keeping him going. I've offered to help, but he wants to do everything himself.'

'Okay. I'm going to have a chat with him.'

They walked into the lounge together and David Selwyn glanced up.

'Would you like me to get you a tea or coffee?' Caroline offered.

'Coffee would be great,' Whitney said, hoping another injection of caffeine would help the headache, as she'd forgotten to take any pills. 'How are you coping?' she asked David, once the FLO had left the room.

'How do you think?' he replied, the pain in his eyes almost tangible. 'I still can't believe it. I keep hoping Rita's going to walk through the front door as if nothing has happened. But I know she won't. Not after seeing her at the morgue.' He leant forward and rested his head in his hands, emitting a low groan.

Whitney's insides clenched. She wanted to reach out

and give him a hug, tell him that it would all be okay, and he'd get over it. But she knew nothing of his life. And it wouldn't be professional. However unlikely it seemed he could be Rita's killer.

'What about the children, how are they handling it?'

He sat upright and for the first time made eye contact with her.

'It's difficult to say as they're spending a lot of time in their rooms, on their laptops. Normally we limit their screen time, but this is far from normal, so I'm letting them stay on there for as long as they want. What else can they do? I don't want them to go back to school until after the funeral. But I don't know when that will be,' he said, his jaw clenched.

'Unfortunately, it's out of our hands. You have to wait until the coroner has released Rita's body before the funeral can be arranged.'

'I understand,' he said, emitting a painful sigh.

'During our investigation we came across a man called John Hawkins. He was a customer in the pub where Rita worked. Did she ever mention him to you?'

'She hardly ever talked about her work. It's not like it was her career. Just a way of bringing some money in.' He frowned slightly. 'Actually, she did mention one guy who she thought fancied her. Is that who you're talking about? He sent her some flowers.'

'She told you about that?' Whitney asked, surprised he'd taken it so calmly.

'Yes. Why wouldn't she? We had that kind of relationship. No secrets. She said he was harmless.'

'And you didn't mind?' She couldn't hide the surprise in her voice. Most men she knew wouldn't take it so well. What did it mean? George would know.

'I didn't *like* it, but the fact she told me was proof it didn't mean anything.'

'I'm sorry to tell you, but we have reason to believe he'd been stalking Rita. He knows where you live.' She left him to draw the inevitable conclusion.

'You think it's him?' He lifted his trembling palm up to his chest.

'We're still investigating, but he certainly had more than a passing fancy for her. Did Rita complain about anything going missing recently?'

She hated having to broach this.

'What do you mean?'

'Did she lose any underwear? Possibly off the washing line.'

'Not that I know of. She hardly ever hung it out, preferring it to go into the dryer.'

Not what Whitney wanted to hear. If Hawkins hadn't got it from the line, there was only one other place.

'Does anyone have keys to your house? Or had you or Rita lost your keys recently?'

'What?' His whole body tensed. 'You think he came in here?' He stared at her, his eyes like saucers. 'Did he have underwear belonging to Rita? Is that why you're asking?'

Whitney took out her phone and pulled up a photo of the two pairs of white lacy knickers they'd found in Hawkins' bedroom. She sat beside David on the sofa.

'Please look at this photo. Do you recognise these?' She held her phone out and he stared at it.

'Oh. My. God.' The colour drained from his face. 'Those are Rita's. That means he's been here. I'll kill the bastard if I see him,' he said, his eyes flashing.

'We don't know for certain that he came into your home uninvited,' she said, wanting to placate him.

'Rita would have mentioned if he'd turned up. As far

as I know, she had no idea he knew where we lived. Rita was home during the day, so if he came in, he must have waited for her to go out.'

That made sense. But how would he have got into the house?

'Assuming he did come in while Rita was out, could he have got in at all?'

'Yes. It's possible,' he said leaning forward and clutching his head in both hands. 'Ever since the time Rita locked herself and the children out, we've kept a set of door keys hidden in the front garden. He must have known. How though?'

'Maybe she mentioned it in the pub. Or he'd been watching her. You said she didn't usually hang underwear on the line but in this instance, maybe she did.'

'I guess so,' he said.

'Let's go and check to see if the key is still there,' Whitney suggested.

He got up and she followed him out of the front door and into the garden. He stopped beside a row of flowerpots.

'It's here.' He lifted the one that was third from the path and under the living room window. There was nothing there. 'It's gone. He must have taken it.'

'Check under the other pots,' she said.

'It won't be under any of them. The reason we chose the third one is because both the children were born on the third of the month.'

'Let's just check,' Whitney said, bending down and lifting up the pots. The keys were under the sixth. 'Here they are.'

'We didn't put them there.'

Whitney pulled out an evidence bag. 'I'll take the keys and get them dusted for prints.' They headed back inside –

David like a zombie at the realisation someone had been inside their home – and returned to the lounge.

'Are you sure Rita wasn't concerned by his behaviour when she was at work?'

'Yes. She was used to customers liking her. It had happened in other pubs she'd worked.'

'Where were these?'

'In Birmingham.'

'Did she always tell you what happened at work?'

'Yes, of course. People would come into the bar and confide in her. Usually men.'

'And you didn't mind?'

'You've already asked me this. I trusted her. She'd said her boss watched out for all of the staff, so I knew nothing was going to happen… Except it did.' He collapsed in on himself and let out a large groan. 'I'm never going to see her again. She'd worked in pubs for years with no problems. She felt safe because she drove herself there and back. How are we meant to carry on without her?'

The door opened and Caroline came in carrying a tray with three mugs of coffee.

'I've been explaining to David that we're aware of someone who'd been following Rita and knew where they lived. We'll be investigating further and will keep him up to speed.'

After finishing her coffee, Whitney walked to the door with Caroline following.

'We've arrested someone, but I don't want David to know until we've confirmed our suspect's guilt. But it's looking most likely.'

She dismissed the nagging doubt in her mind that George's comments had caused.

'I won't mention anything,' Caroline said.

'Stay with him. He's in a bad way and appears about to

break. Try to convince him to call some family.'

'Yes, guv.'

'If you can't, find out why. Is he running from something? Or someone? We haven't yet got her computer back from forensics. There might be something on there which might point to any family issues.'

Whitney drove back to the station, thoughts of David Selwyn and his family at the forefront of her mind. On her way to the incident room, she caught sight of Jamieson heading towards her. She inwardly groaned.

'Sir,' she said, giving a nod.

'I understand you've been to see the victim's husband and mentioned to him about the stalker who's now in custody.'

How did he know? She hadn't briefed him yet. Which one of the team had blabbed?

'Yes, sir, we've arrested someone and I've put in a request to keep him in custody for ninety-six hours. It gives us time to get everything lined up.'

'I'll chase it up and make sure it comes through pronto. Excellent work. It's about time we managed to solve a murder straightaway instead of having it hanging around until we're faced with another one.' He flashed a self-satisfied smile.

What had made him so cheerful?

'Well, sir, if this is down to who we've got in custody, then there won't be any more murders. But we do need to find out his motive and why he murdered in that particular way. His guilt is not a foregone conclusion.'

'You know what these stalkers are like. Maybe he asked her to leave her husband and she turned him down flat, making him look an idiot in front of others in the pub?'

'It will all be part of the investigation,' she said, her hands clenching into fists at her side. He nodded his dismissal and she stalked back to the incident room. The usual chatter filled the room and she jumped on the table, standing with her hands on her hips.

'Right,' she shouted. They went silent. 'Who's been talking to Jamieson?' She scanned her team, searching for the guilty person.

'What do you mean, guv?' Matt said.

'I've just bumped into him and he knows everything, despite me not having briefed him yet. He knew all about Hawkins being in custody. He also knew that I'd been around to see David Selwyn. How?'

'It's not me,' Matt said, vigorously shaking his head.

'Nor me,' Frank added.

The others all muttered the same.

'How the hell does he know then?' she growled.

'He must have some other way of finding out,' Doug said. 'Someone who knows the victim's family.'

'The only person there was Caroline, the FLO.'

'Has she got a hotline to Jamieson, do you think?' Doug asked.

Had she? Jamieson had been interested to know which FLO was on the case. He'd also been sprucing himself up. Were they …? She supposed it could be possible. But why would Caroline want to be with him? Whitney would sooner walk over hot coals than consider a relationship with him. She shook her head and relegated those thoughts to the back of her mind.

'From now on, things stay within these four walls. I will inform Jamieson when we have anything to report, so as to keep misinformation from spreading.' She clambered down from the table and walked over to Matt, pulling out the bag containing the door key from her pocket. 'Get these dusted for prints. I'm going to my office. Let me know when the duty solicitor arrives.'

Chapter Twelve

George tapped her foot on the gravel path as she waited to be collected from work. She'd give it a couple more minutes and if Whitney still wasn't there, she'd walk to her own house. Staying somewhere else and being held to ransom by the media had grown extremely tiresome.

She glanced up as an ancient Ford pulled into the car park. Whitney drove up beside her and she got in.

'Sorry I'm late. I was interviewing John Hawkins.'

'And?' George strapped herself into the car and frowned.

She still wasn't convinced they'd got their murderer. He hardly seemed capable of such scheming.

'He denied the murder and said it's nothing to do with him. We do know he'd been into the Selwyns' house. His prints were on the spare set of keys they kept outside, so whatever happens he'll be charged with unlawful entry. We need to track his movements, and go through his house again, looking for something else to connect him to Rita. The team's working on it. Let's get home. I could do with a drink.'

'I'll cook dinner, as I didn't last night.'

'That sounds great, thanks.'

'What have you got in?'

'Not a lot. You know, the usual, some five-minute noodles. Tins of beans. Some pasta,' Whitney said.

George grimaced. It sounded like something her students might eat. How could anyone live like that?

'Let's stop off on the way and pick up some real food. What do you fancy?'

'Surprise me,' Whitney said, as they headed to the supermarket.

Back at the house, George busied herself in the kitchen, cracking eggs and chopping spinach for a green frittata. The last time she'd made it was when she was with Ross.

She paused and rolled her shoulders. There had been several text messages from him since her father's name had been splashed across the papers.

If you need to talk, I'm here.

She hadn't replied, though. Unsure if it was because she *did* want to see him, or because she *didn't*. All she knew was there were too many other things on her plate to think about it.

She finished cooking and after they'd eaten and cleaned up, they sat in the lounge with a glass of wine.

'I'm going back home tomorrow,' she said.

'Why?' Whitney asked.

'I can't thank you enough for allowing me to stay here, but I need to get back to some sort of normality. I doubt they're still hanging around waiting for me. There have been other stories in the media now. My father is old news.'

'It's up to you,' Whitney said. 'You're welcome to stay here as long as you'd like. It's no trouble.'

'Thank you for your offer, but I'm looking forward to

spending the weekend at home, unless you want me in tomorrow.'

'No, we won't need you. The team are on top of the investigation and there's nothing more you can add. I'll call you if anything changes. You've got your parents to worry about, anyway. Have you decided whether you're going to London to see them?'

'Not yet. They haven't asked me to. In fact, I haven't yet spoken to either of my parents, although my brother is keeping me up to date. After the initial arrest, my father has been let out on bail.'

'At least he's not in custody. It could have easily happened. Though I'm guessing he's got a hotshot lawyer in his corner.'

George didn't know who her father's lawyer was but could say with certainty it would be a well-known legal expert.

'He's hardly a flight risk,' she said.

'Some wouldn't agree. With his money, he could easily hire a private jet and take off somewhere with no extradition treaty with this country.'

'He's not a gangland criminal. If he took off, it would be the end of his illustrious career. He'd want to fight this,' she stated in an authoritative voice.

'Good. I'm here if you change your mind about being alone at home. Or if the media are still there.'

'Thanks. I'll remember that.'

She wouldn't be hounded out of her own house by the press any longer. They wouldn't be able to see her once she was firmly ensconced inside. Which was exactly where she intended to stay for the weekend.

'But more to the point, I can't decide what to do about tomorrow night,' Whitney said, biting down on her bottom lip.

'What's happening?' She didn't remember her friend mentioning anything.

'I've got a school reunion which, foolishly, I decided to attend. But now I'm not sure.'

She couldn't think of anything worse.

'Have you been to one before?' she asked.

'No. Usually I discard the invites as soon as they arrive in my inbox. For some reason, this one I kept, telling myself that if I went it would show people I'd made something of my life, despite leaving school when I was seventeen and pregnant. Although they didn't know about the pregnancy. I kept that from everyone.'

'You might enjoy it.' George said.

'It's not like I need to impress any of them. I must have been having a bad day when it arrived. Probably missing Tiffany.'

George glanced at her friend. Most of the time she hid how much she hated her daughter not being there by burying herself in her work.

'Go, and show them,' she encouraged. 'You can't work on the murder case twenty-four-seven, especially now you have someone in custody. You'll have fun.'

Well, she assumed Whitney would have fun. She'd never been to a school reunion herself and didn't intend to. Her school days were best put to the back of her mind. Her best friend had committed suicide while they were at boarding school and George had been the one to find her. It was indelibly etched on her mind. She'd never forget it.

'I'll think about it,' Whitney said, taking a sip of wine. 'Just to change the subject, I must tell you about Jamieson. It's most odd. Two things. First of all, he was almost nice to me regarding solving the case. Also, he knew details about having Hawkins in custody before I'd told him. He knew I'd been to see David Selwyn and his family, and what the family liaison officer had told me, even before I got back. When I asked the team if any of them had blabbed, they all denied it. I believe them, they had no cause to lie.'

'Apart from you going off on one for them speaking to him,' George said, a wry smile on her face.

'They're used to my occasional outbursts,' Whitney said, waving her hand dismissively. 'Anyway, it hit me. Jamieson is having a fling with Caroline, the FLO. What else could it be? Can you imagine? What on earth does she see in him?'

'How would I know?' George said, laughing. Whitney in gossip mode was a delight and always amused her.

'I'll keep an eye out for any more telltale signs and let you know. Even if you're not interested. But, one thing's for sure. From now on I'll be very careful what I say in front of her.'

Chapter Thirteen

Whitney peered at herself in the mirror. Where the hell had all those wrinkles come from? She really should embark on a skincare regime. In an ideal world, maybe, but nowadays she hardly had time to dab on some face cream every morning.

What should she wear? She had no idea what people wore to a school reunion. She flicked through the clothes in her wardrobe, throwing anything on to the bed which seemed remotely suitable. Standing in front of the mirror, she held up each garment in turn and eventually decided on a sleeveless cream shift, with tiny green flowers. She teamed it with a cream cardigan and a pair of heels. Was it too matronly? She was going to be forty in a couple of years and, as well as not wanting to dress too young for her age, she didn't want to look like an old fuddy-duddy.

After spending longer than usual on her make-up, she chugged back a glass of wine and left. She needed to be careful not to drink too much as she didn't want to be over the limit. She drove to the venue, a hotel in the centre of the city. Outside was a six-foot sign saying 'North

Lenchester Academy Reunion in the Wellington Room'. The only time she'd been to the hotel was many years ago when she was on the beat and she'd been called to a fight.

The Wellington Room was long and wide with white walls and dim lighting. It was filled with people laughing and chatting. She stiffened. This was a mistake. She had no difficulty speaking to anyone while doing her job, but when faced with a room full of people she hadn't seen for years…that was different. She swallowed hard and was about to leave when a voice called out.

'Are you Whitney Walker?' a woman sitting at a table full of badges asked, giving a beaming smile and flashing a set of brilliant white teeth.

Veneers? Or false? Definitely not her own.

'I am, yes.'

'It's me, Charlotte Long. You knew me as Charlotte Potter.'

Whitney wracked her brain and couldn't remember the name. Why hadn't she looked back over her old school photos before coming, to remind herself who everyone was?

Because she was too busy with the murder enquiry.

'Great to see you,' she said, returning the smile. 'How are you doing?'

'I'm a stay-at-home mum. I have three boys aged nine, seven, and five. They're such a handful, but I'm lucky I don't have to go out to work. My husband, Darren, is an architect,' Charlotte said proudly, in what clearly had to be a cultivated accent. No one from their school spoke like that.

Whitney just about managed not to roll her eyes. So *this* was a school reunion. An evening of one-upmanship.

'That's nice. Do you still live in Lenchester?' she asked.

'Yes, in Pennington Grove.'

Of course she did. The really posh part of the city.

'I know the area,' she said.

'What happened to you? All I remember is you left school after the first year of A-levels.'

'Yes, that's right. I was fed up and decided to leave.' She wasn't going to tell her the real reason.

'Do you work?'

'I'm a police officer.'

Not impressive compared with being an architect, and the money certainly not enough for a property in Pennington Grove.

'Super. That must be interesting. Have you done it for long?'

'Over twenty years.'

'You must see all sorts of things in your line of work. I'm not sure I could do anything like that.' She wrinkled her nose. 'Are you a constable?'

Why did she assume that? Because anyone who'd dropped out of school was bound not to have a high-flying career.

Stop. This isn't a pissing contest.

'No. I'm a detective chief inspector.'

The woman's eyes widened. 'Goodness. You have done very well for yourself, haven't you?'

'Yes, I like to think so. Where's the bar?' She'd had enough of this conversation.

'At the back of the room,' Charlotte said, pointing. 'I'm sure you'll recognise lots of people on the way. Obviously, once they find out you're a police officer, they might clam up a bit.' She gave a false laugh.

'I'm well used to that,' Whitney said flatly as she walked away.

She headed over to the bar and ordered herself a soft drink. She'd save her single glass of wine for later. That's if she stayed much longer because, from where she was standing, it was unlikely. She'd claim to have been called away to work.

She took a sip of her drink and scanned the room. There were plenty of people there, all standing in small groups. Despite what Charlotte had said, she didn't recognise any of them. How come they seemed to know each other? Had they all kept in contact over the years?

'Is it Whitney?' She turned at the sound of the male voice.

It belonged to an attractive man of medium height, with dark curly hair. There was a small scar above one eye and a familiar smile tugged at his mouth. Her stomach dropped. It was Martin Finch.

Tiffany's father.

'Y-yes.' Heat rushed up her cheeks. Thank heavens the lights had been dimmed. She didn't want the embarrassment of him seeing her cheeks bright red.

'Do you remember me?'

She gave a hollow laugh. 'How could I forget,' she said. And then she remembered he didn't know about her being pregnant with Tiffany because she hadn't told him. It was the result of a drunken night she'd chosen to forget.

'What are you doing here? I couldn't imagine this being your scene,' he said, smiling.

His brown eyes twinkled and suddenly she was seventeen again, remembering just why she'd slept with him. She shook her head. No. She couldn't think anything about him. She'd always referred to him as a waste of space. But, then again, he'd been a kid back then. They both had. Was he actually like that? It didn't matter as it had all happened twenty-one years ago.

'It's the first one I've been to and will definitely be the

last. I'm not quite sure what was going through my head when I decided to come. You?'

'I don't travel to Lenchester often, and then only to visit my mother. Unfortunately, she died recently, and I came back to arrange the funeral and sort out her things.'

'I'm sorry to hear about your mum,' she said.

'Thank you. I had nothing planned for this evening and remembered the invite so decided to stick my head in. Although I got reprimanded by *Charlotte* for not letting them know, as there was no badge for me.'

He seemed nicer than she'd remembered. Not that she'd known him well at school because although they were in the same year they were in different forms and took different subjects, so their paths seldom crossed.

'Oh dear,' she said, grinning. 'What do you do now?' she asked, immediately wanting to kick herself for being the same as the others who were there.

'I work in banking, in London.'

A banker? She didn't remember him being one of the clever ones at school.

'Away from Lenchester.'

She'd wanted to leave the city once, but circumstances were never right for her to do so. Now, she couldn't imagine living anywhere else.

'After school I took a gap year and travelled all around South America, and Asia. Then I came back and studied commerce at university in London. After that I went into finance.'

'Are you married?' Where the hell did that question come from and why did she want to know? This wasn't a police interview.

'I was. My wife died several years ago.'

'I'm so sorry.'

'Thank you.'

Did Tiffany have any brothers and sisters? What if the answer was yes? Should she tell her daughter? Ask Martin if they could meet up? Perhaps it was best if she didn't find out.

'Do you have any children?' she asked, unable to stop herself. Clearly her mouth was ignoring her head.

'No. We couldn't have any.' A dark shadow clouded his face for a second, then it vanished as quickly as it had arrived. 'What about you? What job do you do?'

How much was she going to tell him? She couldn't be rude and say mind your own business, considering she'd just grilled him.

'I'm in the police force.'

'That doesn't surprise me,' he said, a wry smile on his lips.

'Really?' That she didn't expect. 'You must be the only person. Most people don't believe it when I tell them,' she said, not adding that it was because of her height. Or lack of it.

'You always had that *don't mess with me* air about you.'

She leant against the bar, trying to appear casual when in fact she was finding his comments disturbing.

'How do you know that? We hardly knew each other?'

'You stood out among the other students.'

What?

'Me?' She gave a hollow laugh.

'Yes, but I was too nervous at that age to do anything about it.' He gave a small shrug.

This was doing her head in. She was face to face with Tiffany's dad who was turning out to be the total opposite from how she'd firmly planted him in the recesses of her mind.

'Well, not quite,' she said, not quite able to return his gaze.

'I'm sorry about that.' He flushed. 'I do remember we'd had rather a lot to drink that night.'

'You could say,' she said, taking a large swallow of her soft drink and wishing it was something stronger.

'Afterwards…I'd thought maybe we could go out. But you ignored me every time I was anywhere close.'

That wasn't how she'd remembered it. Then again …

'Water under the bridge now,' she said, wincing at the cliché she'd trotted out.

'Are you married? Children?' he asked.

'I've never been married, apart from to my job.' She gave a laugh at her attempt at humour, which sounded false. 'But I do have a daughter, Tiffany.'

She has your eyes.

'Pretty name. Does she go to school locally?'

'She was at university studying engineering, but she dropped out during her third year and now she's travelling in Australia.'

'At university?' His eyes narrowed. 'You must have had her when you were very young.'

Whitney's insides clenched. This was getting too close for comfort.

'It's been lovely catching up, but I've really got to go. Just before you came to talk to me, I had a text from one of my team. We're working on an important case at the moment that needs my attention.'

Okay, it was a lie. But it could easily be the truth.

'Can I see you again while I'm here?' He locked eyes with her, and her heart did a triple flip.

'I don't think that's a good idea.'

'For old times' sake. I'm not here for long.' He smiled and two dimples appeared in his cheeks. It was so tempting.

'I'm not sure we'd have anything to talk about,' she said, dismissively.

'We might.'

Did she want to see him again? What about Tiffany?

'Here's my card. Give me a call and we'll see.' She handed it to him, and he looked at it, slowly nodding.

'Detective Chief Inspector. You've done very well.'

'Thanks. I worked hard to get there.' Was she trying to impress him?

'I don't doubt it. I'll call you,' he said.

'No promises, though,' she said, immediately regretting it as she sounded so dumb.

She hurried away.

What the hell just happened?

Chapter Fourteen

Whitney hung her bag on the back of the chair in her office, determined that today she would concentrate on work and not let her attention be diverted by thoughts of Martin Finch. Yesterday was meant to have been her day off, but with Hawkins in custody she'd decided to come in. She hadn't achieved much as most of the time she'd spent going over in her mind the conversation she'd had with Tiffany's father, and then oscillating between wanting to meet up with him again, to deciding that no way on this earth would she. She was still no closer to an answer.

She slipped off her jacket as Matt burst through the door and marched towards her.

'What is it?' she asked.

'We've got another body, guv.'

'What?' She swallowed as Jamieson's words rang out in her mind.

'A woman found in the woods. The exact same spot.'

Her heart sank. It was exactly what she didn't need first thing on a Monday morning. Then something else occurred to her. Hell. 'We've still got Hawkins in custody. You know what that means, don't you?'

'He couldn't have done it. Shall I arrange to have him released?' Matt asked.

'Not until he's charged with illegally entering the Selwyns' house and stealing Rita's underwear.'

'I'll arrange for that to be done.'

'Thanks. Also, contact SOCO and the pathologist and inform them of this latest murder. I'll see if George can meet me at the scene. '

'Do you want me there as well, guv?'

'No. You can coordinate everything from here.'

'Will do.'

'By the way, you didn't tell me the results of your appointment at the hospital. Is it good news?'

'Yes. Very.' He grinned.

'I'm thrilled for you. Let me know when you decide to share the news, so we can have a celebration.'

'Okay,' he said, turning and heading back to the incident room.

Whitney pulled out her phone and hit the speed dial for George.

'Where are you?' she asked, not even bothering to say hello.

'About to leave for work.'

'How was it over the weekend?' She was safe asking because George wouldn't think to ask her about Saturday. She always waited for Whitney to volunteer information.

'Fine. I managed to get plenty of work done and didn't go out. The media seem to have left me alone for now. Thank goodness. Why are you phoning? It sounds urgent.'

'It is. We have another body, left in the same place as the first.'

'It couldn't have been Hawkins as he was in custody,' George said.

'You've got it in one. I'm going to the scene. Can you meet me there?'

'Yes. Do you want me to pick you up?'

'It's quicker if we go separately,' Whitney said.

Which wasn't the actual reason. She still wasn't sure whether she wanted to discuss Saturday night, and she knew that as soon as she was with George she wouldn't be able to stop herself from blurting out everything. She needed to devote her attention to this latest body.

'As you wish. I'll meet you there shortly.'

'Okay.'

Whitney ended the call and then left for the woods. She was there within fifteen minutes. The area was cordoned off and a uniformed officer, Constable Murray, stood at the entrance. She walked over and signed herself in.

'Who found the body?' she asked Murray.

'We did. PC Smith and I arrived earlier. We were asked to check on the area during our patrol and we came across it.'

For such a new officer she seemed remarkably calm after what she'd witnessed.

'What time was that?' Whitney asked.

'A few minutes after eight this morning, guv.

'Is this your first body?'

Murray hadn't been in the force long. Whitney could remember in graphic detail the first time she'd been to a murder scene. Luckily it was outside, as she'd spent half an hour throwing up behind a tree.

'No, guv. I interned at the morgue before choosing to join the force. At the time I was thinking about going into pathology.'

'That explains your reaction, or lack of, to finding the body,' she said.

'Yes,' Murray agreed. 'Plus, there's no blood or anything gruesome down there.'

'Okay. I want a report from you and Smith as soon as possible.'

'Yes, guv.'

The sound of a car engine distracted her. It was George.

She headed over to meet her. 'Hi.'

'What do we know about the victim?' George asked.

'Nothing yet. We'll find out more when we get there.'

They walked into the woods, keeping to the footplates, until reaching the clearing which was surrounded by blue-bells. The victim was lying on the ground, her head resting on a red cushion. It was just possible to make out the sides of the coat of arms on it.

'No sign of being stabbed,' Whitney said. 'Yet, the cushion and everything else is the same. What did she die of? She looks perfectly healthy to me.'

'She might have been poisoned,' George said.

'What makes you say that?'

'The pink colour of her face. Some poisons can do that to a person, in particular cyanide.'

'Let's have a look around the scene before Claire gets here.'

'Step back. Step back,' the pathologist called from behind.

Too late.

'Good morning,' they both said as Claire headed towards them.

'Is it? Is it really? Another body found first thing in the morning. This is getting to be a little too repetitive. Let me get on.' She strode past them. 'What do we know? Let's have a look,' Claire muttered to herself, as she put her bag on the ground and took out her camera.

'It seems to be the same as the last one,' Whitney said.

'Here we go again. Stop trying to assume things without me having gone through the proper procedures,' Claire replied.

'At the moment, we've got another red cushion and a dead body in about the same place. It doesn't take the *Brain of Britain* to work that out,' Whitney snapped.

Claire stopped what she was doing and stared at her open-mouthed, as did George.

'What?' Whitney said, pressing her lips into a thin line.

'Is something wrong?' George asked.

'No. Why?' she bristled.

'For all your idiosyncrasies, it's not like you to speak to me like that,' Claire said.

'What did I say?' Had she been rude? She didn't think so, at least not in comparison to how the pathologist was to her.

'You can't remember?' Claire said, shaking her head.

'I'm sorry. I've got a lot on my mind. Let's just get on.'

Claire and George shared a puzzled glance.

'That's what I'm trying to do,' Claire said, moving to the side of the body and beginning to take some photos.

'We need to identify the victim, so we can inform the family. Does she have any ID on her?' Whitney asked.

She glanced at the victim. She was tidily dressed in a black skirt, which came a couple of inches above her knee, and a checked shirt. Diagonally across her body was a small, tan coloured handbag.

'Look inside the bag. It will be there if anywhere,' George said.

'Let me take some more photographs before disturbing it and then I'll investigate,' Claire said.

'We'll take a look at the place where we believe the last victim was brought in, to see if there's any evidence there.'

They headed down the path towards the edge of the woods.

'Are you going to tell me what's wrong?' George asked.

'It's nothing. I've got a lot on my mind.'

'Anything you're prepared to share?'

Whitney's brows knitted together as she stared at George. It was unusual for her to offer. She really must have been behaving oddly.

'There is something,' she admitted.

'I thought as much. I'm so much better at interpreting your behaviour than previously.'

'It was Saturday night.'

'Saturday night?' George frowned. 'Oh, the reunion.'

'Yes. The *reunion*.'

'Did you have a good time?'

'No. I left after twenty minutes. But something happened that I didn't expect.'

'It's all sounding very theatrical,' George said. 'It was only a school reunion. Did someone take exception to you being a police officer? Was it someone you'd arrested?'

'No, nothing like that. I met someone I hadn't seen for over twenty years.'

'Hardly surprising because you knew them from school.'

'Except this someone wasn't a person I wanted to meet again. Ever.'

'Stop talking in riddles. Tell me.'

She drew in a calming breath. 'I met Martin Finch.'

'Who's he?'

'Tiffany's father.'

'Oh.' George paused. 'That must have been awkward.'

She could always rely on George for the understatement.

'You could say.'

'Did you tell him about Tiffany?'

'No, of course I didn't. What do you take me for? But he did ask to see me again.'

'Oh.'

'Is *oh* all you can say? Normally you're not backwards in coming forwards with your comments,' Whitney growled. 'Sorry, I didn't mean to be rude. It's just …'

'No problem. Are you going to see him again?'

Whitney ran her fingers through her hair. 'I don't know. I just don't know. We've got too much on at the moment for me to take the time to decide. I'll have to park it and make a decision later.'

Or never. That would be the sensible thing to do. Except there was something about him. Something …

They reached the entrance to the woods and walked around, both of them bending over and scrutinising the area.

'Here are some bark chippings that appear to have been moved,' George said. 'It could be a wheelchair, if we're still assuming that was the way the body was brought through. It's too dry to tell properly, though.'

'I'll get SOCO to take a look. Let's get back to the scene.'

'You can come over here now,' Claire called out, as they came in sight of her. 'In the purse there was a staff photo ID card for the university. Her name was Josie Potts and she worked in the library.'

'Do you know her?' Whitney asked George.

'No, I don't recognise her, but that's not surprising as there are so many people working there.'

'Thanks, Claire. We need to find out where she lives

and inform the family. We'll be in touch once you've completed your post-mortem.'

'Wait a minute, I haven't finished.'

'Sorry. Time of death?' Whitney said, pre-empting her.

'Between midnight and six this morning.'

'Thanks.' Whitney turned to go.

'I still haven't finished, for goodness' sake,' the pathologist growled.

'Well, stop with the drama and tell us,' Whitney said.

'I'll ignore that on account of you not being your usual self. There was a note pushed into the pocket of her shirt.'

'From the killer?'

'That's for you to work out. I've taken a photo and it's now in an evidence bag.' Claire passed it to Whitney.

She glanced at it through the see-through bag. Damn, it was typed. No handwriting to analyse.

'*A second body for your delight. So tranquil in death. A beautiful sight.* What the hell is that meant to mean?'

'That the murderer is a godawful poet?' Claire said.

'What do you make of it?' she asked George, handing her the evidence bag and ignoring Claire's sarcastic comment.

'The use of language makes it most likely the murderer is male.'

'Why?'

'Women tend to use colourful, emotive words, whereas men tend to express themselves more factually.'

'The word *tranquil* is emotive,' Whitney said.

'It is, but as with most things, there's a continuum. You have to look at the note as a whole and see where it fits within the range.'

'Okay, I get it. Anything else?'

'The note also implies that there are more deaths to come.'

'How did you work that out?' Whitney asked.

'He used the word *second*. It's not final. I suspect we've got another serial killer on our hands.'

Whitney threw her hands in the air. 'And here we go again. Jamieson is going to go off on one big time, and our lives are going to be put on hold.'

'But you love it,' Claire said. 'You're never happier than when having to solve serial killer cases.'

'That's ridiculous. Anyway, we still need to speak to this victim's family.'

She pulled out her phone and called Ellie.

'Yes, guv,' the young officer said.

'Our victim is called Josie Potts and she works in the library at the university. Please find me her contact details as soon as possible, so we can inform the family.'

'Yes, guv.'

'Also, ask Frank to check CCTV footage and cars, to see if there are any matches from the first murder.'

She'd let him go back to doing what he liked best.

'You want me to ask him?' Ellie said, a nervous tone in her voice.

For all of the officer's genius on the research front, she was extremely shy when having to deal with others in the team.

'It's okay. Is Matt there?'

'Yes.'

'Call him over.'

'Hello, guv,' Matt said after a few seconds.

'Our victim's name is Josie Potts and Ellie's finding me her contact details. I want you to ensure that Frank checks the CCTV footage to see if we've got any similar vehicles close to the woods around the time of both murders. Also, we need to check whether the victims were linked in any way and—'

'There's something else,' George said, interrupting.

'Hang on a minute, Matt.' Whitney turned. 'What?'

'The paper this note is typed on comes from Porters Conference Centre in Worcester.' She held it up and Whitney saw the cream embossed logo.

'Matt, ask Ellie to research Porters Conference Centre in Worcester. There was a note left on the body and it was typed on some of their paper.'

'I'm on to it. When will we see you?'

'After I've been to see the victim's family.'

'Okay. Ellie's here, she's got the details you requested. I'll pass you over to her.'

'Hello, guv. Josie Potts is single and lives on her own at 28 Russell Street. Her parents, Len and Iris Potts, also live in Lenchester at 365 Dorchester Road.'

'Thanks. We'll go there now.' She ended the call and turned to George. 'Do you have time to come with me to the victim's house to see her family?'

'Yes. But after that, I really need to go to work as I've got a few things on.'

Chapter Fifteen

George pulled up outside the 1930s semi-detached house on Dorchester Road. The garden was neat and tidy, and the outside looked recently painted. Whitney arrived five minutes later, and they headed for the door.

Whitney rang the bell, her face tense, and an older woman, who appeared to be in her early seventies, answered.

'Mrs Potts?' Whitney asked.

'Yes,' she said, looking puzzled.

'I'm Detective Chief Inspector Walker and this is Dr Cavendish.' Whitney held out her warrant card. 'We'd like to come in and have a word with you.'

'Is it about the neighbours? I did call the police, but we didn't expect someone to come around straightaway. It's not an emergency, but we do need it dealt with. I—'

'No, it's not about that,' Whitney interrupted. 'If we could come inside, please. Is your husband here?'

'Yes. He's out in the garden, where he always is.' She fiddled with the single strand of pearls which hung around her neck.

'Could you ask him to come inside, please?'

'Is this serious?' She bit down on her bottom lip.

'We would like to speak to both of you together,' Whitney said gently.

George admired the officer's skill in handling such difficult circumstances. Whitney never faulted in her compassion, despite having had to undertake the task of delivering devastating news on numerous occasions.

'Okay. If you'd like to go into the sitting room, I'll fetch him.' She ushered them into the house and opened the door leading to a square room, which had cream flock wallpaper and was traditionally furnished, with a sand coloured high-backed sofa and matching chairs. Blue patterned cushions added a splash of colour. A large dark-wood sideboard with claw foot legs stood against the back wall.

In keeping with the exterior, it was very clean and tidy, though obviously lived in. George walked over to the fireplace and looked at a photo of the victim in her graduation gown. She stood between two others, one being her mother and the other, George assumed, was her father. There were other family photos, but always only the three of them.

Whitney joined her. 'Only Josie here. Do you think she was an only child?'

'She appears to be,' George said.

'Their lives are going to be destroyed.' Whitney let out a long sigh.

After a few more minutes, Mr and Mrs Potts came into the room. He was tall, slim and alert, with a shock of white hair and pale grey eyes. He, too, looked to be in his early seventies.

'What's all this about?' he asked, looking at each of them in turn.

'Please sit down,' Whitney said.

The couple sat next to each other on the sofa, and Whitney and George sat opposite on the easy chairs.

'Well?' he said.

'We've come to speak to you about your daughter, Josie,' Whitney said.

Mrs Potts' hand clutched at her chest. 'What's happened? Has there been an accident? Is she okay?'

'We found a body in the woods this morning and believe, from the identification she carried, that it's Josie.'

Mrs Potts let out a moan and Mr Potts remained frozen, staring at them as if he hadn't understood what had been said.

'What happened?' Mrs Potts asked.

'We don't have the exact details, but we're treating her death as suspicious. We're waiting to hear back from the pathologist for confirmation about what took place,' Whitney said.

'This sounds like the other death I saw on the news. A woman was murdered and left in Bluebell Woods. Is it the same?' Mrs Potts said.

'Yes, I'm very sorry.'

'Are you sure it's Josie? She doesn't live anywhere near the woods. Surely, it's got to be a mistake,' Mrs Potts said.

'We don't believe it is.' Whitney paused for a few seconds. 'Do you feel up to me asking you some questions?'

Mrs Potts looked up at her husband, who was blinking away some tears. 'Yes,' he said nodding.

'I understand Josie lived on her own.'

'Yes. She moved out of here a couple of years ago to live with her boyfriend. She also wanted to be closer to the university where she worked,' Mrs Potts said.

'We have no record of her living with someone,' Whitney said, frowning.

'She doesn't any more. They split up.'

Could they have an aggrieved ex-boyfriend on their hands? If so, how do they account for the first death? Unless it was a copycat. Except Josie didn't appear to have been stabbed and drowned. But worth investigating, none-theless.

'Do you have his name? We'd like to speak to him,' Whitney said.

'His name is Terry Archer. We don't have his details because he moved overseas. He got a job in Canada last year. He left about six months ago. That was why their relationship ended. He wanted her to go with him, but she wouldn't leave us on our own. We told her to go and that we'd be fine, but she wouldn't. If only she'd gone, she would still be alive.' She began sobbing and tears streamed down her cheeks. Mr Potts placed his arm around his wife's shoulders and pulled her close.

That ruled out the ex-partner.

'When was the last time you saw Josie?' Whitney asked, after Mrs Potts had calmed down a little.

'She came over on Saturday. It was my birthday and we had a family tea, just the three of us. Josie brought a birthday cake she'd made,' Mrs Potts said, sniffing.

'Did she mention seeing anyone suspicious hanging around? Or had she noticed anyone following her?'

'No, she didn't say anything. But she probably wouldn't because we'd worry, and she wouldn't want that. As far as we knew, everything was going well for her. She said now the students had broken up she was getting the library back in order. She'd been looking forward to going on holiday with a friend. They were going to Marbella. She …' her voice broke and she let out another groan and began to shake.

'That's enough,' Mr Potts said, holding up his hand, gesturing for them to stop.

'I understand,' Whitney said. 'We'd like to take a look around Josie's house. Do you have a key we can borrow?'

Mr Potts pulled a set of keys from his pocket and took one off, which he gave to Whitney. 'This is to her front door.'

'Thank you. We'll need someone to formally identify Josie for us. Would you be able to do that?'

'Yes,' Mr Potts said. 'When do you need me to go?'

'Today or tomorrow is fine. Here's my card. Give me a ring when you're ready and I'll arrange for someone to collect you.'

'I want to go too,' Mrs Potts said.

'I don't think that's a good idea,' her husband said, shaking his head.

'I have to see her one last time. How does Josie look? Can we tell it's her? H-has she been—'

'Her face is unharmed,' Whitney said, interrupting. 'As soon as the pathologist has more for us, we'll let you know. We're very sorry for your loss.'

They left the house and walked down the path to where their cars were parked.

'I hate this part of the job,' Whitney said. 'It's so hard. We've totally wrecked those lovely people's lives.'

'No, *we* didn't. The killer is the one who did it. You did your job very well,' George said. 'Nothing can change what happened, but you delivered the news in the best way possible.'

'It still doesn't stop me from feeling like shit,' Whitney said. 'I'm going back to the station.'

'Keep me up to date with the case. I'm quite busy over the next couple of days, but I have pockets of time if you need me.'

'I'll be in touch once we hear back from Claire and know the exact cause of death. I'll need your input then.'

'Or if we get another body,' George said.

Whitney glared at her. 'I'll pretend you didn't say that.'

Chapter Sixteen

Whitney glanced around at her team working. 'I've just come from the parents of our second victim, Josie Potts,' she said as she headed over to the board and wrote the name of the second victim next to the first. 'Matt, did you find any links between the two of them?'

'So far nothing, apart from they were both connected to the university. Rita Selwyn was a part-time student and Josie Potts was a librarian.'

'Rita may have used the library for her studies, so that's another potential link,' Whitney said.

'Yes, guv.'

She wrote up *University* and *Library* on the board.

'Josie lived on her own after splitting up with her boyfriend. He's been in Canada for the last six months, according to the parents. Ellie, I want you to look into it. Make sure that is the case. His name is Terry Archer.'

'Yes, guv,' Ellie said.

'This is a copy of the typewritten note left on this second body. It was written on paper from the Porters Conference Centre in Worcester.' She stuck the copy she'd made to the board. '*A second body for your delight. So tranquil in death. A beautiful sight*,' she read out.

'It sounds like something from a Christmas cracker,' Doug said.

'Yes, even I could do better,' Frank said. 'There was a young man with a bucket, who wanted to try out a—'

'Frank,' Whitney warned. 'Concentrate on the case and not your attempts at poetry. Focus. Dr Cavendish believes it indicates our killer is male and we are to expect more deaths.'

'Does that mean more overtime?' Frank asked.

Really? That was all he was concerned about?

'Maybe. Have you found anything on the CCTV footage of the main roads heading in the direction of the woods?'

'Not yet, guv. But it's hard because of the lack of cameras around there.'

'Keep checking. If it's someone who knows the area well, they could be using back streets, and not appear on camera. But if it's someone who doesn't know the area, they will be on the main roads.'

'But if it is a serial killer, didn't Dr Cavendish once say they very often work in areas familiar to them?' Frank said.

Whitney stared at him open-mouthed.

'Bloody hell, Frank. What's happened to you?' Doug said.

'What do you mean?'

'Since when do you recall anything told to you like that?'

Frank scowled in his direction. 'I'm not totally stupid, you know.'

'No one said you were. But even the guv's jaw dropped,' Doug said, laughing.

Whitney quickly clamped her mouth shut. She didn't

want to be seen belittling the older officer. 'It's something we do have to consider, Frank. But to be sure, check all of the roads coming in and out of the city.'

'Will do,' he said, letting out a sigh.

'Ellie, anything on the conference centre?'

'I've contacted them and asked for a list of all the conferences held this year, together with names of anyone from Lenchester who stayed there. The problem is the centre doesn't keep a record of all conference delegates, so unless they actually used the accommodation, we won't have a complete list. The person I spoke to told me their stationery is left in all of the meeting rooms *and* in the bedrooms. It could be months before we're able to trace every attendee for all of the conferences and meetings they've held there.'

'If you don't hear back from them soon, get in touch again.'

'Yes, guv. They did say it could take a few days, because their conference manager is on holiday.'

'Okay. Keep on top of it. Matt, the parents gave me a key to Josie's house. I want you to go there and see if there's anything that might give us an indication of why she was chosen as a victim. Take Sue with you.'

'Okay,' Matt said.

'I'm going to see Jamieson. He needs to know about the latest body. He'll no doubt want to arrange a press conference.'

She went upstairs to Jamieson's office and knocked on the door. He called out for her to come in.

'Morning, sir.'

'I understand there's been a second death. I read it in the dailies.'

Whitney had to force back her shocked expression. So

often he seemed to miss what was going on until she'd told him. Or his *confidante* did.

'Yes, sir. Another body has been found in Bluebell Woods.'

'Stabbed?'

'We're not sure of the cause of death until we hear from the pathologist, but it didn't appear to have been a stabbing.'

'I thought I said we're not to have any more serial killers.'

'Well, it's not like I've arranged it. Anyway, we need a third death for it to be classified as the work of a serial killer.' She rolled her eyes before she could stop herself.

'There's no need to be facetious, Walker. What do we know so far?'

'Our victim worked at the university library. She lived on her own. I've been to speak to the parents, and at the moment, members of my team are searching her house to see if there's anything that might help us.' Her phone rang and she glanced at the screen. 'I better take this. It's the pathologist.'

'As you wish,' he said, giving a flick of his hand in his usual dismissive way.

'Walker,' she said, answering.

'When are you coming over? I've got some preliminary findings,' Claire said.

'Now,' she said, ending the call and planning to use it as an excuse to leave his office. 'Dr Dexter wants to see me. She has some information regarding this latest death.'

Jamieson stood. 'I'll come with you. I haven't been to the morgue before.'

He had to be kidding. Seriously, that was all she needed. Then again, maybe she could get Claire to subject him to some of her *treatment*. That would prevent all future accompaniments, for sure.

'Okay, sir.' She bit back a smile, as she envisaged his face after Claire had done her worst.

'We'll go in my car.'

She certainly wasn't going to complain about that as she didn't want him in hers.

'Are you ready to go now?' she asked.

'Give me five minutes. I'll meet you in the car park.'

She went downstairs to collect her bag. On her way back through the incident room she said, to no one in particular, 'I'm going to see the pathologist and Jamieson's going to be with me.'

Frank looked up and laughed. 'I'm sure he'll enjoy it.'

'Especially if Dr Dexter is on form,' Whitney said, grinning. 'I'll see you later.'

By the time she reached the car park, Jamieson was already sitting in his car, waiting for her. It was a top of the range Lexus. Typical. Everyone had nice cars apart from her.

They drove out of the car park and headed in the direction of the hospital.

'So, Walker. What's going on in your life at the moment?'

Whitney glanced at him. Why was he acting interested? It didn't make sense. Unless he was trying to catch her out. Looking for an excuse to take her off the case. That wouldn't be unheard of.

'Not a lot, sir. Busy dealing with the murders, as you know.'

'Do you still go to choir?'

She'd mentioned once to him that she was part of the local Rock Choir. She was surprised he'd remembered.

'When I can make it, but I often miss rehearsals.'

There was no way she'd make it this week, which was a shame as she could do with something to take her mind off the crap going around her head. As in, Martin Finch. She loved singing. Her mum must have had a premonition, naming her Whitney. At one time she'd thought about a career as a professional singer. Having Tiffany meant that was out of the question, but she wouldn't change it for the world. Her daughter was everything to her.

She wondered what her mum would make of Martin. She'd love to talk to her about him, but with the dementia how much would she understand?

'It's always good to have something to do aside from work. That's what I say. You can't work twenty-four-seven.'

She was desperate to pinch herself but couldn't in case he noticed. It was like she'd stepped into an alternate universe. He'd gone from being as grumpy as hell over the last few months, because of not getting promoted, to being all happy and chatty. Which he'd never, ever been. He was messing with her head.

Was it all down to Caroline?

'Yes, I agree, sir, but sometimes it's not always possible.'

'I like to play golf and go to the theatre when I can.'

'That's nice, sir.' What else could she say? Apart from ask him who accompanies him.

'What about Dr Cavendish? What does she do in her time off?'

She certainly wasn't going to gossip about George.

'I've no idea.'

'Is she related to Edward Cavendish, the surgeon who's been in the media recently because of the tax evasion charges?'

No way was she going to answer that.

'I'm not sure what you're referring to, sir,' she said, knowing it made her sound stupid, and ill-informed.

'Get out of the bloody way,' Jamieson shouted as some-body walked in front of the car, distracting him from their conversation. He slowed down and waited as the old man crossed. From then on, he continued moaning about drivers and pedestrians, which saved further conversation about George.

They reached the hospital and parked outside the morgue. Once inside, they walked down the corridor and he screwed up his nose.

'What a smell,' he said.

'You get used to it,' she said, unsure why she'd lied, because it still affected her.

When they entered the lab, Claire was sitting in the office area, looking at the computer screen.

'I'm here,' she said.

Claire looked up and nodded. 'Good.'

'I've brought Superintendent Jamieson with me.'

Knowing he was standing behind her and couldn't see what she was doing, she winked at Claire, hoping she'd recognise it as a sign for her to be on her *best* behaviour. Although there was no discernible change in Claire's behaviour, Whitney spotted a slight twinkle in her eye.

Occasionally, Claire would show her fun side, though in the main she tended to be a pain in the arse. She knew Whitney's feelings about Jamieson, so hopefully she'd oblige and pull out all of the stops.

'Good morning, Dr Dexter,' Jamieson said.

Claire stood. 'Follow me,' she said in her usual officious tone, grabbing her white coat on the way and not responding to Jamieson.

Whitney grinned to herself. It appeared Claire was going to play ball.

'Stand over there.' Claire led them to the body, which was laid out on the stainless-steel table, and pointed at the spot where she wanted them, about a foot away from the victim's head.

Whitney glanced at Jamieson, who was going a delicate shade of green. Was this his first body? She sincerely hoped so.

'What's that smell?' Whitney asked.

'A clue as to the death,' Claire said as she pulled over the light to illuminate the body showing where she'd made her incisions and sewn them back up. 'The victim was poisoned. My findings suggest it was cyanide, but that will be confirmed by toxicology. All of the outward signs are there, including the almond smell. Although not everyone is able to smell it.'

'What are the other signs?'

'See the black on her lips?'

'Yes,' Whitney said, peering in.

'That's vomit.'

Whitney grimaced. She'd never seen black vomit before.

'Would you like to take a look, sir?' Whitney said, as she stepped to the side.

'I'm fine here,' he said.

'You're not squeamish are you, *Superintendent*?' Claire asked.

'No. I can see from where I am, that's all.'

'You'll get a much better view from over here,' Claire said.

'Thank you. But no.'

'Any other signs?' Whitney asked, biting back a smile.

'The skin and internal tissues were a reddish colour.'

'Did the victim swallow the poison?'

'No. It was much more interesting than that. Which is why I wanted you to come in to see.' Claire turned the victim's head until the left ear was showing. 'Do you see the cut inside the ear?'

'Yes.' Whitney inspected the tiny cut, not much wider than one caused by paper.

'It's my belief the victim was cut, and poison tipped into her ear, which was then quickly absorbed into the bloodstream through the open wound.'

'How can you make that assumption?' Jamieson said, taking a step closer and peering at the ear.

He'd clearly got over his problem with the body.

'Are you questioning my judgement?' Claire asked, her clipped tone a sure indication he was treading on dangerous ground.

Whitney moved to the side. She wanted to enjoy this. She'd love to record it on her phone so she could play it to George but wasn't able to do it by touch alone.

'Why would someone poison a person by making a cut in their ear? How do you know the cut hadn't already been there for some time?'

'Where shall I begin. First, I can tell from my training and experience when the cut was made. The wound tells me that. Second, the reason *why* the poison was adminis-tered in this way doesn't come under my remit. I tell you my findings and it's up to you to use them to catch the killer.'

'And it's definitely cyanide?' he said.

'As I've already told you, I'm waiting for confirmation from toxicology. Then we'll have a conclusive answer. Also—'

'When will that be?' Jamieson said.

'Stop interrupting,' Claire barked. 'The results will be here when they arrive. What I was about to say is it appears the victim was restrained before being poisoned, as there are marks on the wrists and ankles.' She pointed to the red lines where the skin had been bruised.

'Do you know what was used to restrain her?' Whitney asked.

'Similar restraints were used on both wrists and ankles. Judging by the depth and pattern of the marks, I believe it to be nylon rope. I'll check and let you know.'

'Were there any signs of a struggle?' Whitney asked.

'If you look at the wrists, the marks aren't uniform, indicating she struggled a lot.'

'I'm assuming you can tell when the restraining marks were made, which means you can give us an idea of how long it was between her death and the time she was restrained?' Jamieson said.

'You assume right,' Claire said. 'It will all be in my report.'

'Any trace evidence?' Whitney asked.

'Under the fingernails there were traces of soil and skin. I've sent it to the lab for identification.'

'Does that mean we can get the DNA of the person responsible?' Jamieson asked.

'It's not necessarily skin from the assailant, but we can check to see if they're on the database.'

'What about the soil, do you think it came from the woods?' Whitney asked.

'I don't believe so, but I'll know more once the test results are back.'

'Was there any sexual interference?' Whitney asked.

'No. There was no bruising around the outer genital areas.'

'What you're telling us, is that the victim was tied up and poisoned in the ear,' Jamieson said. 'But at the moment, you can't confirm what the poison was or give us any indication as to who the assailant is?'

'That is correct. We'll have a fuller picture once we have the lab results.'

'So why did you call us in?' Jamieson said. 'This could all have been done on the phone.'

'In theory, yes. It could.' Claire looked at Whitney and rolled her eyes. Jamieson must have seen it. 'I view my role here as primarily to perform the post-mortem, but also to educate. When officers actually see what happens, they're better able to understand the findings and put together a picture of the offender. This is how we work.'

'Thank you for putting me right,' Jamieson said, a steely tone to his voice.

'If that's all, we'll go now,' Whitney said.

'You'll get my report in a few days,' Claire said, turning her back on them and covering the body with a sheet.

Whitney and Jamieson left the lab.

'She can be a bit of a madam,' Jamieson said, as they headed down the corridor.

'It's just Claire being Claire.'

'And what's with her attire? Isn't there a dress code?'

Whitney choked back a laugh. Claire's *attire* had been quite tame compared with how it usually was. A plain navy pleated skirt, and red and brown V-necked jumper, teamed with some short green and brown striped socks.

'Dr Dexter is the best pathologist we have. Probably the best in the country. She was right when she said seeing the body and understanding what occurred is invaluable. It gives us a much greater insight into the crime.'

'If you say so,' Jamieson said. 'Make sure you use it to solve the case.'

Chapter Seventeen

'Listen up, everyone,' Whitney said as she called the team together for their morning briefing. 'It's been two days since the latest body was found and I want to go over everything we've got so far.' She was interrupted by the phone ringing on the table. She picked it up. 'Walker.'

'There's been another body found in the woods,' one of the officers from downstairs said.

Whitney inwardly groaned. Not another one. It was official. They now had a serial killer on their hands.

'Okay. Thanks for letting me know.' She replaced the phone. 'Change of plan,' she said to the team. 'There's been a third body found in the woods. Matt, you can come with me to the scene, the rest of you, keep going and I'll meet you back here later.'

She headed to her office to pick up her bag and jacket. On the way she called George.

'Whitney,' George answered after only one ring.

'I don't suppose you can come in today, can you? We have another body.'

'I'm not surprised. I'm going to be stuck in a departmental meeting this morning, but after that, I can be with you. I take it the body was found in the same place?'

'Yes. I'm on the way to the scene now, so I've no idea of cause of death. This isn't good. Only two days between the second and third deaths. That's a ridiculously short amount of time.'

'Agreed. The killer has halved the time between deaths.'

'Does that mean we should expect another one tomorrow?' she asked.

'Let's not jump to any conclusions,' George said. 'I'll see you later.'

Whitney collected her bag and jacket before returning to the incident room for Matt.

'Let's go,' she said to him.

When they arrived at the scene, she checked that correct security procedures were in place, and then headed towards the clearing. Claire was already there taking photos and walking around the body. Whitney waved when she glanced up.

'Stay where you are,' the pathologist called out.

They stopped a few feet from the body. The victim was male, and his head and face were covered in dried blood and his clothes were ripped.

'What the hell happened to him?' she said. She glanced at Matt, as he turned away. His face was grey. However many times he saw mutilated bodies, it always affected him. Whitney, on the other hand, had developed a coping mechanism, whereby in most cases she could distance herself from what she was looking at.

'It's very different from the others,' Claire said.

'Apart from the body being laid out on a cushion. What do you think happened to him?' Whitney risked asking, seeing as Claire had already engaged in conversation.

'I'm not committing to anything, but it looks remarkably like he'd been dragged along the ground. There's an indentation in the skull which I need to examine.'

'Do we know who the person is?' Whitney asked.

'There was a wallet in his back pocket.'

'Have you finished with it?' Whitney said.

'Yes. You can step forward and take it.'

Whitney opened the wallet and found a student ID card with his name on it. Despite the blood on his face, she could clearly see it was the victim in the photo.

'Matt, call Ellie and ask her to find contact details for Owen Baxter, a student at Lenchester University.'

'Yes, guv,' he said, as he stepped away from the body and pulled his phone from his pocket.

Whitney stared at the body. 'This is crazy. We've got three different victims, three different deaths. The only similarities being the location at which the bodies are left and the cushion. Is it the same cushion with the same coat of arms as the other two?'

'From what I can see, yes. I believe so.'

'All these differences. What do they mean?'

'Ask George,' Claire said.

'Was there a note?'

'I didn't find one.'

The killer was playing with them.

'I'm going back to the station. I'll catch up with you later, Claire.'

'Not today. I've got a lot on. Come and see me tomorrow.'

'First thing tomorrow morning okay?' There was no point in trying to persuade the pathologist. If she said she wouldn't see them, she meant it.

'Yes, that's fine,' Claire said.

'Can I take the cushion?' Whitney asked, pulling out an evidence bag.

'Yes. I'll remove it from under his head.'

Claire passed it to her.

'It's remarkably clean considering the state of him. Some dirt and a little blood, but that's all. Do you think it was a while between when he was killed and when he was placed here? So, the blood had time to dry?'

'It doesn't take long for blood to dry, and until I'm back at the lab I'm not prepared to make that call. I can tell you from the body temperature that death took place between 6 p.m. and midnight yesterday.'

After putting the cushion in the bag, she walked over to Matt who was standing with the phone to his ear.

'I've got Owen's details,' he said, after finishing the conversation with Ellie. 'He comes from Leicester and was a second-year student here.'

'Did she have any other information?'

'The parents, Gwen and Melvin, own a florist shop. He has a younger brother and sister. He's twenty.'

'We'll drive out there now to inform them. I thought the students had finished. What was he still doing here?'

'I guess we'll find out when we speak to his parents.'

'We'll try their shop first, as they'll probably be at work.'

The drive took them thirty-five minutes and when they reached the shop, she breathed a sigh of relief as there were no customers in there.

A bell rang as they walked inside and a woman in her forties, with auburn hair pulled back into a ponytail, came through a door behind the counter.

'Good morning. How can I help you?' she said, smiling at them.

'We'd like to speak to Mrs Baxter,' Whitney said.

'That's me.'

'I'm Detective Chief Inspector Walker, from Lenchester CID, and this is Detective Sergeant Price.' She held out her warrant card for the woman to check. 'Is your husband here as well?'

'Yes. He's out the back sorting through the flower delivery we've just had.'

'We'd like to speak to you both somewhere quiet, if we may.'

'Why? What's happened?'

'I'd like you to close the shop for now, and we'll talk to you both together.'

The woman clutched the edge of the counter. 'Tell me what it is. Please, just tell me.'

'Matt, turn the sign to closed.'

'Yes, guv.'

'Is there somewhere we can talk through the back?' Whitney asked, her insides clenching like they always did.

The woman nodded and they walked around the counter. Once there, she ushered them through the door.

'Melvin, the police are here,' Mrs Baxter called to her husband.

'What is it?' He rushed over.

'Is there somewhere we could sit down?' Whitney asked.

'We've got a staffroom,' Mrs Baxter said.

They followed her into a small room with a sink, kettle, microwave, table, and chairs. They all sat. Frightened eyes stared back at her.

'I'm sorry, but we're here to see you about your son, Owen.'

'Why? What's happened?' Mr Baxter's face drained of colour.

'We've found a male body in Bluebell Woods in

Lenchester, and we believe it to be Owen. He had his student photo ID on him.'

'W-what happened?' Mrs Baxter asked, her voice hardly audible.

'We're treating his death as suspicious. I can't tell you any more until we've heard back from the pathologist. I'm very sorry for your loss,' Whitney said.

She hated those words. They were instructed to say them, but they always stuck in the back of her throat. It wasn't that she didn't feel sorry for them. She couldn't imagine anything worse than to lose a child. But those words, so often trotted out, seemed trite in these circumstances.

'Is this related to the other bodies found in the woods?' Mr Baxter asked.

'Yes, it is.' She nodded.

'How did he die?'

'As I mentioned, we're waiting for the pathologist's report, so we can't give you an answer. We will need someone to identify Owen.'

They both stared at her, eyes wide, like deer caught in the headlights.

'I-I can do that. When?' the father said.

'Could you come to Lenchester tomorrow?' Whitney asked, gently.

He sucked in a breath. 'Yes.'

'Is there anyone we can ask to be with you?'

'No. Thank you.' Mr Baxter gave a low groan. 'We've got to tell our other two children. They'll be devastated.'

'Where are they?'

'At school.'

'Would you like me to send an officer to collect them? We can bring them here or take them to your home,' Whitney suggested.

'We'll do it. It's going to be bad enough for them without the shock of having the police fetch them from school,' Mr Baxter said, clearly struggling to keep it together.

They were reacting typically as a couple. One stunned from shock, Mrs Baxter, and the other trying to put on a brave face by thinking of the logistics, Mr Baxter.

'Would you mind answering a few questions before we leave?'

'Okay,' he said giving a sharp nod.

'I wondered why Owen was still in Lenchester, as the students had broken up from university.'

'He was due to come home at the end of the week,' Mrs Baxter said, sniffing. 'He had some outstanding work to finish that he'd got an extension on, because he'd been sick. He had glandular fever earlier in the year and he'd fallen behind with his work.'

'Where does he live in Lenchester?'

'He was in a large student house. The lease finishes at the end of the week. His flatmates have all gone home, except one who comes from Lenchester but prefers to live-in with other students and was also staying until the lease ended. Oh, my God. I can't believe what's happened. If only he'd come home sooner. Why would anyone do this? I-I don't understand,' Mrs Baxter said.

'I'm sorry that I can't give you any more answers. We're investigating at the moment. When was the last time you spoke to Owen?'

'A couple of days ago,' Mr Baxter said.

'Did he mention anything strange happening?'

'No, not at all. He was looking forward to coming home. He'd got a job for a few weeks in a local DIY centre. He always worked there during the holidays. He'd planned a holiday with some friends next month. They were going to Greece …'

His words hung in the air.

'Do you know the name of the flatmate still there, so we can contact him?'

'I'm not sure. He wasn't one of Owen's close friends. There were eight of them in the student house, and rooms were allocated by the university,' Mr Baxter said.

'I think it was Piers, but I don't know his surname,' Mrs Baxter said.

'That's fine. We can find him. If you do think of anything we ought to know, please contact me,' Whitney said handing him a card.

'Thank you,' Mr Baxter said.

They left the shop and Whitney turned to Matt. 'We need to get back to the incident room straightaway.'

Chapter Eighteen

George walked down the corridor and out of the Victorian building where her department was housed. As she headed towards the car park her phone rang and she pulled it out of her bag. She did a double take. It was her father. The first time she'd heard from him since everything had blown up.

'Hello.'

'Georgina, it's your father.'

'Yes, I know,' she said.

Only he would feel the need to introduce himself when calling on a mobile phone.

'I want you to come to London.'

Typically, he goes straight to the point. He wouldn't possibly consider asking how she was.

'Why?'

'Because of all this trouble I'm in. It's important we get together as a family to present a united front to the media. They haven't stopped hounding me since it happened. It's been the same for your mother and brother.'

'They camped outside of my house for a while, too' she

said. If she didn't volunteer the information, he wouldn't ask.

'What did you say to them?' Panic echoed in his voice.

'Nothing. I didn't speak to them. I stayed with Whitney for a couple of days initially. Now they've gone.'

'Good. Make sure you refuse to answer any question if anyone approaches.'

'Are you guilty of what you're being accused?' So far, he'd said nothing about being innocent.

'Georgina, I'm not prepared to discuss anything on the telephone. You should know better than to ask me to do that. The conversations we have will be in private and not for anyone else to hear. Where are you at the moment?'

'I'm just leaving the university.'

'It's early to be finishing for the day.'

'I'm going to the police station.'

'You're not still working with them, are you?'

'Yes. We're investigating a series of murders. You might have seen them reported on the news. They're—'

'This is more important,' her father interrupted. 'I want you here straightaway to be with the rest of the family supporting me.'

'I've already explained—'

'Your brother and mother haven't refused, and I don't expect you to, either. I'm going to be fighting these accusations. I'm giving a press interview late tomorrow morning and you are to be here.'

'I'm not sure that's going to be possible, Father. I have this case to consider.'

Why did she feel she was fighting a losing battle?

'I think you need to reflect on where your priorities lie, young lady. It's not often I ask you for your assistance. Family comes first and you should be cognisant of that.

I'm sure the police force can manage without you, while you're supporting me in a time of crisis.'

Words were cheap. Where was he when she went through the *crisis* of having to leave medicine and find another career? All she'd received from him were the words: it was for the best because she wasn't clever enough to follow in his footsteps.

'I can't discuss it now. I'll let you know later.'

She wasn't prepared to make a decision on the spot. If the murderer had now reduced the time between kills, there could easily be another death in the next day or so.

'Don't bother to contact me. Be at the house by ten o'clock tomorrow morning. The media interview will be at eleven.' He ended the call without even saying goodbye. His behaviour was to be expected but, even so, it still irritated. Then again, there wasn't much he did that didn't annoy her.

When she arrived at the incident room, Whitney was standing by the board, engrossed in conversation with Matt.

She walked over to them and stared at the board which showed nothing other than names and photos.

'Hi, George,' Whitney said.

'What have I missed?' she said.

'This case is getting stranger by the minute.'

'Explain.'

'Yet again, the mode of death is different. But unlike the other deaths, this person was so badly injured you could hardly make out who he was. His face was cut up. His clothes were ripped and dirty. It wasn't pleasant. Matt couldn't even look, could you?' Whitney grinned in his direction.

'You know me and dead bodies,' he said.

'Was there a cushion?' she asked.

'Yes, identical to the other two.'

'Hmmm. Interesting. A note?'

'No.' Whitney put her hands on her hips and stared at the board.

'Was there anything else that was different about this murder, aside from the actual mode?'

'Not that I know of. What are you thinking?'

'He's straying from a common serial killer pattern. It's like he's playing with us. Changing some things and keeping others the same. The similarities are the body dump site and the cushion.'

'The victim's a student at Lenchester Uni, so that's another similarity.'

'Have you had anything from Claire yet?'

'We're awaiting confirmation from her as to what killed him. It appeared he'd been dragged around, as he had a big dent in his skull. I'm going to see her first thing in the morning.'

'Do we have the cushion?' she asked.

'It's with forensics. I've got a photo here.' Whitney handed her the photocopied image.

George stared at it. 'Three identical heraldic cushions. Have you had any luck finding out where they can be purchased? It would have to be somewhere that could incorporate the design of the crest.'

'Ellie,' Whitney called out. 'Have you got any information on where the cushions were bought?'

'I've been tracking various sites online. You can have similar cushions custom-made, incorporating a family crest, or you can buy them ready-made from a shop and the crest can be applied later. I'll have a list put together soon, and will then follow up on each one.'

'Great. Keep me up to date with what you find. Matt, I want you to start a background search on Owen Baxter.

We need to know if there are any links between the victims, other than the university.'

'Yes, guv,' he said turning and heading towards his desk.

'Whitney, can I have a quick word in private?' George asked.

'Yes, of course. Let's go to my office.'

She followed Whitney and closed the door behind them.

'My father called earlier,' she said, letting out a frustrated sigh.

'That explains the long face. Has he said any more about the charges?'

'He wouldn't talk about it. He implied he didn't trust that his phone wasn't being tapped. A bit far-fetched, if you ask me.'

'Is it?' Whitney said.

'You think it could be?'

'I don't know, but I wouldn't be surprised.'

'That's illegal.' As soon as she spoke, she realised how naïve her words sounded. There had been plenty of scandals reported where celebrities had had their phones hacked.

'But it doesn't mean it isn't done,' Whitney said.

'Irrespective of that, he wants me to go to London tomorrow morning in time for him to give a statement to the press. He wants the whole family there as he thinks we should present a *united front*.' She did quote marks with her fingers. 'I wouldn't commit and said I'd let him know.'

'What did he say to that?'

'He told me not to contact him as he expected me to be there. He wasn't going to take no for an answer.' She folded her arms tightly across her chest.

She wouldn't be dictated to like that. Did that make her like him? She hadn't thought of it in those terms.

'What's your issue with going?'

How could she put this without coming across like a spoilt child?

'You need me here. We've got three bodies and no answers.'

'I think you should support your family if that's what he wants. He doesn't ask much of you, normally.'

Since when was Whitney so philosophical? And since when was George ruled by her emotions? The answer to that was simple, as far as her parents were concerned, her usual level-headedness flew out of the window.

'No, he doesn't. But even so, I don't know whether I should go or not. It's not like they support me in anything I do.'

'Do you ever ask them for support?'

Good question.

'No.' She shrugged.

'If you want my opinion, and I think you do or you wouldn't have told me about it, you should support him. We only have one family, and once they're gone, you can't get them back.' A wistful expression crossed Whitney's face.

How would she feel if she had no family to call on? Even though Whitney's mother and brain-damaged brother were still around, they were both living in care homes and dependent on her, not the other way around.

'You may be right,' she acquiesced.

'Good. It's not like you're going to be away for long. Take an early train and come back in the afternoon. I'm going to see Claire first thing, so by the time you've returned we might have more to work on.'

'You're right. I'll go. It will keep the peace.'

'I'm glad you're taking my advice, for a change. Contact me once you're back.'

'I will. Thank you for your help.'

'My pleasure. Let's go back to the team. I'd like you to speak to them regarding the type of person we could be dealing with.'

'Now we have three bodies, I can talk about the dichotomy between the different deaths and the resting of the heads on cushions.'

'Excellent. Walk this way.' Whitney opened the door and she followed her out into the main area. 'Attention, everyone. Dr Cavendish is going to talk to us about the deaths and what conclusions we can draw from them.'

'The murderer is bipolar,' Frank shouted out.

Whitney shook her head. 'Enough.'

George stepped forward. 'What made you say that, Frank?'

'Two reasons. First of all, the killer uses a cushion as if trying to make them comfortable. But he kills them. It's like going from one extreme to another.'

'Yes, that is an interesting feature,' George said.

'Plus, the murders are all different. That's unusual,' Frank continued.

'That's not going to make someone bipolar,' Doug said.

'You're right,' George said. 'But there is a misalignment between each victim being murdered in a violent manner, and then rested on a cushion. Like Frank said, it's as if the killer is trying to make them comfortable in their death.'

'Told you,' Frank said to Doug, puffing out his chest.

'Give it a rest. It was luck you came up with that,' Doug said, laughing.

'Do you think the killer is sending a message?' Whitney asked.

'It's something I've been giving some thought to. Is it religious? Maybe, if the arms had been crossed over the chest as if the killer was sending them to their maker. But that's not the case here.'

'Is he telling us he's really nice, and that's why he's trying to make people comfortable?' Whitney suggested.

'Possibly, in a perverse way. It could also be because he feels no ill will towards the victims, if they were chosen quasi-randomly, and he wanted to show it.'

'So, he kills them but really cares about them. That's just plain weird,' Frank said.

'Could our killer be someone who works in the caring profession?' Doug asked.

'It's a bit of a leap, but we can't discount it,' George said. 'It's likely they have links with the university. Our biggest clue is still the use of the heraldic cushions.'

'Do you think our murderer teaches history at the university?' Doug asked.

'It's certainly worth investigating.'

'Is there anything else you can add?' Whitney asked.

'Not at present. When are you holding a press conference?'

'I've got to speak to Jamieson about it,' Whitney said.

'Has SOCO found any evidence around the crime scene? Considering all of the bodies have been left in the same place there might be something?'

'We're waiting to hear back. I'll give them a nudge after I've seen Jamieson.'

'Is it worth having a police guard in place at the scene, as there have now been three bodies?' George asked.

'Officers have been patrolling several times a day since the first death, but that hasn't been successful. As the budget won't stretch to a twenty-four-seven watch, I'll request a secret camera is installed.'

'That should help. If you don't need me, I'm going back to work to finish off something that I'd planned to do tomorrow. Now I'm going to London, I need to do it today.'

'Good luck. I'm sure it will be fine.'

'I doubt it will be, but I'll return as soon as possible. Let's hope there isn't a fourth body while I'm away,' she said, ignoring the way Whitney glared at her. 'Don't mention jinxing, I'm not in the mood for it,' she warned, before turning and leaving.

Chapter Nineteen

Whitney hurried down the corridor towards the lab where she was due to meet Claire. She hoped the pathologist would have something for her because despite further door-to-door enquiries they'd received nothing useful, nor had any of the press conferences generated anything worth following up on. It was like this murderer operated in a vacuum.

Claire was standing in the centre of the lab. She was wearing a white coat which didn't hide her spotted, navy, wide-legged trousers. Whitney had an inward bet with herself that the top Claire was wearing would be clashing and patterned.

'Morning, Claire,' she said.

Claire turned around. Whitney had won her bet. She was sporting a mustard and brown paisley blouse with a bow at the neck.

'Hello,' Claire said, smiling broadly.

She did a double take. It wasn't yet nine-thirty in the morning and Claire was cheerful. In all of the years she'd known the pathologist, those two things had never gone together.

'You seem happy,' she said, deciding to broach the subject.

'That's because I enjoy my work.'

'I thought you always enjoyed your work, but we rarely get a smile from you, especially early in the morning. In fact, very often you don't smile at all, whatever time of day or night.'

'I'll accept that,' Claire said. 'But despite the hour, I was anxious to get in today because these bodies are proving extremely fascinating. So much so, deliberating on them is keeping me up at night. I couldn't wait to get to work this morning.'

'You've lost me,' she said shrugging.

'Come over here and take a look at the latest victim. I'll explain everything.'

Whitney stepped forward and stared at the body lying on the table. It had the usual Y-shaped incision from where Claire had done her work and there was dried blood all over the victim's stomach, head, face, feet, and hands.

'He's a mess,' she said, shaking her head. She hoped Claire would clean him up before his father came for the formal identification.

'I've never come across anything like this,' Claire said.

Whitney frowned. 'What do you mean? Surely there isn't much you haven't seen in your years of undertaking post-mortems.'

'As we discussed yesterday at the crime scene, the victim appeared to have been dragged along the ground and this caused some serious damage. All his clothes were ripped, and his body had taken a severe beating. But he was also stabbed.' She pointed to a wound on the stomach. 'I didn't see that until he was on the table.'

'And that's what killed him?' Whitney asked.

'No. I don't believe so. Have a look around the neck.' She pointed to the dark brown ligature mark, with a red band either side. 'This mark is what we'd expect to see on a person who'd been hanged with a rope.'

'So, you think someone hanged him before dragging and stabbing him?' Whitney asked.

'No, I don't believe that was the cause of death, either. But he did have a noose around his neck and the dragging is what caused the raised imprints. See, they're pointing upwards? That's a result of him being pulled along at speed.'

'What was this noose made of?'

'The fibres suggest it's a nylon rope.'

'The same rope the other victims were restrained with?'

'It's likely. I've sent the fragments off for testing so will know soon enough.'

'Was this victim tied up first?'

'Yes.'

'If it wasn't the stabbing or the noose which killed him, what did?'

'That's the puzzle. Look at his skull.'

Whitney swallowed hard. She was okay viewing most things. But there was a huge gash and she could see his brain. She covered her mouth with her hand in case she vomited. 'Ugh,' she said.

'Don't go all squeamish on me,' Claire said.

'I'm fine,' Whitney said, swallowing back the bile that had shot up into her mouth.

'Good. I didn't have you down as being a wuss. See the hole in the skull?'

'Yes,' Whitney said, peering through half-closed eyes.

'Look at the shape of it. It suggests that the head hit

something hard, like a rock. There are also particles of mud and rock in the wound.'

'So, it was *this* which killed him?' Whitney asked. It was beginning to feel like one of those never-ending B-movies, when all you want is for them to get to the point.

'Maybe. But the post-mortem also showed he'd had a heart attack. I suspect there was so much adrenaline being released into his body, during the assault, that his heart couldn't cope. Boom. It gave out.'

'*Boom?*'

'Sorry, my nephew has been staying with me for a few days. It's what he says all of the time.'

Whitney stared at Claire. This was the first she'd mentioned any family. She was worse than George for keeping things to herself.

'What you're now saying is that our victim was stabbed, had a noose placed around his neck and was dragged around, injuring his head. At some point during these proceedings he had a heart attack, which may, or may not, have been the cause of his death.'

'In layman's terms, yes. Also, to create this amount of damage to the body the rope would have been attached to a vehicle.'

'A tow bar?' Whitney suggested.

'Yes, that would be most likely. The injuries are consistent with the vehicle having been driven around in circles, resulting in the body being lifted off the ground and dropped down with some force. The body would have ended up shooting out in all directions and it was during this time, I suspect, he hit a rock causing the damage to his skull.'

'Shit. Could there be a worse way to die?' Whitney said, a shiver going down her spine.

'It certainly would have been painful and not instantaneous,' Claire said.

'What about time of death? Do you have something more specific?' Whitney asked.

'Between 11 p.m. and midnight.'

'There must be plenty of trace evidence. Anything that will help us?'

'I've sent off some soil and dust samples from the hands and feet, to see if it was somewhere close to the wood.'

'Was the victim wearing shoes?' Whitney asked. She couldn't remember from when she saw him at the scene.

'No shoes. Other than that, he was dressed.'

'It's amazing his wallet stayed in the pocket. We'll have to check how deep the pockets of his trousers were.'

'As fascinating as your deliberations are, I have something else to tell you.'

More? Surely not.

'About this body?' Whitney said, her brow furrowed.

'No. I've heard back from toxicology regarding our second victim. This is why I'm finding these deaths so interesting. Every day brings something I haven't encountered before.'

'What are their findings?'

'As I suspected, the victim was poisoned with sodium cyanide that had been placed into the ear. But what is interesting is *how* the poison entered the ear.'

'You said it was through the cut.'

'It's what I originally believed, but that's not what happened. The murderer dissolved the cyanide in DMSO and syringed it into the ear, bypassing the cut. From there it got absorbed into the bloodstream.'

'What's DMSO?' Whitney asked.

'Dimethyl sulfoxide. It's a chemical compound used in the treatment of pain and the healing of wounds.'

'Why not put the cyanide straight into the ear without this DMSO?'

'It served to increase the effects of the cyanide, so the victim died quickly.'

'I think I understand,' Whitney said, her head spinning with everything she'd learnt so far.

'Yet again, another very strange way to kill someone. And nothing I've come across in the past.'

'We've got three deaths, all of which are bizarre. The first death, stabbing *and* drowning. On their own not uncommon. But why use both methods? The second, poison through the ear. Again, strange. And the most recent death could be from one of three causes. What the hell is going on?'

'That's for you to work out,' Claire said.

'I need to discuss it with George. Have you got anything else for me?'

'Surely you have enough to work on?' Claire said, shaking her head.

'I just wanted to check.' She grinned at Claire.

'You can go now as I'm busy. I'm expecting a body to be delivered shortly and I want some breakfast. I'll let you know once I've got the soil and dust findings.'

Chapter Twenty

George paid for the taxi and stood outside her mother and father's stunning London home in Belgravia. Their neighbours were both wealthy and famous, and were frequently entertained by her parents. She hadn't been back there since December. It had been the usual traditional Christmas with her parents, her brother, and his wife. She had to force herself to attend. Her parents had staff who prepared the meal, and everything was very formal. Ross hadn't come with her. He'd spent the day with his family.

It was in total contrast to the Boxing Day she'd spent with Whitney. They'd visited her mother in the care home, and taken her brother, Rob. Tiffany had been in Australia, so she wasn't there. Ross had joined them later and they'd had a very chilled and laid-back time.

She drew in a breath and walked up to the front door of the cream painted terrace. She didn't have her own key, so she had to ring and wait for someone to answer. The door was opened by her parents' housekeeper who'd worked for them for over twenty years.

'Hello, Miss Georgina.'

'Good morning, Alice. I hope you're well.'

'Yes, thank you.'

'Are they all in the drawing room?'

'Yes. They're expecting you. Can I get you anything?'

'A coffee would be lovely, please.'

When she reached the drawing room, her father was standing by the fireplace looking like a character from one of Dickens' novels, and her mother was seated on the cream and mink striped sofa looking very elegant in a navy pencil skirt, pink blouse, and navy shoes with a kitten heel. Some pearls hung around her neck. Very conservative, compared with her usual Vivienne Westwood outfits. Clearly her father had instructed her on what attire was suitable. Her brother was standing by the window, a younger version of her father. Yes, definitely a Dickensian scene.

'Good morning,' she said as she walked in and sat beside her mother.

'Finally,' her father said, making a tutting sound with his tongue against his teeth.

'You said you were giving your statement at eleven.' She glanced at her watch. 'It's only a few minutes after ten, so there's plenty of time.'

'You've still cut it fine. We need to decide exactly how we're going to play this,' he said.

'How are you, Mother?' she asked, turning to face her.

'Fine, thank you,' her mother replied. She was a human rights lawyer and spent most of her time travelling all over the world, fighting causes. 'I've put everything on hold for now. It's only right.'

Was that a dig at her? Not usually her mother's MO.

'And what about you, James?' she said to her brother.

'We have to stand with the family. I've cancelled my surgeries.'

Her brother was a surgeon like her father. He was fortunate in that he didn't have her aversion to blood. She tried not to think about it, as for her entire childhood and into her teens she'd planned on having a career in medicine.

She turned her attention back to her father. 'Perhaps you could actually tell me what it's all about. I'm assuming what's been reported in the media isn't accurate.'

'I'm not prepared to go into the finer details now. It's not necessary. All you need to know is my lawyers are working on it.'

'But what they're accusing you of. Did you do it?' Her question wasn't unreasonable.

'It's more complicated than that, Georgina. And not something you'll understand. It's pointless me going into it.'

Her insides clenched. Why the hell did he always treat her like she was some idiot? She had a PhD and was very well qualified. But she'd never amount to anything in his eyes. He'd always felt that she'd let him down, from when she was a small child, and she had no idea why. But she didn't want to go into it. She was beyond looking into the psychological make-up of her parents, especially her father. Although her mother wasn't much better, as she let him get away with it.

'Why do you want me here if it's something I won't understand?'

'Because we're going to present a united front. I want people to see me as a solid, upstanding family man.'

Oh yes, the *united front* that both her brother and father kept mentioning.

'I don't see why that's necessary. It's not as if you've had some torrid affair. That's when you normally see families sticking together in public.'

'We have to be proactive. If this does get to court, and I'm in front of a jury, people have to be on my side.'

George shrugged. It was pointless saying anything. 'Right. You said you wanted to sort things out. Where are you actually giving this statement?'

'I've invited one media person to the house. They're having an exclusive interview, directed by me. I've approved the questions. It's going to take place here, in the drawing room. It gives a sense of informality which will work well in photographs.'

'Has it affected your work?' she asked, assuming it would have.

'What do you think? My private practice virtually dried up overnight. Non-stop cancellations. That's another reason the public should see me as a family man. I need my patients to return. It would be impossible to rely solely on the National Health Service for my income. That's not going to pay for all this, is it?' he said, gesturing around him.

He was right about that. He'd made his money from his private work, which involved celebrities, government ministers, and heads of state. Anybody who was anybody came to him if they needed a cardiac surgeon. Her parents would certainly have to change their lifestyle if his work didn't pick up.

'I hope your idea will work and patients will return.'

'I'm not going to sit back and *hope* for the situation to be resolved. I'm going to be taking action to ensure it does. As I've always said: men at some time are masters of their fates.'

George stared at her father; her eyes wide. 'That's it,' she muttered. 'Why didn't I think of it before?'

'What is it?' her father said, staring at her blankly.

'*Men at some time are masters of their fates.* It's part of a speech from *Julius Caesar.*'

'Is that where it comes from? It's something I've said for years. Why is it important?'

'It's been staring me in the face all of the time. Shakespeare,' she said, her mind whirling as pieces of the puzzle shifted into place.

'Georgina, you're talking nonsense,' her father said. 'Pull yourself together. This is important and I need complete focus from you.'

George shook her head and stood up. 'I've got to get back to the station. We're working on a triple murder case and I've finally figured out the pattern.'

'You can't up and leave.' Her father glared daggers at her.

'You don't need me,' she said. 'You've got it all in hand.'

'Georgina. I'm warning you. If you go, you can forget being part of this family.'

She chewed on her bottom lip. She shouldn't leave them when they needed her, even if she didn't believe they did. Whitney was right. She toyed with calling the detective to tell her but decided against it. She could use the train journey to draw her thoughts together.

'Okay. I'll stay, but that's it. As soon as it's over, I really have to get back.'

'What about lunch?' her mother said. 'Alice has already prepared it.'

'I'm sorry, Mother, I can't stay. After the interview I'll be leaving for the station.'

'I fail to see why working with the police is more

important than being with your family,' her brother said, looking down his nose at her.

Trust him to join in and take her parents' side.

'It's not,' she said. 'I've agreed to stay and won't change my mind. But after the interview, I'm leaving. And that's final.'

Chapter Twenty-One

Whitney glanced up as the door to the incident room opened, startled as George came striding through, with great determination, making a beeline for her at the board.

'What on earth are you doing here? I thought you were in London until later.'

'I managed to catch the fast train back immediately after my father's ridiculous family charade, which included photographs in the drawing room.' Her upper lip tightened.

'What's not to love about *photos in the drawing room*?' Whitney quipped, hoping to defuse the situation, as her friend appeared so uptight.

'What *is* to love about it?' George said, giving a dry smile, the tension easing in her face.

'That aside, there was no need to rush back. You could've stayed for lunch with your folks.'

Though knowing what George thought of her family, it was hardly likely to be a fun time.

'I know, but while I was there, I had an epiphany.'

'Ouch. Did it hurt?' Whitney said, laughing.

'What?' George frowned.

'It was a joke. Tell me about this *epiphany*?'

'This is not the time for joking,' George said.

'Excuse me for having fun,' Whitney muttered under her breath, though not quietly enough because George glared at her. 'Sorry. Carry on, don't mind me.'

'It's the murders. I can't believe I didn't see the link before.'

Her eyes lit up, and Whitney's skin prickled. Finally, a break.

'Tell me.'

'It's Shakespeare. It came to me when my father quoted *Julius Caesar* earlier.'

'Your family quotes Shakespeare during a normal, everyday conversation? Bloody hell, it's like *Downton Abbey*.' She tried to stifle a giggle but failed.

George didn't seem to mind, though.

'It suddenly dawned on me that our murders have got a Shakespearean theme to them.'

'In what way?' she asked, paying attention, all thoughts of joking gone.

'The first victim was both stabbed and drowned. It's exactly like George, the Duke of Clarence, from the play *Richard III*. He died from being stabbed and drowned, although he was drowned in a vat of wine and not water.'

'How do you know this? Actually, forget that. You know everything. But drowned in wine? I guess there could be worse ways to go.'

'Drowning in any fluid would be decidedly unpleasant,' George said.

'What about the second murder?' Whitney asked. 'Oh, by the way, Claire confirmed sodium cyanide was used to poison the victim. It was dissolved in DMSO before being tipped into her ear and absorbed into the bloodstream.'

'That makes sense, it would speed up the process,' George said, nodding.

'Of course, you'd know that, too.'

'The second death relates to *Hamlet*. In the play, Claudius killed Hamlet the King of Denmark by pouring poison into his ear.'

Whitney sucked in a breath. 'Holy crap. You're right. Shakespeare has got to be the link. What about this last one?'

'You haven't told me yet how the victim died,' George said.

'This one is a doozy and has Claire very intrigued. In fact, I've never seen her so obsessed with a series of murder cases before. It seems the victim was stabbed and pulled by a vehicle from a noose which was tied around his neck, and in the process hit his head on a rock. You should have seen the wound. I nearly threw up after catching sight of his brain. To top it off, the victim had a heart attack, which the killer couldn't have planned. Claire can't be sure which of the events was the final nail in the coffin, so to speak.'

'I'm not sure.' George paused and her brow knitted together. Then her eyes widened. 'Of course. It's Hector from *Troilus and Cressida*. He was stabbed and then his body tied to a chariot and dragged around the walls of Troy. Obviously not by a vehicle, but by horses. This third death confirms it. Someone is replicating Shakespearean deaths.' She folded her arms and gave a self-satisfied smile.

'That's brilliant, George. You're a genius,' Whitney said in awe.

Under each of the victims' names she wrote the play associated with them.

'I only wish I'd made the connection sooner,' George said, giving a heavy sigh.

'Don't be so hard on yourself. You've already worked it

out after only two deaths, and you need at least two or more to establish a pattern. You didn't even know about the third when you came to your conclusion.'

'You're right,' George said, nodding.

'What's most important is we have this information and it's going to lead us to the killer,' Whitney said. 'How do the heraldic cushions tie in?'

'The answer to that will undoubtedly become apparent as we go further. I'd be very surprised if it doesn't involve the killer being steeped in tradition, as I mentioned before.'

Whitney turned to face her team. 'Listen up, everyone. Dr Cavendish has done it again.' She flashed a smile in George's direction. 'We suspect the murderer is copying deaths from Shakespeare's plays, which explains why each time the mode of killing has been different. We need to find someone who's a Shakespeare aficionado, and interested in heraldry. Where's the best place to start?'

'I suggest a two-pronged approach,' George said.

'Go on,' Whitney said nodding.

'There's a world-renowned expert working at the university who is the go-to person for anything relating to Shakespeare. Professor Benedict Hamilton. It would make sense to speak to him as he might be able to give us more insight into the murders and also he may be able to explain the link with the cushions.'

'Right. We'll go to the university and see him straight away. Do you know him?' Whitney asked.

'Not personally, but that's not an issue. I can get us in to see him, providing he's on campus.'

'You mentioned two prongs. What's the second?' Whitney asked.

'The Shakespeare plays which have been emulated, so far, are well known. It would indicate that although our murderer has more than a passing interest in the playwright's works, they're not necessarily an expert. If anything, our murderer is showing a moderate amount of knowledge, which could have been readily accessed online or in textbooks. We should check any events on Shakespeare that have been put on in the area recently. Also, let's look in more detail at students at the university, considering that's the place which links the victims. I suggest starting with the English department,' George said.

'Doug. You can check the events put on. Go back six months,' Whitney said.

'I'm on it,' Doug said.

'Ellie, contact the university and ask for a list of students in the English department and the courses they've taken. Take a look and see what you can find.'

'Yes, guv.'

'We'll be back later.' She turned to George. 'Come on, we'll grab a coffee on the way to take with us.'

Chapter Twenty-Two

'Thank goodness you came up with the Shakespeare connection, otherwise we would have been absolutely stuck,' Whitney said, as George was driving them to the university.

She took a sip of coffee, enjoying the warmth of the brown liquid as it slipped down her throat. This was only her second caffeine fix of the day, and she'd been getting withdrawal symptoms.

'It's certainly an unusual case. No wonder Claire's been so fascinated by it.'

'Now we're on our own, tell me more about your trip to London and what happened with your dad.'

'There's not much else to tell.' George shrugged and kept looking ahead.

'Did you ask him about the charges?'

'I did, and he told me nothing. Said I wouldn't understand.'

'You're kidding, right? You're the cleverest person I know. How could you not understand something like tax evasion? Even I know about it.'

'You and my father have differing opinions on my ability.' George glanced in her direction, her face set like a mask. Was she doing her usual and compartmentalising what she didn't want to think about?

'All I can say is he can't know you very well.'

'Hardly surprising, as I spent my younger years at boarding school, and now only see him twice a year.'

How could parents be like that? Where was the love and support every child should have? George might have had all the benefits of wealth, but Whitney wouldn't have swapped her upbringing with her friend's for all the money in the world.

'I'm sorry.'

'Why? What have you done?' George frowned.

'For you having been brought up the way you were. It's sad.' Tears formed in her eyes and she blinked them away before George spotted them. She wouldn't understand why it affected Whitney so much.

'I'm not complaining.'

Because she didn't know what she'd missed out on. To George it was the norm. Shipped off to boarding school with others from similar backgrounds. They probably thought it happened to every child.

'You missed out on so much. We might have been poor, but my parents were always there for me. Just like I am for Tiffany.'

'I'll never know what that's like,' George said, a tinge of wistfulness to her voice.

'You've always got me. Anytime you need it. Me and Tiffany.' Whitney rested her hand on George's arm.

'Thank you. Much appreciated.' George's tone was flat.

'What did your mum and dad say when you told them

you were coming back here straight away?' She'd have loved to have been a fly on the wall to witness it.

'They weren't happy, obviously, but my father had done his interview with the press, so he could hardly complain. They only wanted me there for show. This was far more important. When I actually came up with the Shakespeare connection and everything slotted into place, I knew I had to get back to explain it to you as soon as possible.'

'I'm glad you did.'

George drove through the black wrought-iron university gates and turned into a car park signposted *Staff*, which was only half full.

'How much are you going to tell Professor Hamilton when we see him?' George asked, as they came to a halt.

'I want to focus on making a connection between the deaths and the cushion, but will probably ask hypothetically, if that's the word, rather than mention the exact nature of the deaths.'

George took her to the English department, and they stopped at the administration office.

'I'm here to see Professor Hamilton. Is he in?' George asked the woman behind the desk.

'I saw him earlier. His office is number sixty-three.'

'This is a lovely building,' Whitney said as they headed down the high-ceilinged long corridor, which had a series of large paintings on the walls.

'I agree. Many of these paintings are hundreds of years old and were donated by alumni going back decades.'

They reached the professor's room and knocked on the door which was slightly open. He was sitting at his desk staring out into space. He was overweight and had thinning grey hair combed over his head in an attempt to disguise baldness.

'Can I help you?' he asked, when he noticed them.

'I'm Dr Cavendish from the Forensic Psychology Department,' George said.

'Oh, yes, I thought I recognised you. We don't usually see scientists here.' He smiled and revealed a set of yellowing teeth.

'We've come to ask for your opinion on a certain matter. This is Detective Chief Inspector Walker from Lenchester CID.'

He sat up straight; his eyes bright. 'Come on in. I've never been asked to help the police before.'

His eagerness to assist didn't sit right. Whitney couldn't put her finger on it, but something was off.

They walked in and closed the door behind them, sitting on the chairs facing his desk.

'I understand you're an expert on Shakespeare,' Whitney said.

'Yes. I am renowned in the field,' he said, a patronising tone to his voice.

He looked conspiratorially at George, a supercilious expression on his face. Was this some sort of private academic club she'd entered?

'We're interested in your opinion on the relationship between deaths in Shakespeare's plays and heraldry.'

'Hmmm,' he said as he leant forward on his desk and stared intently at them. 'That's an odd question, and not one I've encountered before.'

Did that mean he didn't know anything? Was this visit going to be a waste of time?

'Let's first of all start with deaths in Shakespeare's plays. What can you tell us about them?' Whitney asked.

He visibly relaxed and sat back in his chair, resting his hands on his stomach.

'Death is an important theme in his plays.' His voice had totally changed, as if he'd suddenly gone into lecturing mode. 'This is because, in Elizabethan England, death was much more a part of everyday life than it is today. Life expectancy was much lower. People expected to see plenty of death in his plays and would have been disappointed if there wasn't any. That doesn't make Shakespeare macabre, but more a product of his time.'

'If someone was interested in learning more about death in Shakespeare's plays, where would you suggest they look?' Whitney asked.

'They could come to one of my lectures,' the professor replied, giving a creepy smile.

'Would that be of more use than, say, looking online?' she asked.

'That goes without saying. I'm an expert. I go into more detail than you'd find in a basic internet search. I examine the plays and Shakespeare's use of language and how he plays to the audience of the day. His most violent plays were the most popular in his lifetime. *Titus Andronicus* is a prime example of this. Today's audiences find the brutality in this play difficult to stomach, yet it was regarded as brilliant at the time he wrote it.'

'Could—' She was interrupted by her phone ringing. Ellie's name was on the screen. 'Excuse me, I'm going to take this,' she said, realising it must be important for the officer to disturb her. 'Walker,' she said answering it.

'Guv, are you with Professor Hamilton?' Ellie asked, sounding concerned.

'I'm going to take this outside. I won't be a moment,' she said to the professor and George. 'What is it?' she asked once she was in the corridor and out of earshot.

'Sorry, to interrupt but I thought you would want to know this. I've just heard back from Porters Conference Centre, and they recently hosted a series of lectures on Shakespeare, and guess who was one of the presenters?'

She'd known there was something suspect about him. George might not believe in gut instinct, but she was about to be proved wrong.

'Thanks, Ellie. I'm going to get him down to the station. Good work. Look into our professor. Ask Frank to find out what car he drives and to check for it on the CCTV footage. You can ask Matt to instruct Frank, if you'd rather.'

Matt and Ellie were close, and she wouldn't mind asking him.

'Thanks, guv.'

Whitney ended the call and returned to the office. George and the professor stopped talking when she entered.

'Sorry about that,' she said. 'An admin issue I had to deal with.'

George stared at her, a quizzical expression on her face. Whitney turned her head slightly so the professor couldn't see and winked.

'I understand,' the professor said.

'Professor, thank you for your input so far. What I hadn't yet mentioned was we're currently investigating three murders which took place recently. Each murder was different, as the killer copied deaths found in Shakespeare's plays.'

He rubbed his chin. 'How did you make the connection between the deaths and Shakespeare?'

'Dr Cavendish thought there could be a link, but we wanted to check with an expert.'

'Well, you've come to the right place,' he said, flashing a smug smile.

'Rather than discuss it here, if it's not too much trouble, I wondered if you'd be prepared to come to the station and take a look at some photographs we have, to confirm our suspicions and see if there's anything we've missed,' Whitney said.

'I'd be delighted to. I have to make a quick phone call and then I can be at your disposal. Shall I meet you at the station?'

'We'll take you and bring you back later. You make your call and we'll wait for you outside.'

'Okay, that would suit me. Driving through the city isn't my favourite occupation.' He laughed and his stomach shook.

They left his room and walked a little way down the corridor.

'I take it you're going to explain what's going on,' George said, quietly.

'The phone call was from Ellie. She'd heard back from the conference centre. Remember, the note on the second victim was typed on their paper? It seems your professor recently gave a lecture there. I want to bring him in, but not have him suspect we believe he could be involved.'

'I didn't detect anything suspicious from him, although it's not unusual for an offender to want to assist in an investigation. It gives them a sense of superiority, imagining they're untouchable.'

'Exactly. Let's get him out of his comfort zone and we can interview him properly. I need to ask the Super to arrange a search warrant.' She pulled out her phone and called.

'Jamieson.'

'It's Walker here, sir. I'd like you to arrange a search warrant for a Professor Hamilton from the university. We have information linking him to the note left on the second body.'

'What information?'

'The note was typed on paper used at a conference

centre he attended. He's also an expert on Shakespeare, and we believe the murders have a Shakespearean link.'

'Leave it with me.' He ended the call before she could reply.

'Right. That's done,' Whitney said. 'Let's hope the warrant comes through while he's with us. I don't want to give him a chance to get rid of any evidence, which is why I said we'd take him.'

Chapter Twenty-Three

Whitney left Professor Hamilton in one of the interview rooms with a cup of tea, saying she'd been called away and would be back soon. She positioned an officer outside the door to make sure he didn't leave. She needed to see Jamieson about the warrant.

'Sir,' she said, knocking on his open door and walking in.

'Yes, Walker?' He looked up from the papers on his desk.

'I came to see where we are on the search warrant for Professor Hamilton's accommodation and office at the university.' She remained standing, not wanting to stay any longer than necessary.

'I hope you're right, Walker. I'm not happy with a distinguished professor being subjected to a search if it's based on a hunch.'

'As I've already explained, sir. We can link him to the note. At the moment he's waiting in one of the interview rooms.'

'Have you arrested him?'

'No. He believes he's here to help us with the case, that we're using his expertise. He doesn't yet know about the note. We'll introduce it during the interview.'

'I'll chase up the warrant and let you know.'

'Thank you.'

She left his office and went to the incident room to collect George and pick up her case folders.

'Guv,' Matt said as she walked in. 'Professor Hamilton has been complaining about being left alone and wants to leave. They're not allowing him to.'

'We'll be on our way shortly. Ellie, what have you got on the professor?' she asked, walking over to the officer's desk.

'He's divorced, aged fifty-six, and lives alone in one of the staff apartments at the university. He lectures all over the world on Shakespeare.'

'Excellent. Keep going with your research. Frank, got anything?'

'The professor drives a 1964 blue Triumph Spitfire, but there's no sighting of his car anywhere close or leading to the woods.'

'Nice car,' George said. 'But definitely not large enough to transport a body and something to move it with, though. I don't suppose there's another vehicle registered to him, is there?'

'No,' Frank said.

'He could have hired a car. Frank, get in touch with local car hire firms and check.'

'Will do, guv.'

'Okay, let's go down to interview him.'

'Do you want me outside watching?' George asked.

'No. He knows you and I don't want to put him on his guard by bringing in someone else.'

They went downstairs and walked into the room. Professor Hamilton was sitting quietly, staring at his phone.

'Sorry to have kept you,' Whitney said. 'Do you mind if I record our conversation?'

'Umm…I suppose it's okay.' He glanced at George, an anxious expression on his face.

Did he think the academics were going to stick together? Mistake.

She started the recording equipment. 'Interview, on Thursday, July the second. Those present: Detective Chief Inspector Walker and Dr Cavendish. Please state your name,' she said, nodding at the professor.

'Professor Benedict Hamilton.'

'Thank you, professor. I'd like you to confirm for the recording that you're here voluntarily to assist us in our enquiries.'

He blinked fast several times. 'Yes. You asked me to help because of my expertise.'

'I'd like to show you photographs from the three murder scenes. Please could you let me know if anything in particular stands out?'

She took from the file three photographs of the victims at the scene and slid them over to him. He placed them beside each other and stared, his eyes wide.

'What am I looking for?' he asked.

'Do you recognise where the bodies are?'

'No. Other than it appears they're in a wood.'

'That's correct. They were left in Bluebell Woods. Have you ever been there?'

'No,' he said shaking his head. 'I can't say I have.'

'Are you sure?'

'Not one hundred per cent. But I don't believe so. Why?'

'I just wanted to check.'

'Can you identify what the victims' heads are resting on?'

He picked up the first one and stared at it. 'A heraldic cushion.'

How did he know that so readily? Hardly any of the crest was visible.

'You have very good eyesight, if you can deduce that.'

'You mentioned earlier you were investigating deaths to do with Shakespeare and heraldry. I made the assumption that's what the cushion was.'

Whitney pulled out a copy of the note from the folder on the table in front of her and slid it over to him. 'Recognise this?'

He picked it up. 'No. Should I?'

'Look again.'

'It's a badly written piece, which I assume purports to be poetry.'

'Does the paper it's printed on look familiar to you?'

He stared at the note, twisting his lips. 'No.'

'It comes from the Porters Conference Centre. You were there recently.'

He placed the note on the table and pushed it back towards Whitney. 'Several weeks ago, I gave a lecture there. But …' His voice faded away.

'This note was found on the second of our murder victims. Can you see where I'm going with this?' Whitney asked.

'I came here to help you and now you're accusing me of murder.' His eyes bulged.

'No one has accused you of anything, we're simply asking questions,' Whitney said in a cool voice.

'That's not how it appears from this side of the desk.'

'Professor Hamilton, where were you on Wednesday the twenty-fourth, Sunday the twenty-eighth, and this

Tuesday just gone?' She leant forward and locked eyes with him.

'I'm not saying anything else without my solicitor present.' He folded his arms and sat back in his chair.

'That is your prerogative. Interview suspended.' She stopped the recording.

'I want to leave,' the professor said, pushing his seat back and standing.

'That's not possible. Call your solicitor and we'll resume questioning when they arrive.'

He pulled out his phone and keyed in a number. 'She can't be here for another two hours,' he said after ending the call and placing his phone on the table.

'We will wait until then,' Whitney said.

'What am I meant to do now?'

'You can stay here. We're waiting for a search warrant for your apartment and office.'

'I want to be with you when you go through my possessions,' he said.

'That won't be possible. But if you let us have your keys, it will save us having to force the lock.'

'This is ridiculous. I came here of my own volition to help and this is what you do. No wonder the police have such a poor reputation. How could *you* work with them, someone of your professional standing?' He shot George a filthy look as he pulled out the keys from his jacket pocket and gave them to Whitney.

'Thank you. We'll return once your solicitor is here.' She gathered up her folders and left the room. George followed.

'He's a conundrum,' George said. 'His body language suggested shock when he studied the photographs, but also he was intrigued by what he saw. I'm reserving judgement as to his guilt or not.'

They returned to the incident room and Whitney stood in the middle.

'Listen up, everyone. The prof has clammed up and won't speak until his solicitor arrives. She's going to be at least two hours. Have we heard yet about the warrant?'

'Yes, guv,' Matt said. 'Jamieson's assistant phoned down a few minutes ago to say it had come through.'

'Good,' Whitney said. 'You and Doug can come with George and me.'

They drove to the university and walked across the grounds, keeping to the paths because of the *keep off the grass* signs, until they came to a large Victorian building standing in its own gardens.

'This way,' George said, as she led them towards the main entrance of the three-storey building.

'How come you don't live on campus?' Whitney asked.

'I like my privacy. This is far too open for me. Also, I have my own house. Professor Hamilton only rents these rooms from the university.'

George took them up the stairs to the next floor and stopped outside number six. Whitney took out the key and opened it. The four of them went inside. It was shabbily furnished with what appeared to be antique furniture. There were piles of books and papers everywhere.

'George and I will take the bedroom. Matt and Doug, you can take this mess.'

She handed George a pair of disposable gloves and they walked through to the bedroom. It was as messy as the rest of the place.

'Clearly he wasn't expecting visitors,' George said.

'You can say that again.'

George went over to the bedside table and pulled open the drawer, while Whitney opened the dressing table drawers and began to look through. There wasn't much in there, apart from a watch and a Stephen King novel. She then went to the wardrobe. It wasn't very full, a selection of trousers and shirts along with two jackets. On the floor were two pairs of shoes, one in brown and one in black, and two pairs of trainers.

'Nothing so far,' George said.

'Same here,' Whitney replied. 'Did you look under the bed?'

'No.'

'I'll look.' Whitney ducked down and found a shoebox which she pulled out. She opened it and did a double take. There was a lipstick, a pair of women's black leather gloves, which looked like they'd seen better days, and a small plastic photo wallet. 'I've got something.'

'Interesting,' George said, once she was standing beside her.

Whitney pulled out the plastic wallet and opened it. Each insert had two photos of the same woman which, judging from the angles, appeared to have been taken without her knowledge. There were twenty different shots in total.

'I know this person,' George said. 'Her name's Jenny Fowler. She's a lecturer in the English department. She could be the next victim. Do the lipstick and gloves belong to her?'

'Maybe. Or they could have belonged to Rita, or Josie.' Whitney put everything from the box into an evidence bag. 'We need SOCO here to check for anything linking him to our victims.' They returned to the sitting room where the others were searching. 'Found anything?'

'There's some seriously dark shit here,' Matt said. 'Books on death and satanism. As well as more books on Shakespeare than you'd find in a library.'

'Guv,' Doug called out. 'Look what I've found.'

She walked over to the kitchen area. 'What?'

'A notepad from the conference centre. I found it in the kitchen drawer.' He held up the A5 pad for her to see.

'Put it in an evidence bag and we'll see if the note at the scene matches.'

'Will do, guv.'

'Leave everything now. I'm bringing in SOCO,' she said returning to the lounge area. 'We need to get back to interview him. His solicitor will soon be there.'

'Before we go, you should look at this,' George said, glancing up from a book she was studying on the table.

'What is it?'

'A text discussing Shakespeare's sonnets. Beside each one there is a handwritten note referring to a particular woman.'

'Jenny Fowler by any chance?' Whitney asked.

'I believe so, as she's named several times. We need to find out more.'

'Agreed. Put it in an evidence bag and we'll take it with us. Professor Benedict Hamilton has a lot to answer for.'

Chapter Twenty-Four

They returned to the interview room and Professor Hamilton was shifting awkwardly in his seat, rubbing his hands together. Beside him was a woman, in her fifties, with dark hair cut into a short bob.

Whitney placed her folder on the table and turned on the recording equipment. 'Continuation of the interview with Professor Hamilton. Those present are Detective Chief Inspector Walker, Dr Georgina Cavendish. Also, present is …' She nodded to the woman opposite.

'Veronica Coles, solicitor.'

'I would like to confirm that you are not under arrest and you're here voluntarily,' she said, leaning forward and locking eyes with the professor.

'That's not what you said earlier when I asked to leave,' he said.

She gave a small shrug and peered at her folders, taking out the typed note found on the second victim. 'Professor Hamilton, I'd like to return to the note which was found at the scene of one of the murders.'

He glanced at his solicitor and back to Whitney. 'I've told you, it's nothing to do with me. I can't be much plainer than that.'

'Please confirm to us that you're an expert on deaths in Shakespeare's plays and that you lecture extensively on the subject.'

'Yes. You know that. She knows that, too.' He glared at George.

'We have three murders which are based on some of his most famous deaths. Dr Cavendish will go into detail.'

Were they the most famous? She'd assumed they were but knowing George they could be more obscure. Then again, they wouldn't be unknown to an expert on Shakespeare like the professor.

'The first involved the victim being both stabbed and drowned.'

'Duke of Clarence in *Richard III*,' he said, a smug smile replacing his worried frown. 'Was the person drowned in wine?'

'Water,' George said.

'Hardly authentic, is it?'

'Authenticity isn't the point. The second victim was poisoned, via the ear,' George said.

'*Hamlet*.'

'The latest victim was stabbed and dragged across the ground from the back of a vehicle.'

'Hector in *Troilus and Cressida*. I don't suppose a horse was used, by any chance?' He smirked again.

Nerves?

'Professor Hamilton, this is no laughing matter,' Whitney said.

'I'm sorry.' He bowed his head. 'I didn't commit the murders.'

'Returning to the note on the body, which was typed on paper from the conference centre. We—'

'You can't pin the murders on me because I happened to attend a conference there. Hundreds of people go in and out of the place every day.'

Whitney exchanged a knowing glance with George and arched an eyebrow as she pulled out of her folder the evidence bag containing the notepad. 'Do you recognise this?'

His eyes darted from Whitney to George, panic etched across his face. 'Umm…I …' He turned to his solicitor.

'We found this in your room. It will be going to forensics for confirmation that the paper used in the note found on the second murder victim was taken from it.'

'This is crazy. Why would I want to murder anyone? I'm not that sort of person. I'm a law-abiding citizen. Whatever you think I did, I can assure you I didn't.'

'Do you consider stalking to be legal?' Whitney asked.

He frowned. 'Stalking? What's that got to do with the murders?'

Whitney pulled out the plastic wallet of photos they'd found in his room and held it up. 'Do you recognise this?'

'No.'

'These are photographs of a lecturer from your department. Jenny Fowler. Why do you have them?'

He glanced sideways at his solicitor, who shook her head.

'I've never seen them before in my life.'

'Was Jenny Fowler your next victim? What particular Shakespearean death had you lined up for her?'

His whole body tensed. 'I'd never want to hurt Jenny. We're in a relationship.'

'Will she confirm that?' Whitney pushed. 'Because you

understand we will be asking her to corroborate your story.'

'Umm …'

'And why are there no photos of the two of you together?' she asked, not giving him time to answer. 'These look to have been taken secretively.' She opened the wallet and pushed it to the middle of the table, turning the inserts so he could see each one of the photographs.

He leant in and whispered to his solicitor, 'No comment.'

'Don't start that.' A frustrated sigh left her lips.

'You're not listening to me. I've never stalked Jenny. I've never seen those photos and I have no idea how they ended up in my room.'

'I'd like to ask you again. What were you doing on Wednesday the twenty-fourth from the evening into Thursday, Sunday the twenty-eighth into early hours Monday, and last Tuesday from late afternoon onwards?'

'I've already told you, I had nothing to do with these deaths.'

'Please answer the question.'

'I'll need to check my diary to confirm my movements.'

'Is it on your phone?'

'Yes,' he said, taking it from his jacket pocket and pressing the keys. 'I was at home on the twenty-fourth and twenty-eighth. Last Tuesday we had a department meeting which went on until five-thirty and then I went for a drink with a colleague. I arrived home at around seven-thirty and didn't go out until the next morning.'

'During the times you were at home, can anyone vouch for you?' Whitney asked.

'No, they can't. Not in person. Although I did attend an online meeting at ten on Tuesday talking to some people overseas. I'm sure you could check my computer for proof of that.'

'What was the meeting about?'

'An international conference being held in Greece next year. I'm on the committee. They can vouch for me.' He wiped away the perspiration which had formed on his forehead.

'I'll need the names and contact details of the people who were on this conference call.'

'That's no problem. I have an alibi, so can I go now?'

'No, professor, you can't. We haven't finished. Your alibi for only one of the dates in question is weak, at best, as it covers a very short period out of the time in question.'

'But I keep telling you. It's not me.'

'What is it about Shakespeare's deaths you find so fascinating?' She leant back in her chair and stared at him.

'Shakespeare makes astute observations on the human condition in a way that no other playwright has, before or since.'

She wasn't sure she understood that, but no doubt George could enlighten her.

'You understand why we might suspect you of being involved in these murders, as they replicate Shakespeare's deaths, on which you're an expert, and we found the notepad in your possession?'

A resigned expression crossed his face. 'Okay, yes. I admit it looks suspicious, but you have to believe me, I don't know anything about it.'

'Also, the victims had a connection to the university. A place where you both live and work.'

'As do hundreds of other people.'

'Not people who are Shakespeare experts.'

He slumped in his chair. 'But I've already told you it's got nothing to do with me. I came here to help. I admit to being an expert, but that doesn't mean I'm going to replicate his murders. This is just plain ridiculous.'

'Let's go back to Jenny Fowler.'

'Why?' he said, not able to look at her.

'As well as the photographs we found a lipstick, and a pair of women's leather gloves. Do they belong to her?'

He leant in and had a brief conversation with his solicitor. 'I have no idea.'

'It's not going to help your case if you don't tell us what you know,' Whitney continued.

'I don't care. I'm not prepared to answer any further questions about her.' He folded his arms, resolutely.

'Okay, we'll come back to that later. I understand you're divorced.'

'Why is that relevant?'

'What happened?'

'My wife left me for somebody else and moved to the States.' His top lip curled, it clearly still rankled.

'Who was this *somebody else*?'

'A librarian at Oxford University.'

A librarian. Victim two worked in the library. Did he have a vendetta?

'Was this recently?' Whitney asked.

'Five years ago.'

'Do you have any children?'

'A son. But I haven't seen him for years as he went overseas with his mother.'

'To clarify, currently you live alone and work at the university.'

'Yes, and that's been perfectly fine for me. I spend all my time writing articles and lecturing.'

'Is there anything else you wish to ask my client? Because at the moment, this interview seems to be going around in circles,' the solicitor cut in.

'We need to investigate further. We'll be holding you in custody.'

'Can they do that?' he asked his solicitor.

'Yes. Initially for twenty-four hours,' she replied.

'We can apply to hold you for up to ninety-six hours in cases of this nature,' Whitney added.

'This is ludicrous,' he said banging the table with his fist. 'You conned me into coming to the station to *help* and then used it to keep me here. I'm being framed. There's no other explanation.'

'I require details of the person or persons you claim to have been online with on Tuesday. Please write them down.' She passed over her notebook and he took it and scribbled down names and email addresses from his phone.

'Here,' he said pushing the notebook back at her. 'Check these.'

'Wait here and an officer will escort you to one of the cells,' Whitney said. 'Interview suspended.'

She left the interview room with George and headed back to the incident room.

'His reactions were consistent with someone who's innocent,' George said. 'There were no cracks in his facial expressions when he was denying his involvement, not even the slightest one. He also didn't fidget in the way a guilty person proclaiming their innocence might. The only time he displayed any sign of dishonesty was when he said he was having a relationship with Jenny Fowler.'

'He could have studied body language and know how to react.'

'That's a possibility, but it's hard to control every aspect of behaviour, especially when in a stressful situation like a police interview,' George said.

'I can't believe there's nothing connecting him to our victims, though. There's too much evidence.'

'I agree, there's definitely something linking him,' George said. 'But it could be that he's being framed, as he suggested.'

'Which leads to one big question. Why?'

'That's what we need to find out. Where are we going next?'

'To visit Jenny Fowler, after I've given his alibi details to Ellie for checking.'

Chapter Twenty-Five

George drove them back to the university and they returned to the English department. It was quiet without the students milling around. She missed not seeing them.

'I've no idea if Jenny is going to be around but we'll soon find out,' she said, as they walked up the steps into the building.

'How do you know her if you're in different departments?' Whitney asked.

'We're both on the university research committee. She's an astute researcher, and her contribution is excellent.'

They walked along the corridor to her room. The door was closed, so she knocked and waited.

'Come in,' Jenny called out.

'Hello,' George said as they walked in.

Jenny Fowler was in her late thirties and had a mass of dark curly hair which hung a couple of inches below her shoulders. She was seated at one of the two desks in the large square office, which had high ceilings and a big picture window facing the university grounds.

'Hello, George.' She smiled and it lit up her face.

'I wasn't sure whether you'd still be here,' George said.

'I'm catching up on the never-ending admin. What can I do for you?'

'This is Detective Chief Inspector Whitney Walker. We'd like to have a word with you about Professor Hamilton.'

A shadow crossed her face. 'Oh, him.'

'He claimed that you and he had a relationship?'

'What?' she said, her nostrils flaring.

'I take it that's not the case,' Whitney said.

'Too right it isn't. I can't believe he said that.' She sighed. 'Actually, come to think of it, it would be the sort of thing he'd say.'

'Would it be fair to say that he's infatuated with you?' Whitney said.

'Yes. But I thought I'd put a stop to it. Although I did decide I was going to report him to HR if anything else happened. But nothing did.'

George gave a knowing look in Whitney's direction. Had he stopped because of his involvement with the murders?

'We'd like you to go through the whole situation with us,' Whitney said, as she pulled out her notebook and pen.

'Of course, take a seat.' She gestured for them to sit at the circular table situated in the centre of the office. 'Would you like a coffee?' she offered, nodding towards the coffee machine sitting on top of the wide window ledge.

'That would be great,' Whitney said. 'I drink enough coffee as it is, if I had one of those in my office, I'd be on a permanent caffeine high.'

George smiled to herself. Was it possible for Whitney to consume any more coffee than she already did?

'I brought it in from home. I couldn't bear what the

university provides. Good coffee is imperative to get you going.' She handed them both a mug.

'I'll second that,' Whitney said. 'How long have you worked here?'

'I came as a mature student twelve years ago. After completing my degree, masters, and PhD, I was offered a lecturing post.'

'How long have you known Professor Hamilton?'

'Since I was an undergraduate. I took one of his courses.'

'Did he have a *thing* for you then?'

'Not that I'd noticed.'

'What changed?'

'He sent me some congratulatory flowers four years ago, when I passed my PhD. On the card he'd written a Shakespearean sonnet because, you know, he's absolutely obsessed with the man.'

'And after that?'

'A Christmas card every year, each with lines from a sonnet in them. Then, one evening, maybe six weeks ago, I was out with friends in a local pub, and I noticed him sitting at a table in the corner on his own staring at me.'

'What did you do?'

'I waved, thinking it was a coincidence. The next day he sent me some roses, again with lines from a sonnet. I hadn't intended to encourage him. I was being friendly.'

'Was it after then that you had a word with him?'

'Yes. I went to his office and thanked him for the flowers and told him it wasn't appropriate and not to send any again.'

'What did he say?'

'He asked me out on a date, and I turned him down.'

'What about more recently? Have you had any contact with him?' Whitney asked.

'Not directly with him, but a couple of weeks ago I got the feeling I was being watched, especially while I was here at work. It was weird, and only a feeling. I never actually saw anyone, maybe an occasional shadow.' She shuddered.

'Did you report it?' George asked.

'How could I? I had nothing concrete to tell.'

'Did you suspect the professor?' Whitney asked.

'It did cross my mind,' Jenny said.

'Going back to the flowers. When you thanked him, what did he say exactly?' Whitney asked, looking up from writing notes.

'He told me they were a late birthday gift.'

'He knows the date?'

'That wouldn't be hard to find out as I'm in the student database.' She picked up a pen from the middle of the table and turned it around in her hand.

'Do you have a partner?' George asked, hoping the answer was yes and she wasn't living alone.

'Yes. We live a couple of miles outside of the city.'

'Does Professor Hamilton know your address?' Whitney asked.

'He could've got it from the database. I'm fairly sure he does, as one time I thought I saw him in his car parked close by.'

'And you didn't think to do anything about it?'

'Well, like I said, I was going to report it, but I didn't want to cause him any trouble, and he seemed harmless.'

'We're investigating a series of murders that have taken place locally which have a Shakespearean theme to them.' Whitney said.

'You think it's him?' she asked, raising a hand to her chest.

'It's a lead we're following.'

'I can't believe he'd do anything like that. For all his

eccentricity and oddness, he doesn't come across as someone who would commit murder.'

'Contrary to public opinion, most murderers blend in very well with their surroundings.' Whitney said.

'What made you come to see me? Has he mentioned my name?'

George glanced in Whitney's direction. Jenny was going to be extremely upset once she knew the full extent of the professor's infatuation.

'We found photographs of you in his belongings. They'd been taken from a distance. Possibly at the time when you thought you were being watched. Had you noticed any items of yours missing, anything of a personal nature?'

'What sort of things?'

'Lipstick? Gloves?'

Jenny paused for a moment. 'My favourite lipstick disappeared not so long ago. But to be honest, I didn't think anything of it. I thought it might have fallen out of my bag.'

'We did find items in his possession.' Whitney took out her phone and showed a photo of what she'd found.

'Oh, my God. Those things are mine. The disgusting creep.' She ran a shaky hand through her hair. 'Can you charge him for it?'

'We'll definitely be looking at it.'

'I'm going to HR to put in a complaint. Can I ask them to contact you to verify what I've said is correct?'

'If you could wait until our investigation is over, then it won't muddy the waters,' Whitney said.

'Okay,' she said, nodding.

'Thank you for your help. If you think of anything that might help with the enquiry, here's my card,' Whitney said, handing it to her.

They left Jenny's office and headed outside.

'This is going to affect her greatly,' George said, as they walked towards the car. 'Going from thinking someone had an interest in you, to discovering he'd been stalking is a huge issue to deal with. He should lose his job over it.'

'If he's our killer, he'll lose his job anyway,' Whitney said.

'*If.* I'm not yet convinced.'

'He's certainly weird,' Whitney said. 'But whether that makes him a murderer, I don't know. This is the second stalker we've dealt with on this case. First there was Hawkins and now we have him. What are the odds?'

'Well, if you take the—'

'I don't really want to know, it's just a figure of speech.'

'That aside, it all seems too clean. We know he's a stalker and he's a Shakespeare aficionado, but we have no motive. He's a clever man. If he was to murder, why type the note on a pad that could be traced back to him? Plain paper would have been the most obvious choice. Also, why now begin to murder? There are too many unanswered questions.'

Whitney's phone rang and she pulled it out of her pocket. 'Walker.' She glanced up at George, her eyes sparkling. 'Okay. I'll see you later.' She ended the call and stared at her phone; her face difficult to read.

'What was that about?'

'That was Martin. Tiffany's dad who I met at the reunion. He wants us to meet for a drink later. As you heard, I agreed.'

'Why?'

'I don't know. He took me by surprise.' Whitney grinned, 'I couldn't say no. It's crazy, but after all these years it's almost like we have some unfinished business.'

'But you'd never thought that before, though.'

She wasn't convinced it was the right course of action for her friend. It could become extremely difficult for her.

'None of my thoughts have had anything to do with him for years. But now he's here, I'm wondering whether there are things which need discussing.'

'Does that mean you're going to tell him about Tiffany?'

'I don't know. I really don't know what to do.'

'I'd better get you back to the station straight away so you can get yourself ready,' George suggested.

'There's nothing to get ready for. It's just a quick drink after work. Perhaps he wants to say goodbye before he goes back to London. In which case there will be no need to mention Tiffany to him.'

Chapter Twenty-Six

Whitney stared at herself in the bathroom mirror. She'd brushed her hair and touched up her make-up, but she still looked dreadful. Probably from lack of sleep, which was usual during a murder enquiry. Was she right in agreeing to go for a drink with Martin? It was too late to change her mind. They were due to meet in fifteen minutes and she didn't want him to think she was flaky by making a last minute cancellation.

She left the station and drove to the pub where they'd arranged to meet. She had no idea what car he drove so couldn't work out whether he was already there. After taking one last look at herself in the car's mirror, she sucked in a breath and headed towards the entrance.

He'd chosen an olde worlde pub on the edge of the city which was comfortable and never rowdy. She scanned the bar and saw him sitting on his own at a table towards the back of the room. A pint of beer was sitting on the table in front of him. He glanced up as she was looking in his direction, smiled and waved. He started to stand, and she gestured for him not to, assuming he was going to come over and buy her a drink. She would do that herself.

She ordered a glass of wine and made her way over to where he was sitting. Her heart was practically pumping out of her chest.

'Hello,' she said, trying to force herself to sound natural and failing miserably.

'Glad you could make it.' He smiled.

Wasn't he at all nervous? He didn't seem to be.

'I didn't expect to hear from you again,' she said, taking a large sip of wine, hoping it would relax her.

'Bumping into you at the reunion took me back to a time when we were at school.'

'Hardly surprising as that was the intention of the evening,' she said, flippantly.

Was she being too sarcastic? It wasn't intentional, it had just slipped out.

'Well, yes. I realised that.' He laughed, showing his perfect white teeth. 'Before I go back home, I thought it would be fun to have a proper catch-up.'

'Okay,' she said. 'What do you want to know?'

'You're not making this easy,' he said arching an eyebrow.

'It feels weird. We were kids when we last met. Now we're strangers. You know what I do for a living. I know what you do. We know each other's marital status. What else is there?'

Crap. She was sounding as direct as George.

'If it was going to be a pointless meeting, why did you come?' he challenged, his brown eyes flashing in amusement.

'I don't know. Probably the inquisitive police officer in me was slightly interested.'

'Only slightly?' He grinned. Damn those bloody dimples.

'Sorry. Work's stressful at the moment. I shouldn't take it out on you.'

'Apology accepted. Let's drink to a pleasant evening together.' He picked up his glass and clinked it against hers. 'What's keeping you so busy?'

'There's a serial killer on the loose.'

'A serial killer,' he repeated.

'Yes, which is why I can't stay too long.' She didn't want him to think she was out with him for the whole evening. Her nerves couldn't stand it.

'However long you can stay is fine with me. Why don't you tell me about your daughter? You must be very proud of her going to university. Although didn't you say she'd dropped out and gone overseas?'

'Yes, I am. Tiffany may go back to studying after her travels. Whatever she decides is fine by me. It's her happiness which is my main concern.'

'That's how it should be. Do you speak to her often?'

'Why do you keep asking me all of these questions?' she asked, her faculties on full alert. Did he know? Had someone at the reunion told him? That was ridiculous. They couldn't have. She was convinced no one at school had known she was pregnant when she'd left. And as for who Tiffany's father was, she thought she'd be taking that secret to the grave.

'No reason. I'm just curious.'

'Yes, we text or Skype most days.'

'You're very lucky. I'd always wanted a daughter.' He shrugged. 'But it wasn't to be. How old is Tiffany now?'

'She's twenty-one.'

He locked eyes with her for what seemed like an eternity. 'Is that why you dropped out of school, because you were pregnant?'

She sucked in a deep breath. In her heart of hearts, she'd known their conversation was going to end up here, but she'd tried to pretend it wouldn't. Now …

'Yes. But no one knew the real reason why I left. After I'd had Tiffany, my parents helped me, and I went into the police force.'

'And have done exceptionally well.'

Perhaps he wasn't going to put two and two together, or he'd have pushed her more on it.

'Thank you,' she said.

He smiled warmly. He seemed nice.

Whenever people had asked about Tiffany's father, she'd told them it was a one-night stand when they were both drunk. It was true, up to a point. He'd never seemed interested in her, prior to that night. But what she'd never admitted to anyone was that she'd always found him attractive. Being with him now, made her realise she still did, which was not a good situation to be in.

'I'm going to ask you outright,' he said, cutting across her thoughts. 'I hope you're going to be honest with me.'

She stiffened. 'What?'

'Am I Tiffany's father?'

She swallowed hard. Should she tell him? Should she not tell him? Did it matter? Now Tiffany was in her twenties it wasn't like he could do anything. He couldn't try to take her away. He'd said how much he'd always wanted a daughter and all this time he already had one. How would he react? Might he take it out on her? What should she do? Thoughts were screaming at her from all angles.

'Whitney?' he said softly. 'Is Tiffany my daughter?'

'Yes.' She paused and studied her hand, not daring to look at him. 'Yes, she is.'

The silence hung ominously in the air. She glanced up. He was staring at her, his expression unreadable. Where was George when you needed her?

'Why didn't you tell me?' he finally said.

'Look, we had one night of drunken sex. We—'

'It was more than that to me,' he interrupted, his voice flat.

Her eyes locked with his. No way. She didn't believe him. It couldn't be true.

'Really? Afterwards, you didn't speak to me. It was as if it never happened.'

'I think if you remember, I did approach you. And you totally blanked me.'

Was he right? Is that what she'd done? Even though she'd liked him, she'd been so embarrassed the next day. She'd never intended to lose her virginity that way.

'Maybe I did, but you shouldn't have accepted it. You should have made more of an effort. Why didn't you try to speak to me again?'

'I did. But you made it perfectly plain you wanted nothing to do with me. What was I to do?'

She leant forward on the table, running her hands through her hair. In a million years she'd never have imagined having this conversation with him.

'We were seventeen for goodness' sake. At that age nothing we do makes sense,' she said, offering a lame excuse.

And nothing made sense when heading towards forty either, if this was anything to go by.

'How would you feel if I said I'd like to meet Tiffany?'

She stared into his warm brown eyes as they pleaded with her. How could she refuse? She'd had over twenty years with her daughter, while he'd believed he was unable to father a child. It wasn't fair not to let him see her.

'You can't at the moment because she's in Australia.'

'I know that, but what about when she comes home? Has she ever asked about me?'

'No, because I told her the same as I told everybody. It was one drunken night with a waster …' Damn. She hadn't meant to use that word.

'Is that how you saw me?'

Silence bounced between them before she finally returned his gaze.

'No. That was what I told everybody, to stop them from asking further questions,' she admitted.

'Good. I want you to understand that if I'd known I would have stood by you.'

Really? That would have been no good for either of them. They wouldn't have their careers if that had been the case.

'What happened was for the best,' she said, firmly.

'May I see you again, after tonight?'

'I thought you were going back to London?'

'I am, but it's not that far away. We could see each other occasionally, and when Tiffany comes home, you can introduce me to her.'

Nausea washed over her. Introduce him to Tiffany? Talk was cheap, but when push came to shove, could she do it?

Did she even want to? It was too much to think about. But she'd have to respond.

'I'm sure we can sort something out.'

Whitney left the pub, her head spinning. What the hell had she agreed to? Suddenly, Tiffany's father was back in her life and she'd agreed to see him. She glanced at her watch.

It was only nine. Would George still be up? She had said to call if she wanted. Before she could change her mind, she pulled out her phone and hit speed dial.

'Whitney?' George said, answering almost immediately.

'I need to talk. Are you free?'

'I've almost finished my work. Would you like to come here?'

'Thank you.' A huge exhalation of pent-up breath left her body. 'I'll be there soon.'

She barely kept to the speed limit and was soon pulling up outside. George opened the front door and stood on the doorstep as she ran down the short path.

'What's happened?' George asked, panic etched across her face.

'I need a drink.'

'I have some wine in the fridge.' George stepped to the side to let her through and closed the door behind them.

'Great. Pour me one.'

'Are you sure you're not already over the limit? I can smell it on your breath.'

'Look, you're not my mother. I'm fine. I can have one more drink. I need something.'

'As you wish,' George said, shrugging.

She followed George into the kitchen and watched her friend pour them both a glass of wine which she placed on the table.

'Thanks,' Whitney said, taking a huge slug.

'Are you going to tell me what's wrong?' George said.

'I've just been out with Martin, as you know.'

'You didn't stay long. Was it really awful?'

That depended on her definition of awful.

'I stayed long enough for the damage to be done.' She took another large mouthful of wine.

'What on earth happened?' George strummed her fingers on the table.

'He knows about Tiffany.'

'You told him? But …'

'He guessed.'

'Why is it such a problem? Tiffany's grown up.'

'That's not the issue. I like him.'

'And?'

'I mean, *really* like him.'

'I still can't see the problem.'

She didn't understand. Hardly surprising. This was George after all.

'You don't get it,' she said, clenching her fists and resting them on the table. 'I've spent the last twenty-one years claiming he was a piece of shit and it all happened on one drunken night. A night I couldn't forget soon enough.'

'Isn't that what occurred?' George frowned.

'In a way, yes. I was drunk and the next day highly embarrassed. I thought he didn't want to know me, but he said he tried to talk to me, and I blanked him. Several times, in fact.'

'That sounds like something you would do,' George said, nodding.

'I was only seventeen. I don't even remember him trying to speak to me. Or I've conveniently forgotten. After discovering I was pregnant, I thought that was it. I mean, no way would someone aged seventeen want to be saddled with a child. He said had he known he would have stuck by me. But I know for certain that wouldn't have worked.'

'You can't say that because it's conjecture. What has he been doing since you last saw him?'

'He's actually done really well. He went to university and now works in finance.'

'Is he married?'

'His wife died a few years ago.'

'That can't have been easy for him. Does he have any children?'

'No, they weren't able to. Which makes him knowing he now has a daughter even more important to him.'

'That's understandable.'

'I get it. I really do. But what am I going to tell Tiffany?'

'The truth.'

'You make it seem so easy, but I'm not convinced. I've agreed to see him again before he goes back. Although I'm not sure how I'm going to fit it in with the case on the go.'

'Could he stay a bit longer?'

Typical George making everything seem possible.

'I don't want him to. It puts too much pressure on me. Anyway, we don't know when the case will be over.'

'You have to play it by ear and see what happens,' George said.

'Trust you to be so philosophical when my insides are jumping around like a jelly bean.'

'You know me.' George shrugged.

'I'd better be going,' she said as she finished her wine. 'Thanks for the talk. I needed to sound off. We've got an early start tomorrow. Can you come in?'

'Yes. I'm not sure when, but I'll be there as soon as I can.'

Chapter Twenty-Seven

George made it to the station by eight, having stayed up late the previous night to finish her work, knowing Whitney needed help. She suspected further evidence against Professor Hamilton was required to make any charges stick…if it was him. And if it wasn't, they needed to re-examine all of the evidence they'd collected to see if they'd missed anything.

She pushed open the door and was greeted by the noise of everyone at work. Whitney was standing by the board and she headed over to her.

'Oh, good. I'm glad you've arrived,' Whitney said. 'I was about to start the briefing. Attention, everybody. We've got a lot to do if we're going to nail Professor Hamilton. All we have is the note, which is clean of fingerprints, and some evidence of his infatuation with one of his colleagues. None of his fingerprints appear at any of the scenes, and there was nothing incriminating at his home and office, other than the notepad, and forensics are unable to tell if the paper used for the note was actually taken from that particular pad. We need to start looking more carefully. So, where are we?' The phone on the desk rang, interrupting her. She picked it up. 'Walker.'

The team watched as Whitney's jaw dropped. 'What the…Okay. Thanks.' She ended the call. 'You're never going to bloody well believe this. We've got a fourth victim. And you know what that means.'

'That the professor didn't do it,' Doug and Frank said in unison.

'It's like déjà vu with Hawkins. Two stalkers, both of whom are innocent of the murders. Is the killer playing a game with us? Is he leading us to these men? What the hell do we have to do to solve this case?' She looked at George. 'You said everything was too easy for us and, as usual, you were right.'

'I wasn't certain but did have reservations.'

'I'm going to the scene. The rest of you keep on with what you're doing until I get back. Are you okay to join me, George?'

'Absolutely.'

She waited while Whitney collected her bag and they headed out to the station car park.

'Let's think this through,' Whitney said, while George drove them to the scene. 'If the killer had been observing Rita Selwyn, he would have known about Hawkins. So, by carrying out the murder after she'd worked a shift at the pub, he would know that we would most likely be questioning him.'

'That makes sense,' George said, mentally going through everything they had.

'The note on Josie Potts was designed to lead us to Professor Hamilton, and it just so happened that following her murder we contacted him. Was that intentional? Did the killer expect us to go to him as an expert?'

'You're assuming the killer knew we'd made the

connection with the murders and Shakespeare,' George said.

'True, but let's park that for now. The killer must have known about the professor's infatuation with Jenny Fowler and could have planted the box containing photos and her possessions. The professor did claim to know nothing about it.'

'That's entirely possible.'

'Also, why was Owen Baxter killed and not Jenny Fowler? That makes no sense. She would have been the logical person, if the professor is being framed.' Whitney thumped the dashboard. 'What is going on here? And where does John Hawkins fit in? There's no point in trying to frame two people.'

'What has been intriguing me about these murders is the lack of any discernible pattern, except the dump site and the cushion. This is an integral part. He's toying with us. Leading us in different directions.'

'Basically, what you're saying is until we capture him, we might not know how it all fits together?'

'It's a possibility,' she said, tensing. The longer it took to catch the killer, meant more people were at risk.

'Don't forget the university. All of our victims had a connection there, as does the professor,' Whitney said.

'But when you take the number of students, both full and part-time, together with staff, we're looking at over twelve thousand people. Far too many for us to investigate, even if we can whittle it down a little. There's got to be something we're missing.'

For the remainder of the journey they sat in silence, both of them engrossed in their individual thoughts. As they pulled up at the woods, Claire arrived in her sports car. George stared longingly at the pathologist's MGC, having serious car envy. She had to drag herself away and follow Whitney over to the officer standing by the entrance and sign herself in.

'Thank goodness it's Claire,' Whitney said. 'Mind you, she's so fascinated by this case she'd have fought off any other pathologist who wanted to take it. You'd have thought one dead body was much the same as another when it came to post-mortems, but clearly not. Then again, what do I know.' She chuckled.

'These deaths are as much of a puzzle for Claire as they are for us. The harder the puzzle, the greater the satisfaction when it's solved,' she said.

'Why are you two here, already? Can't you give me any time to myself,' Claire said as she joined them on the footplates.

'We all heard about this latest death at the same time. Come on, let's get down to the scene and see which of Shakespeare's murders we've got this time,' Whitney said.

'What?' Claire said.

'George made a connection between the mode of death and Shakespeare. They've been ripped off from his plays.'

'Nice work,' Claire said, nodding in George's direction.

They arrived at the scene and found the latest body had been left in the same place as the others. A woman who looked to be in her forties was lying with her head resting on a red cushion which looked identical to the others. Her arms were by her side.

George peered at her face. Her harried expression indicated there had been nothing peaceful about her demise.

'Same as before,' Whitney said. 'What's that around her mouth?'

'It appears to be saliva stains from where it pooled during death,' George said, as she focused on the marks on the victim.

'Does that mean anything?' Whitney asked.

'That the victim was poisoned is my guess—'

'Guess away. Obviously, you don't need my help,' Claire said. 'If you think you can solve it, perhaps you'd like to do the post-mortem as well while you're at it.'

'I can't undertake a post-mortem, as you well know,' George said, frowning.

'But I can. So, please get out of my way because I need to get on.'

'How come we haven't erected tents around the bodies found here?' George asked, moving to the side and allowing the pathologist to walk past.

'We don't need to as the bodies are moved fairly quickly after Claire and SOCO have been here. It's not like there are any people around. They only use them to protect the body from the weather and prying eyes. Or if they're going to need to spend significant time at the scene. This is awful, George. It's like we're back to square one. The professor's in custody, so he's in the clear.' Whitney began to pace. 'SOCO will be here soon and they can check in more depth, but if it's anything like the other murders, the scene will be clean.'

'It's part of the killer's profile. He's very methodical in what he's doing. He makes sure everything's spotless, and nothing is left unless he specifically wanted it to be.'

'Do you think he could have something against stalkers? Bearing in mind he tried to frame both the professor and Hawkins.'

'Except he committed murders while they were in custody, knowing we'd have to let them go.'

'I'm out of ideas,' Whitney said.

'What about the secret camera? Did you get one put up?'

'Yes. I'll ask Frank to take a look when we get back.'

'The key to this is finding out the motive. For all we know, trying to frame both Hawkins and Professor Hamilton could be a red herring,' George said. 'Or it could be that our killer has something against one of them and the other was to confuse us.'

'It's certainly working. I'm confused already by what you've said,' Whitney gave a wry grin.

They returned to Claire, who was busy taking photos.

'Any identification on the body?' George asked. 'I'm assuming there will be as it appears from the previous three victims, the killer doesn't wish us to waste any time discovering who they are.'

'You're right,' Claire said. 'The victim has a driving licence slipped into the back pocket of her jeans.'

'Have you taken a photo of it yet?'

'Yes. You can have it.'

Whitney took out an evidence bag and dropped the licence into it. 'She's Davina Hill. We need to get back to the station to find out more about her.'

They returned to the incident room and Whitney immediately went over to Ellie's desk. 'Here's the victim's driver's licence. I need further details, as we want to visit the family.'

'Yes, guv.'

She then went over to Frank. 'Check the secret camera footage and see if the dump was recorded.'

'I've already done it, guv,' Frank said.

'Good work,' she said, nodding. 'What did you see?'

'Nothing,' he said shaking his head.

'That's not possible. Are you sure?'

'The camera was facing in the opposite direction, so the body drop wasn't caught.'

'How the hell did that happen?' she growled. 'Surely the technicians were informed of the exact location.'

'Yesterday, I checked and the camera was focused on the dump site. I think the murderer must have altered the angle.'

'So much for it being placed in a secret location,' she said.

'It might have been impossible for it to have been completely hidden, because of the trees getting in the way,' Frank said.

'Typical,' she muttered.

'Are you going to let Professor Hamilton go?' George asked.

'Not yet. I want to interview him before we see Davina Hill's family. If our killer is someone who's got it in for the professor, we need to ascertain who it could be, and why.'

Whitney called ahead and arranged for the custody sergeant to take Professor Hamilton to the interview room. She took George with her.

'I'm not saying anything unless my solicitor is present,' he said, as they entered the room.

'That's entirely up to you. I brought you in here to let you know there's been another murder.' Whitney sat opposite him, taking in the instant change in his demeanour once he'd heard about the latest death.

'Which means I can't have done it.' He sat upright a smile on his face.

'That's what we're considering at the moment,' Whitney said.

'Considering? What does that mean? I couldn't have done it.' He glared at her, a vein pulsing in his neck.

'No, but you could have arranged for someone to

commit the murder, so you wouldn't be in the frame. It wouldn't be the first time that had happened.'

He thumped the table. 'That's utter nonsense. I've already told you it wasn't me. Have you contacted the conference committee and checked my alibi?'

'Yes, but there would still have been time for you to commit the murder. Also, how did a note from your pad get to the crime scene?'

She wasn't going to tell him they couldn't prove conclusively that it came from his. There was also the Jenny Fowler stalking to consider.

'I don't know.'

'If it isn't you, then someone must have put it there to frame you. Is there anyone you can think of who might have a grudge against you?'

'How the hell do I know?' He threw his hands up in despair.

'Think about it. Think hard. We've got to catch this person, and at the moment the only evidence we have is the note. Have you fallen out with anyone recently? Any students?'

'Why would students have a grudge against me? My courses are extremely popular. Ask the university administration.'

'Could it be someone who's failed one of your courses?' George asked.

'That's a huge leap to make. Surely failing a paper wouldn't cause a student to commit several murders and then frame me for them. That's a ridiculous suggestion and not one I'd expect from you, considering you're fully acquainted with academic life.'

Whitney glanced at George. Her face was set hard.

'It's our job to investigate every possible lead. I want you to go home and take time to consider every contact you've had recently. Anything that strikes you as odd I want you to let me know,' Whitney said.

'Does that mean I can go now?'

'Yes, you're free to leave, but we will need to speak with you again at some stage. Don't think you're off the hook yet.'

Whitney and George left the room and she arranged for an officer to release the professor.

'You gave him a hard time in there,' George said.

'I don't like stalkers. Not to mention this case is frustrating the hell out of me.' She clenched her fists and knocked them together.

'That doesn't justify you being unprofessional. Don't forget he denied owning the box we found under his bed. That could have been planted.'

George was right. She shouldn't have let her personal feelings show.

'Point taken. But he still sent flowers to Jenny and went to the same pub she was at.'

'Are you concerned he might be in danger, if the murderer discovers he's been released?'

'You're assuming our killer knew that we had the professor in custody in the first place. If the aim was to frame him, then why commit another murder at a time when he couldn't possibly have done it? But, I will arrange for uniformed officers to keep an eye on him. Now, let's go and see Davina Hill's family.'

Chapter Twenty-Eight

George drove them to Great Moreton, a small historic village eight miles out of Lenchester, making sure to drive carefully as the roads were winding. The road curved around the village green and as they reached the bottom, the view across the open countryside was stunning. Ecton Close, where Davina Hill lived, was the last road on the right. She parked outside the Georgian stone detached cottage.

'Are you ready?' she said to Whitney, who'd spent most of the journey staring out of the passenger window.

'As I'll ever be. The victim's husband is Clifford.'

Whitney rang the bell and almost immediately a small, slightly overweight man, in his late forties, with curly grey hair, answered.

'Hello, I'm Detective Chief Inspector Walker, and this is Dr Cavendish. Are you Clifford Hill?'

'Come in,' he said opening the door and moving out of the way so they could walk inside. 'I didn't expect you to be here so soon. I've only just contacted the police. I've been so worried. Davina didn't come home last night. She's never done anything like that before.'

'Is there somewhere we can sit and talk?' Whitney asked.

'Yes, come into the day room.'

They followed him into a large square room with sash windows overlooking the rear garden. A grand fireplace, with fluted pilasters, dominated the area. She sat on one of the bottle-green and cream high-backed wing chairs while Whitney sat next to Mr Hill on the matching sofa. She had turned herself at an angle, so she was facing him.

'Mr Hill, I'm sorry to have to tell you, but this morning a woman's body was found in the woods. We believe it's Davina as we found her driving licence and identified her from it.'

He stared at Whitney, silent for a few seconds. 'D-dead? Are you sure? She might have dropped her licence, and someone picked it up. She can't be dead. She can't …' He slumped forward, wrapped his hands around his head and let out a deep guttural groan, rocking backwards and forwards.

'We're very sorry for your loss. Are you up to answering some questions?' Whitney asked, softly, after several minutes.

'Yes, I think so,' he said, sitting upright.

'Where had Davina been?'

'Out with friends. They went for a drink after a lecture they'd attended and she didn't come home. I called her phone countless times and left messages, but there was no answer.'

'Did you contact her friends?'

He glanced down at his feet, fidgeting. 'I only knew them by their first names and have never met them. Why the hell didn't I get their details from her?' The lines around his eyes tightened.

'How did she know them?'

'They were friends from the course she was taking at the university.'

'What was she studying?' George asked.

'History. She was excited about last night's lecture because it was being given by a visiting professor from Oxford. She did tell me what it was on, but I don't remember. She said they were going out for a drink after, and she didn't think she'd be late. I went to bed before she got home. When I woke at three to go to the bathroom, I realised she wasn't here and panicked.'

'Did Davina notice anyone acting strangely around her recently?' Whitney asked.

'Not as far as I know.' He paused for a moment. 'When you say strange, what do you mean?'

'Whether she thought someone was watching or following her. Anything out of the ordinary.'

'No, nothing like that. I'm sure she would have told me if she was worried.'

'Did Davina have a job?' Whitney asked.

'We worked together from home. I have a graphic design company and she does the administration. But now …' He stared ahead, anguish in his eyes.

'Please may we look at where Davina does her work, there might be something that will help with our investigation.'

'I've already gone through everything on her desk this morning to see if I could find details of the friends she went out with, but there was nothing. It's all kept on her phone. Did you find it?'

'No. All we had was her driving licence. We'd still like to take a look at her desk,' Whitney said.

'I understand. The office is separate from the rest of the house.'

He took them through the house, into the kitchen, and out of the back door into the garden where there was a small converted stable block. Inside were two desks, a light wood table and chairs, and a drawing board.

'Do you still design by hand?' George asked.

'I mainly use software, but if I'm stuck drawing by hand often helps.'

'Which is Davina's desk?' Whitney asked.

'Over there.' He pointed to the one furthest away in the corner, next to a four-drawer filing cabinet.

George followed Whitney, pulling on the disposable gloves she'd been given.

On the desk was a photo of a young boy who looked around ten. Whitney held it up.

'Is this your son?' she asked.

'Yes. That's Erik.'

'Where is he?' George asked, glancing up from looking through the two trays on the desk which were full of paper.

'He's at school. I didn't want him to worry, so I said his mother had stayed at a friend's house last night. Because she could have, if they'd had too much to drink.'

'How did Davina get to the lecture?' Whitney asked.

'Her friend picked her up. Her car is being repaired after a bump she had in it.'

'Did you see the car the friend drove?' Whitney asked.

'No.' He shook his head. 'I was helping Erik with his homework. She came in and said goodbye to us both and left.'

'Is there anyone we can contact to be with you?'

'Davina's parents live in the village, but I'll contact them. They'll be devastated.'

'We do need a formal identification of Davina. Are you able to do that?' Whitney asked.

'When?'

'While Erik's at school it might be easier for you. You can come with us and I'll ask an officer to bring you back home.'

'Does it have to be now?' His voice broke.

'No. Here's my card. Let me know when you'd like to go and I'll arrange for someone to take you,' Whitney said, handing it to him.

'Thank you.' He stared at the card, twisting it over and over in his hand.

'We're going to leave now. Are you sure we can't ask someone to sit with you?'

'No. I'd rather be on my own.'

'We're very sorry for your loss. Please remember you can phone me anytime,' Whitney said.

Once they had returned to the car, George turned to Whitney.

'If we go to the university, I can find out who was on Davina's course. Also, the tutor might be able to tell us which people she spent time with.'

'Good idea.'

'While we're there we should drop into the university library and check if anyone's been borrowing books on Shakespeare's plays and also books on heraldry?'

'Do you really think that would help?' Whitney frowned.

'As we're going there anyway, it might be useful to have a look at the records. Professor Hamilton might not be our killer, but we could see if any of his students had been in there.'

'What about the local libraries?'

'They don't have large academic collections. Let's try

the university library first as it's easier for us to get access to the records.'

'Is this going to be a good use of our time?' Whitney said. 'Surely the murderer can get all the information they need online and wouldn't need to visit the library.'

'I agree,' George said. 'But anyone who's using both Shakespeare and heraldry in committing murders is not only sending us a message but, as I've said before, is also telling us they're steeped in tradition. Deaths in Shakespeare's plays can be researched easily enough. But someone interested in heraldry, using a heraldic cushion they'd designed themselves, is taking it a step further. I don't believe we're looking for an average person. It's going to be someone who has extensive knowledge and understanding about tradition in our society.'

'What sort of person are you thinking about?'

'I'm keeping an open mind, because there could be any number of people with an interest in tradition. It would seem most likely to be someone mature, but not necessarily. First step is to check the university library and find out if anyone has been borrowing books, or signing for them in the reference section. In that instance they would have to read them in the library itself as they're not allowed to take them away.'

'Okay. If you think it's worth it, we'll do it,' Whitney said. 'It would be nice to go back to the station and present Jamieson with some evidence. He's going to be breathing down my neck as soon he hears about the fourth victim.'

'We can park outside the library and, after we've been there, walk to the history department.'

The library was housed in a large, six storey Victorian building on the edge of the campus, separate from the other academic buildings.

'Wow! Look at this,' Whitney said as they walked in

through the large oak doors and she looked around. 'This is amazing.'

'I love it,' George said. 'There's nothing more calming than coming in here and sitting in a corner with a book. It is the largest library in the county. We have an enormous collection of books, some of them extremely rare first editions going back hundreds of years. If we had more time, I'd give you a tour.'

'Another day, when we don't have four murders to solve,' Whitney said.

George took Whitney to the main desk which was in the centre of the ground floor.

'Hello, Rose,' she said. 'This is Detective Chief Inspector Walker. We'd like to have a look at some of your records. We're tracking anyone who has borrowed books on both Shakespeare and heraldry.'

'I can certainly do that if you could give me ten minutes. I'll have a look in the system.'

'Thanks. Can you email me the list, while we go to the reference section?'

'No problem,' the woman said, smiling.

'The reference section is on the fourth floor, we'll take the lift,' she said to Whitney as they walked away.

When they arrived, George headed for the desk. She didn't recognise the person standing behind it.

'I'm Dr Cavendish from the Forensic Psychology Department and this is Detective Chief Inspector Walker, from Lenchester CID. We're investigating a series of murders and would like to know if you have records of anyone who might have signed for books on heraldry and Shakespeare recently.'

'Is this relating to Josie?' she asked, her bottom lip trembling.

'Yes. Did you know her well?'

'During exam time, she'd come and help up here. That's when we're the busiest. I know it's not common knowledge that she'd been murdered, as the police were keeping it quiet, but her dad came into the library to collect some of her belongings. I was on duty and he confided in me. I couldn't believe it.' She sniffed and blinked away the tears in her eyes.

How come she hadn't been interviewed once they knew Josie worked at the library? She'd have to check with Whitney.

'Did she ever mention being worried about someone following her?' Whitney asked.

'No. We had coffee together a couple of weeks ago and she was happy, looking forward to having some time off during the summer break. She was planning to redecorate her house.'

'Back to the records, can you help us?' Whitney asked.

'We keep a book on reception which you're welcome to look at.' She walked to the other side of the desk and picked it up.

'That's a bit archaic,' George said. 'Don't you keep these records on the computer?'

'We used to but we're more likely to get students and staff to sign by having a book. Often, they'll bypass the desk and go straight to the section they're interested in without checking in with us. If we see someone sitting there, we can take the book over to them.' She handed it to George, who flicked through the pages. Whitney stood beside her.

'Stop,' Whitney said, pointing to the page. 'There's someone there called Piers. Do you remember the Baxters mentioned a Piers who shared a house with Owen? I can't read his surname though.' She glanced at the librarian. 'May we take this book with us? It could be evidence.'

'Yes, I can put another one out.'

'Thank you. You've been a great help,' Whitney said.

They headed downstairs and out of the building.

'I wasn't with you when you spoke to the Baxters. What did they say about Piers?'

'He lived in the same student accommodation as Owen, but they weren't friends.'

'Did you check him out?'

'I'm not sure that we did. He was on the periphery of our investigation, and we had other more relevant leads to pursue. We'll find out when we get back to the station.'

'We'll go over to the history department now. It's over there,' George said, pointing in front of her.

Whitney's phone rang and they stopped while she answered it. 'Walker.' Her eyes gleamed. 'Ask him to come into the station. We're on our way back.' She ended the call and smiled as she turned to George. 'Change of plan. Get us back to the station pronto. We're finally getting somewhere.'

Chapter Twenty-Nine

'Professor Hamilton called the office and spoke to Frank. He remembered a student who might have something against him, his name is Piers Bagshawe,' Whitney said as George drove back to the station.

'That's the third time the name Piers has cropped up. You know what I think about coincidences.'

'Exactly,' Whitney agreed. 'The professor is coming in to see us. We'll get all of the details then.'

When they arrived back at the station, they hurried to the incident room.

'Do you want me with you when interviewing the professor?' George asked.

'Definitely,' Whitney replied. 'I want to keep this relaxed and informal, so he gives us as much information as he can. He has no reason to trust us after what happened last time, so we need to put him at his ease.'

'Good strategy. I'm going to check my emails on one of the computers to see if the list has arrived yet from the library.'

'Go for it,' Whitney said. 'Listen up, everyone. We're

waiting for the professor to arrive. Matt, did he say when he would be here?'

'Yes, guv. He won't be long, maybe ten minutes,' Matt said, glancing at his watch.

'Ellie, while we're downstairs interviewing I want you to find out what you can about Piers Bagshawe. All we know is he's a student who lived with Owen Baxter in student accommodation and, according to Owen's parents, he comes from Lenchester. Did anyone check him out after Owen's death?'

'I couldn't get hold of the university accommodation officer to check, and then got sidetracked on investigating the professor,' Doug said. 'Sorry, guv. He was on my list of people to contact.'

'Guv. Front desk has called. Professor Hamilton's arrived. They've put him in interview room two,' Matt said.

'Thanks. We'll have a rundown on where we are when we get back. George,' she called over to the psychologist who was staring intently at the screen. 'George,' she repeated.

'Yes?'

'He's here. Let's go.'

George came over, holding several sheets of paper in her hand. 'I have a list of people who have borrowed books over the last six months.'

She took it from her. 'Thanks, I'll give it to Ellie.' She marched over to where the officer was sitting, her fingers flying across the keyboard. 'When you've completed your search on Piers Bagshawe, please will you go through this list of people who have borrowed library books on either Shakespeare's deaths or heraldry and see if there's anything useful. I've also got the reference library register, please check that, too.' She handed Ellie the paper and book.

'No problem, guv,' Ellie said, placing them on her desk.

Whitney left the room with George and went straight to the interview room where the professor was waiting.

'Hello, Professor Hamilton. Thank you for coming in to see us.' She smiled, wanting to put him at his ease. He visibly relaxed.

'This is confidential. I don't want it recorded.' He nodded in the direction of the recording equipment which Whitney was about to press.

'As you wish,' she said, pulling out a notebook and pen from her pocket.

She needed the information, so if not recording was what he wanted it was fine with her.

'You asked if there was anyone who might bear a grudge against me, and I've been thinking hard about it.' He gazed up to the side, resting his hand on his chin.

Very theatrical.

'That's right,' she said.

'To pass the second year of the English degree course, in the first two terms students are required to submit one piece of coursework, together with two 1500-word essays. In the third term they have examinations. All components of the course have to be passed. I'm sure Dr Cavendish knows all this as it will be much the same in her department.' He nodded at George.

'Yes, ours is similar,' George said.

'Please continue,' Whitney said, forcing herself to remain patient.

'I have a second-year student who didn't submit all of the relevant work and, although he sat the exam and passed, he was informed that he couldn't continue because of it. He claimed he should have been given dispensation as he'd been ill.'

'Did he threaten you?' Whitney asked.

'Not as such.'

'What does that mean?'

'He told me I'd better rethink the decision, or I might be sorry.'

Whitney banged the table with her fist, unable to hide her frustration. 'Why on earth didn't you tell us earlier? I specifically asked you if anyone had it in for you. We're dealing with several murders, one of which it appears you've been framed for.'

'It was the way he did it. With a smile on his face. I thought he was joking. He'd always been a likeable student. To be honest, I was annoyed with him for not completing all of his coursework. I did investigate whether we could do anything, but because he'd missed two pieces of work, and not just one, it wasn't allowed.'

'Did he struggle with the course?' George asked.

'On the contrary, it came very easy to him. Too easy in many respects as he didn't apply himself as much as other students and would often leave his work until the last minute. But even without too much effort, he passed his coursework and examinations last year.'

'How long ago was it that he found out about not being able to continue on the course?' Whitney asked.

'Six weeks. As soon as he'd taken the exam, I told him. I didn't think it fair for him to wait until the final results came out.'

'You still graded his exam even though you knew he wasn't going to continue?' George asked.

'Yes. I wanted to see how well he'd performed and if it was as expected, I'd planned on using it to convince the

Examinations Committee to give him another chance, especially as he'd been ill. They refused.'

Whitney sucked in a calming breath. 'I understand the student's name is Piers Bagshawe. We're currently looking into his background. Is there anything about him we should know?'

'Nothing that I can think of, apart from the obvious.'

Whitney frowned. The obvious? What was she missing?

'You need to be more explicit,' she said.

'The obvious. His name. *Bagshawe*.'

She glanced at George who was nodding.

'You know what he's talking about?' she asked.

'I'm assuming he's referring to *the* Bagshawes.'

'You've lost me,' Whitney said. 'Who are they?'

'Bagshawe is the family name of the Earl of Lenchester. You grew up around here. Surely you knew that,' George said.

Of course George recognised the name. She wouldn't be surprised if the earl was a family friend.

'I've only ever known him as the Earl.'

'Are you saying Piers is related to him?' George said, turning her attention to the professor.

'That's exactly what I'm saying. He's the earl's son.'

'And heir?' George asked.

'No, he's the second son. He has to make his own way in the world without inheriting the family pile. Aka, Havelock Hall.'

Whitney suppressed a chuckle at the thought of what Jamieson would say if he knew they were going after the aristocracy.

'Can you think of a time when he had access to your rooms and could plant the box of items relating to Jenny Fowler and take some of your notepaper?' Whitney asked.

'That exact question has plagued me since remembering his veiled threat. Students are in and out of my office all of the time. I like to keep an *open house* as it were. I usually leave the keys to my rooms on my desk. He might have taken them when I was lecturing and returned them without me realising.'

'Why don't you keep your keys on you?' Whitney asked.

'I don't know. Habit, I suppose. Does this mean you now believe that I didn't commit the murders, nor did I stalk Jenny Fowler?'

'You still sent her flowers and followed her to a pub one evening,' Whitney said.

He flushed and lowered his head. 'But I didn't take photos or steal anything belonging to her.'

'Is it possible that Bagshawe knew about your infatuation with Jenny?' Whitney asked.

'I don't see how, except …' His voice faded.

'Except what?' Whitney pushed.

'If he went to my rooms, he might have seen the invoice for the flowers.'

They'd got more than enough to be working on.

'Thank you for your cooperation, professor,' she said returning the notebook and pen to her pocket. 'You may go now.'

'Before I leave, please clarify that you realise I'm not responsible for any of the deaths,' he said.

'Until the case is solved I'm not prepared to comment, apart from saying you have given us information we can use, which may exonerate you.'

'That's big of you. I don't know why I bother,' he said glowering at her.

'Professor Hamilton, I suggest you leave now before you say anything you might regret.' She stood and opened the door.

'I'm going,' he said, flouncing out of the room.

'Academics can be real dicks, sometimes. Present company excepted,' she said to George.

'You have no arguments with me on that front.'

'You know the Earl of Lenchester. What can you tell me about him?'

'I haven't met him personally, but—'

'And here's me thinking he's a friend of the family.'

George rolled her eyes. 'He's a patron of the arts. The prestigious award for sculpture Ross won a while ago was donated by him. The Havelock Prize.'

'Did you get to meet him at the presentation?'

'No, I didn't. Ross spoke to him on stage but that was all.'

'So, you can't tell me what he's like.'

'No. Other than Ross mentioned he was an affable man.'

'Let's get back to the office to see what else Ellie has found on Piers Bagshawe. I want all of our ducks in a row before we bring him in for questioning, as he's from such a high-profile family.'

They returned to the incident room and she headed for Ellie's desk. The officer glanced up. 'Hi, guv.'

'We know Bagshawe's the son of an earl. What else can you tell me?'

'He's got a record for driving offences. Twice for speeding and once stopped for driving under the influence. Last year he lost his licence for twelve months. It was rein-stated in February. I've printed off his photograph for you.' Ellie handed it to her. 'A good-looking man.'

She glanced at his image. Ellie was right, handsome with a kind face. Could the saying *appearances can be deceptive* be more apt?

'Anything else?'

'He's not particularly active on social media. Maybe posts once every few weeks, if that. He has several hundred online friends but doesn't contribute to their pages.'

'Does he have a partner?'

'Not that I've been able to ascertain. His current address is listed as Havelock Hall.'

'We're going there shortly. Anything else to tell me?'

'Yes. I went through the list from the library and he has borrowed books on both heraldry and Shakespeare. I also looked at the reference library records, and he was in there on the same day as our fourth victim. Do you think that's why she was chosen?'

'It's what we'll be finding out. We have a link between him and the last two victims. See if you can find anything linking him to Rita Selwyn and Josie Potts. Actually, Potts often worked in the reference section of the library. So, there's our link. Just look for Rita.'

'I'll get on to it straightaway.'

Whitney walked over to the board and wrote the name Piers Bagshawe. She put up his photo and drew an arrow from his name to the second, third, and fourth victims. 'Attention, everyone. We've got a strong lead. This guy.' She pointed to the photo on the board. 'He recently failed his university course for not completing work and he threatened Professor Hamilton, albeit in a jocular way. We know he's come in contact with three of our victims. Josie Potts and Davina Hill from the reference section of the library, and he lived in the same student accommodation as Owen Baxter. Ellie is looking for a connection with our first victim, Rita Selwyn. We believe Professor Hamilton has been framed and Bagshawe had the opportunity to have done it.'

'Piers Bagshawe. That's a mouthful of a name,' Frank said.

'He's the son of the Earl of Lenchester,' she said.

'That explains it. All toffs have weird names like that,' Frank said.

Whitney glanced at George. She didn't appear to have taken offence at the comment. Then again, she didn't see herself as a toff. She might not officially be aristocracy, but she knew them all, Whitney suspected.

'Enough, Frank. I'm going to Havelock Hall to speak to Bagshawe. We'll bring him in for questioning. Doug, I want you to see if you can link him to the purchase and manu-facture of heraldic cushions.'

'Yes, guv.'

'The earl will have his own coat of arms. Check that and see if it resembles the one on the cushions in any way,' George suggested.

'Good idea.' Whitney nodded.

'Frank, get the licence plate details for all of the cars registered in his, or his family's, name and check for them on CCTV footage near the scene.'

'Right, guv.'

'George, you can come with me. You're far better able to navigate the aristocratic world than I am.'

'I'm going to ignore that comment,' George said, as she joined Whitney beside the board.

'Why? It's true, isn't it?'

'Contrary to your belief, I do not spend my time in the company of earls, dukes, and barons.'

'Don't tell me there weren't children from aristocratic families at your school.'

'Some. But that was then, and this is now,' George said, coolly.

'Okay, okay,' Whitney said, holding her hands up. 'Let's not fall out. We can't let anything get in the way of solving this case.'

Chapter Thirty

What an idiot I am. How could I not have realised they'd got the snivelling professor in custody when I committed the last murder?

It was inexcusable.

I should have known better than to go away for a couple of days without first checking the status of the investigation.

The question now is how do I fix it?

Only one thing for it. If I can't frame the professor, he'll be my next victim.

I'd loved to have been a fly on the wall when they had him in for questioning. He's so up himself, he'd never have coped with being accused of murder. It served him right. He only had to do one thing, keep me on the course. But that was too much for him.

I warned him, and he should've taken my warning seriously.

Now it's too late.

I'm not worried about being caught. Nothing ties me to the crime scenes. Especially not that ridiculous camera they'd put up. It wasn't even out of sight. Idiots.

Things have changed, so after I've got rid of the professor I'll stop. It's sooner than originally planned, but I've made my point and secured my place in the history books.

No one has ever killed the way I did. That's what makes me unique.

I still picture the faces of Rita, Josie, Owen, and Davina when I told them they were going to die. They all pleaded with me, but to no avail. They'd all slighted me in their own way, and that's why I chose them to be part of my plan to discredit the professor. It was a case of 'double knavery' as Iago from Othello *would say.*

One action with two outcomes.

Now let my family criticise me for being a waste of space. They won't be able to because I've done something they'd never ever have the courage to do. Not in their wildest dreams.

They're not special like I am.

Chapter Thirty-One

George drove them to the Earl of Lenchester's estate, Havelock Hall, which was fifteen miles north-east, out of the city. They passed through the enormous wrought-iron gates and along the windy drive. It was a monumental country home, built in the seventeen hundreds, with gardens designed by the legendary Capability Brown, as evidenced by the distinctive clumps of trees dotted over the landscape.

'Imagine living in a place like this,' Whitney said, as they drove further into the grounds and the vast stone residence came into view.

'It's over three hundred years old, although I believe there have been considerable alterations as it's gone through the centuries.'

'Is it still open to the public?'

'Yes, the hall, park, and gardens are open. I visited last year with Ross. They open at certain times of the year. I imagine it's the only way the family can afford to keep it running. They also hold craft festivals a few times a year.'

'I can't imagine having people wandering through my home, staring at me and my possessions.'

'The family have apartments in the hall which are not open to the public. Although, often the earl can be seen walking around.'

George pulled up outside the front of the hall and parked on the gravel forecourt.

'How do we get in?' Whitney asked, as they got out of the car.

'We'll go through the main entrance and see if we can find the offices.'

They walked up the pale stone steps which were flanked by large ornamental pillars. Once inside the vast entrance hall they followed the signs to the offices. Before they'd gone far a woman came towards them.

'I'm sorry we're closed,' she said. 'Our next open day is Sunday.'

Whitney held out her warrant card. 'I'm Detective Chief Inspector Walker and this is Dr Cavendish. We'd like to speak to Piers Bagshawe.'

'As far as I'm aware, he isn't here.'

George caught the look of resignation momentarily crossing her face. Were they used to trouble from him?

'What about the Earl of Lenchester, is he available?' Whitney asked.

'I'll see if he can be interrupted. He's in a meeting at the moment.'

'Please stress to him that we're here on an urgent matter concerning his son.'

They returned to the entrance, while the woman headed back the way she had come. Several minutes later the earl came marching towards them. George recognised him from the award ceremony. There was no smile on his face. Only worry.

'I'm Humphrey Bagshawe. My assistant, Lesley, tells me you're here about my son, Piers.'

'I'm Detective Chief Inspector Walker and this is Dr Cavendish. Is there anywhere we can talk?' Whitney said.

He looked at George. 'Have we met?'

'You presented a friend of mine with the Havelock Prize for sculpture last year.'

'No, it's not that. It's from further back in time …' He stared at her. 'I've got it. Are you Edward Cavendish's daughter?'

He knew her father? She certainly didn't recall having met the earl in the past.

'Yes, that's correct.'

She tossed a glance at Whitney, who mouthed 'I knew it' behind the earl's back. She wouldn't hear the end of it once they were alone.

'Dreadful mess he's got himself into. I digress. Follow me and I'll take you to my private sitting room.'

They walked down a wide corridor until arriving at a door marked *Private*. He led them to a small room, which had a TV in the corner and a selection of antique chairs, from different eras, situated close to it. A chaise longue upholstered in red, took pride of place adjacent to the large fireplace. He gestured for them to sit.

'Is your son here?' Whitney asked.

'I haven't seen him today. The staff reported to me that his bed hadn't been slept in last night. He doesn't tell me his movements.' He pursed his lips, his body tense.

'We understand your son recently failed the university course he was taking.'

His brows were drawn together in a deep frown. 'That is correct. I'm not happy about it.'

'You're not happy about him failing, or the way it was handled by the university?' George asked.

'Both. Bearing in mind I donate to many of their arts programmes, they could have given him a chance.'

'I believe his tutor tried, but your son failed to submit more than one piece of work without permission, and that's what went against him,' George said.

'I understand. I also realise he's not easy to deal with. Although I'd always hoped his poor behaviour was confined to within these walls, and that outside he acted appropriately.'

'In what respect is his behaviour bad?' Whitney asked.

'He's my second son, and, unlike the first, seems to delight in upsetting the status quo. He's never been easy to deal with. His whole life he's been difficult.'

'Are you sure you don't know where he is?'

'He was living in student accommodation until the end of last week, although he would sometimes stay here. He moved back at the weekend, but I haven't seen him since.'

'Doesn't he tell you where he's going?' Whitney asked.

'No. I'm very busy with the upkeep of the hall, and my other work. I don't have time to keep tabs on him. If he doesn't appear for meals, then I don't know where he is. It's entirely up to him. Just because I don't see him, doesn't mean he's not here. He has his own rooms and I rarely venture into them.'

She knew Whitney wasn't going to understand this behaviour, but for George it was typical of her upbringing and those of others she'd known in her youth. Both her maternal and paternal grandparents came from important families. They weren't aristocrats but moved within their circles.

'Has he plans to work, now he's no longer at university?' Whitney asked.

'He's meant to help me here on the estate, but he's yet to begin contributing. Unlike his brother, who I can rely on. Why do you want to see him? What's he involved in?'

'We're investigating a series of murders, and we believe he might be able to assist with our enquiries.'

The earl's face paled. 'Murders? No. He's many things, but not a murderer.' He slumped into the chair. 'No. Surely not.'

'Your Earlship …' Whitney glanced at George. She mouthed *Lordship*. 'Sorry. Your Lordship, at this stage in our investigation we do not have a suspect. We'd like to speak to Piers because he had a connection with several of the victims. At this stage, he's just assisting us.'

'I see,' the earl said, colour returning to his cheeks.

'We'd like to take a look at his rooms, if we may?' Whitney said.

'I'll arrange for a member of staff to escort you, as I'm in the middle of our monthly financial planning meeting. The upkeep on the hall is astronomical. We're always looking at different ventures for raising money. Otherwise we may have to contact the National Trust's acquisitions team.'

'Would you have to leave the hall if that happened?' Whitney asked.

'No. But the Trust could change things. The hall has been in the family for generations and we employ several hundred people who work in the house, gardens, and on the farmland we own. They too, have been with us for generations. Under the Trust we might have to let some of them go.'

'Hopefully, you'll be able to keep the hall in your possession,' Whitney said. 'You mentioned asking someone to take us to Piers' rooms.'

'Yes. Come with me.'

They returned to the main hall and he left them while he went to find Lesley.

'I didn't realise places like this had financial problems,' Whitney said. 'Did you?'

'Yes, I did.' George's attention was diverted by a large shield on the back wall. 'Look up there at the shield.' She pointed to it. 'That's their coat of arms. It's got the name Bagshawe on the bottom banner. It's not the same as the one on our cushion.'

'That would be too much to ask for,' Whitney said.

'I'm going to take a photo, so I can study it when we get back to the station. It might help.'

Footsteps coming down the corridor interrupted them, as Lesley headed in their direction.

'This way to Piers' rooms,' Lesley said, leading them out of the hall.

'How many does he have?' Whitney asked.

'A sitting room, bedroom, and bathroom.'

She took them up the vast open staircase and around to the right until they reached a door.

'This leads to the private living quarters.' They headed along the corridor and stopped outside one of the doors. She knocked. 'I'm sure he's not here, but just to check.'

There was no answer. She opened it and they went inside to the sitting room. It had floor-to-ceiling windows overlooking the grounds.

'You can leave us now,' Whitney said.

'I've been instructed to wait so I can show you out,' she said.

'Stay outside while we're in here in that case,' Whitney said.

She left and closed the door behind her. Whitney handed George a pair of disposable gloves and she put on a pair herself.

'Look at the size of this room. It's bigger than my whole house and this is just his sitting room. Talk about how the other half live. Let's start in the bedroom.'

They walked into the bedroom which had a large four-poster bed situated in the middle up against the far wall. There were several chests of drawers, a dressing table, and wardrobe.

'Where do you want to start?' George said.

'I'll look through the wardrobe. You take the dressing table.'

'Okay.'

There were stacks of books on the floor and clothes lying around. George's fingers itched to pick them up.

'I'm surprised his room is allowed to be in such a mess. Don't they have cleaners to keep it tidy?' Whitney said.

'Maybe he forbade them from coming in. Having said that, the bed is made,' George said as she headed over to the dressing table, on which there sat a pile of books. 'This is interesting.'

'What have you found?' Whitney walked over to her.

'His reading matter. There's a text here on true crime which is bookmarked on serial killers of the 20th century.' She held it up for Whitney to see. 'There's also a folder with information he's printed off from the internet, all relating to different killers.'

Whitney pulled out some evidence bags. 'Okay, put everything into these.'

'Look, there's also information on poisons.' George held out some printed pages and put them in bags. 'He's obsessed with snakes, judging by the collection of books he has.'

'Ugh.' Whitney shivered. 'I can deal with most things, except snakes. They scare me to death.'

'Most are harmless and are more scared of you than you are of them.'

'Don't be too sure.'

'His laptop is here,' George said, seeing it on the floor beside the desk. She picked it up and showed it to Whitney.

'We'll take that with us, too.'

'Will we have to get permission from the earl to remove all of these items as we don't have a search warrant?' George asked.

'Yes. I'll sort that out when we leave. Let's see if there's anything else of use. When we get back to the station, I'll arrange for SOCO to come over. More importantly, we need to find him and the car he drives. Does he have one which would enable him to drag Owen Baxter around? And, if so, whereabouts did the dragging take place?'

'The hall has extensive grounds, there's bound to be somewhere,' George said.

After continuing their search, and finding nothing else, they returned to the sitting room. Whitney opened the door leading to the corridor. 'There are a few things we'd like to take to the station. Can you please ask the earl if he gives us his permission?'

'Which items in particular?' Lesley asked.

'Books, papers, and Piers' laptop.'

'I'll get in touch with him now. It shouldn't be a problem.' Lesley pulled out her phone and called him, while Whitney waited. 'The earl said it's fine for you to take whatever you want, he'll assume responsibility for it,' she said, after ending the call. 'Is there anything else I can help you with?'

'What car does Piers drive?'

'When he goes out, he borrows one of the estate's cars. There are many for him to choose from.'

'Does he have one he prefers to drive more than the others?' Whitney asked.

'Yes, he does. There's an old Land Rover, four-wheel-drive, which he uses when he can.'

'Does it have a tow bar?' Whitney asked.

'I couldn't be sure, but I imagine so, as it's used on the farm with a trailer.'

'Is the vehicle here at the moment?' George asked.

'I can take you down to the garages and we'll look,' she said.

'Thank you.'

She led them through a different part of the house and into the large kitchen. From there they went through the boot room and out to the rear of the property.

'The garages are over there,' Lesley said as she took them across a small square lawn to some brick buildings.

They walked around the front and Lesley lifted up a double door to one of them. In front of their eyes were at least fifteen vehicles.

George's eyes were on stalks as she took in the array of cars. 'Look at those two. An early Bentley and an early Rolls Royce. And look at that Daimler. What a fantastic collection.'

'This is only a few of them. The earl keeps his rarer cars locked away,' she said.

George would love to be privy to his other cars. She could only imagine what they would be.

'Which is the car Piers likes to drive?' Whitney asked.

'It's not here.' The woman pointed to a vacant spot in the garage next to some more modern cars, a BMW, a Volkswagen Golf, and a Mini. 'I'm assuming he went out in it. It was here yesterday when I came into the garages to fetch something for the earl.'

'Thank you for your help. We're going back to the

station now. If Piers does come back, please contact me immediately. Here's my card.' Whitney held it out for her to take. 'Can we get to the front of the house by walking around rather than going through?'

'Yes, but it will take longer.'

'That's fine. We'll make our own way.'

Lesley left them and returned the way they'd come.

'I thought we were in a hurry,' George said, once she couldn't be heard.

'We are, but I want to take some soil back with us so Claire can compare it to the other samples she has.' She picked up a handful and dropped it into an evidence bag. 'Now we can go.'

Chapter Thirty-Two

On their way back to the incident room Whitney's phone pinged. She glanced down.

'It's a message from Claire. She wants us to drop by the morgue sometime today. That works out well as I have the soil sample for her.'

'Shall we drive to see her now or do you wish to return to the station first?' George asked.

'Let's drop these things off and then we'll go to see her. I'll text to say we'll be there in an hour. That should give us enough time.'

She drummed her fingers on her thighs, excitement coursing through her veins. It was always like this when she made headway on a case. The giddy sensation as frustration gave way to progress.

When they arrived back at the incident room, she went over to Ellie's desk.

'Here's Piers Bagshawe's laptop. Send it to Mac in digital forensics and see what he can get from it. I also have books and papers from his room. George has taken a quick look and they mainly comprise research into murders from the past. Make copies of relevant pieces and send every-thing to forensics.'

'Will do, guv.' Ellie pulled on some disposable gloves, took the evidence bags from Whitney and placed them on her desk.

'Thanks. I'm about to tell the team what happened, so wait until I've done that.' She marched over to the board. 'Attention, everyone. We've just come back from Havelock Hall having spoken to the earl and taken a look around his son's rooms. Not only is he linked to the victims and had a reason to frame Professor Hamilton, but we've also found incriminating evidence. At the moment, he's missing.'

'Shall I put out a BOLO?' Matt asked.

'Yes, get on to that straight away. Frank, you were looking into the registration details for all the cars belonging to the estate. Did you come across an old Land Rover?'

'I'll have to recheck, guv. There are records for over forty cars belonging to them.'

'Do it now. We believe that's what the suspect is driving.'

'I'm on to it, guv,' Frank said.

'Thanks. After that, check the CCTV footage again to see if it's headed in the direction of the woods at any time. Havelock Hall is half an hour away from the crime scene, and he most likely would have taken an A-road as that's the quickest route. Dr Cavendish and I are heading out to see Dr Dexter at the morgue. We won't be long. As soon as we have enough confirmed evidence, we can work out a plan to capture him.'

The morgue wasn't busy as they walked in through the double doors and headed towards the office space, stopping once they saw Claire standing over a body in the centre of the room, her hands on her hips.

'Hello, Claire,' Whitney called out.

The pathologist turned and beckoned for them to come over. 'This case is like the gift that keeps on giving. Come on over and take a look at the latest instalment.'

George caught Whitney's eye and grinned. Claire's fascination with the case was infectious. They hurried over and stood either side of the pathologist.

'What do you want to show us?' George asked, as she stared intently at the victim's body on the slab. The familiar Y-shaped incision showed where Claire had already done her post-mortem but other than that she couldn't see anything out of the ordinary.

'Your latest victim was poisoned.'

'Another poisoning,' she said, unable to hide the disappointment in her voice. 'I was expecting something different.'

'This isn't just any old poisoning,' she said in a mysterious voice.

'Come on, Claire, we don't have all day,' Whitney said.

Both George and Claire glared at her. After all of these years of working with the pathologist, surely Whitney understood the need to play along with her. Even George got it, so it wasn't exactly a difficult concept to grasp.

'Let Claire finish, Whitney,' she said, giving an exasperated sigh.

'Sorry.' Whitney held both hands up in mock surrender. 'Carry on, Claire.'

'This poisoning was the result of a snakebite. Or two, to be precise.'

'A snake?' George said, more to herself. She'd spent last

night brushing up on Shakespeare's most famous deaths and there was one which included two snakebites. 'Were they on her breast and arm?' George leant forward eager to see if her supposition was correct.

'You're one step ahead of me. Look, here.' Claire pointed to the left breast where there were two circular red marks about an inch apart from each other. 'See those small puncture wounds, they're caused by fangs. There's swelling around the entry points, which have slightly discoloured. Further confirmation of a snakebite. Also, I found enlarged lymph nodes in the area, another indicator. If one was needed.'

'That explains the research we found in Piers' room.' Whitney turned to George. 'I take it you know which play it's from.'

'This is based on Cleopatra's death,' George said.

'Exactly,' Claire said. 'One bite would have been sufficient but come around and look at the right arm. An identical set of marks.'

She skirted around the table and saw the fang marks and discolouration on the victim's arm.

'Death would have been almost instantaneous after the initial bite. Her struggle to breathe would have caused the saliva to pool around her mouth, as you pointed out at the scene, and is evidenced by the stains.'

'Tell me about Cleopatra's death. Which Shakespeare play is it?' Whitney said.

George glanced up from staring at the wound. 'It's the final scene of *Antony and Cleopatra*. She dies from the bite of two asps. One to her breast and one to her arm. She committed suicide, believing she would meet Antony again in the afterlife.'

'That's so sad,' Whitney said.

'Yes, it is classed as one of Shakespeare's tragedies.'

'Did you know that it's most likely a myth?' Claire said.

'What is?' Whitney asked.

'Her death. Although she committed suicide, it's believed it was probably from a lethal herbal concoction and not a snakebite.'

'But in Shakespeare's play it was a snake which means this death fits perfectly with the other three,' Whitney said.

'Do you know which snake was used in this instance?' George asked.

'Not yet. I've sent the bloods to toxicology and they'll identify it. As soon as it comes back, I'll let you know.'

'It certainly accounts for the books on snakes we found in Bagshawe's rooms. Although he wouldn't need that many to carry out his mission,' George mused. 'Where would he get the snake? Surely it wouldn't be readily available.'

'There's a thriving black market for reptiles, if you know where to look. It wouldn't be hard,' Whitney said. 'What else have you found, Claire? Was there any trace evidence on the body?'

'Yes. There was some soil under the fingernails which came from a different place. The body was clearly moved post-mortem, as were all of the others.'

'Soil. That reminds me.' Whitney pulled out the evidence bag from her pocket. 'I picked this up in the grounds of the Earl of Lenchester's place. Can you check to see if it's the same as the soil you found here and on the other bodies?'

'Excellent.' Claire took the bag and placed it beside the microscope on the bench along the far side of the room. 'Once you've left, I'll take a look. Who is your suspect? Not the earl, surely.'

'His son, Piers.'

'That's going to be a headline grabber,' Claire said.

'Which is why everything needs to be done by the book,' Whitney said as Claire walked back over to where they were standing. 'Were there any signs of a struggle?'

'The victim was restrained, as you can see by the ligature marks on her wrists and ankles. As with the other cases, the fibres found in the skin were nylon, belonging to a rope. The jaggedness of the marks indicate she would have struggled while tied up.'

'Time of death?'

'Between 10 p.m. and eleven-thirty on Sunday.'

'Thanks. Do you have anything else for us?' Whitney asked.

'No. You can leave now.'

They said goodbye and headed towards George's car.

'I'll say one thing for our killer,' Whitney said. 'He's bloody clever. But not clever enough for you. I doubt we'd have made the Shakespeare connection without your input, and then we'd never have located him.'

'I'm sure you would have,' she said.

'It's not like you to be modest. Admit it. Solving this case was down to you.'

'It doesn't matter who discovered it. This case has been solved through teamwork.'

'Okay. We did it together. But let's not get complacent. We need to apprehend him before another murder is committed. Nothing from what's happened so far leads me to think he'll stop unless we catch him.'

Chapter Thirty-Three

'Listen up, everyone,' Whitney said, once they'd returned to the incident room. 'Claire has confirmed we have another death relating to a Shakespeare play. This time, our victim was poisoned by two snakebites. It's imperative we find Piers Bagshawe immediately. Ellie, I know Mac hasn't had the laptop long, but any chance he's got back to you yet?'

'Actually, yes, guv. He phoned a few moments ago to say he'd found some photos on the laptop which include our victims. I should have them soon.'

'Great. It's all evidence we can use.'

'Anything on the CCTV footage, Frank?'

'Yes, guv. The Land Rover was seen on the main roads heading in the direction of the woods on the night our fourth victim was killed. The footage stops about a mile away from the scene, but it's definitely the same direction.'

'Good work. We're going to interview the earl again. He needs to know we have evidence incriminating his son. He might be able to help us apprehend him. Are the photos here yet, Ellie? It's imperative we discover if he has anyone else in his sights.'

'They've just arrived. As well as our victims, there are also photos of three other people. Two men and one woman.'

'See if you can identify any of them.'

'Will do, guv.'

'George, I'll let Jamieson know what's happening and then we can leave.'

'I'm ready when you are.'

'Actually, I'll give Lesley a quick call to make sure the earl's going to be there.' She took out her phone and keyed in the number.

'Havelock Hall, Lesley speaking.'

'It's Detective Chief Inspector Walker. We'd like to speak to the earl again, will he be available in the next hour? It's urgent.'

'I'm sorry. He left about five minutes ago.'

She clenched her fist. Damn. 'Do you know where he's gone?'

'Yes. He has an appointment in the city.'

'Please contact him and ask him to come to the station. We need to speak to him urgently regarding Piers.'

Lesley gasped. 'Leave it with me.'

Whitney ended the call. 'Listen up, everyone. The earl has gone out. I'm hoping his assistant can track him down and ask him to come to the station. In the meantime, Ellie, pass over what you're doing to Sue, and then continue looking into the background of Piers. Go back as far as you can. I want to know his friends, both past and present. I'll be back after I've seen the Super.'

She hurried to Jamieson's office, knocked on the open door and walked in.

'Walker,' he said, glancing up from staring at his computer screen.

'We've got a suspect for the Shakespeare murders. At the moment, we can't find him, but his father's coming in to see us. I hope. We saw him earlier and he was a great help considering who he is.'

Jamieson frowned. 'Enlighten me.'

'The Earl of Lenchester.'

'What?' he spluttered.

'He explained to us earlier that he's always had issues with Piers, his second son. He's our murderer.'

'Are you absolutely sure? We can't afford to upset someone so prominent in our community by making a mistake.'

'We're ninety-nine per cent certain. Everything points to him. He was kicked out of university for failing his course, which is why he tried to frame Professor Hamilton, who was his course tutor. We've been into his bedroom and found books and internet printouts on Shakespeare and poisons. He also has many books on snakes. We've just returned from the pathologist and the latest victim was poisoned by snakebites. He's our prime suspect.'

'Good work. But remember, we can't afford for this to be messed up. If it is, it's really going to backfire on all of us. I'm holding you responsible.'

She sucked in a relaxing breath. 'I understand, sir. When we spoke to the Earl of Lenchester earlier, he was very cooperative. We're waiting for him to come in so we can interview him further. We need to find out where Piers is and we're hoping the earl can help.'

She left him and went downstairs. On the way her phone rang, it was Lesley.

'The earl is on his way. He'll be with you in fifteen minutes,' she said.

'Thank you.'

Whitney returned to the incident room where George was waiting at the board, tapping her foot impatiently on the floor.

'You're back,' George said as she approached.

'Yes. I got the usual warning from Jamieson about not messing up. The earl should be here in fifteen minutes. You're looking anxious.'

'Excited, yes. Anxious, no.'

Did George even do excited? She'd always been way too level-headed for that.

'What is it?'

'While you were upstairs, I took a look at the Earl of Lenchester's coat of arms and compared it with the one on the cushions the victims were left on.'

'And?'

'What he did was quite extraordinary. I admire his ingenuity.'

'Tell me,' she said, a shiver running down her spine, George's excitement rubbing off on her.

'He's taken the coat of arms and inversed it. Look.' George taped up a photo of the Earl's coat of arms and the one created by the murderer. 'I'll try to keep this simple.'

'I'm not an idiot, you know,' Whitney growled.

'I didn't mean you were, but it's complicated. In principle they are similar. They are made up of a shield and a bird. The earl's bird is an eagle. That represents magnanimity. The killer's bird is a vulture which denotes rapacity. They are opposite. Now look at the shape of the shield. The earl's is a castle which represents safety. The killer's is a bell shape, which represents dispersing of evil spirits and denotes a warning.'

'That's smart.'

'Exactly. Finally, on the earl's shield we have daggers. They represent authority and control. Honour in battle. The killer has foxes—'

'Intelligence, cunning, and refusal to be captured. I remember from before.'

'What the killer is saying is that they won't fight honourably if it means losing the battle.'

'George, you're a genius. This is the final piece to the puzzle. It explains the use of the cushion.'

'Guv,' Matt called out. 'The earl is here.'

'Thanks, Matt.'

They hurried downstairs to the front desk and found him waiting by the noticeboard. When they walked over, he nodded.

'Thank you for coming in to see us, your Lordship. Please, come this way and we'll find somewhere quiet to talk.'

She escorted him to one of the interview rooms, and the three of them went inside and sat. She debated asking if he minded her recording their conversation then thought better of it. In her experience, people were more honest and open if they didn't think they were being recorded. Instead she took out the notebook and pen from her pocket.

'I'm extremely concerned over what's happening with Piers. How can I help?' the earl said.

'Can I get you something to drink?' Whitney asked.

'No, I'm fine. Let's get on with this.'

She sucked in a breath. 'As I explained earlier, we're investigating a series of murders which took place in Blue-bell Woods. They—'

'Yes, I know the murders,' he said, his jaw set in a hard line.

'I'm sorry to have to tell you, but Piers is our prime suspect.'

'What evidence do you have?' He stared back at her like a rabbit caught in the headlights.

Her heart went out to him. How would she feel if she was told Tiffany was a serial killer? She shuddered and forced the thought to the back of her mind.

'There are certain features of the murders that haven't been publicised, including that each murder was replicating one of the deaths in Shakespeare's plays.'

'And you think because he studied English literature at university and did some courses on Shakespeare, he could be responsible?' He was clearly clutching at straws.

'It's a little more involved than that, your Lordship. First of all, some incriminating evidence against Professor Hamilton, your son's tutor, was left at the scene. Although we questioned the professor, one of the murders occurred while he was in custody, so he couldn't have done it. Second, when we searched your son's rooms, we found evidence of his interest in serial killers and deaths in Shakespeare's plays. He also had photographs of all of the victims on his laptop. Finally, the victims were all left lying on a heraldic cushion with a coat of arms which is linked to yours.'

'Linked in what way exactly? Why didn't you come to me sooner? It might have prevented further murders.'

'What we've now discovered is that all of the symbols on the cushions were an inverse of the ones on your coat of arms. This is why we didn't establish a direct link to you. When we researched what was on the cushion, we didn't find a match.'

'In what way is it inversed?'

Whitney turned to George. 'Doctor Cavendish will explain, as she made the connection.'

'The eagle is replaced by a vulture, the castle by a bell, and the daggers by foxes. Using heraldic terminology, I pieced it together. It was the work of a very clever mind.'

The earl leant forward and rested his arms on the table. 'I have always said that he was too clever for his own good. I can't believe this is happening. He's always caused problems, but murder?'

'According to the post-mortem from the latest murder, the victim was poisoned by two snakebites,' Whitney said.

'As in *Antony and Cleopatra*,' he muttered.

'We know from the number of books he had on snakes that he was interested in them. Is there anything else you can add?'

He took a deep breath. 'Piers has been obsessed with snakes his whole life, from when he was around two years old. He was so difficult to manage that I believed if he had something to focus on it would help. We allowed him to keep some as pets from when he was aged eight. He knows how to handle them.'

'Does he still own any?'

'No. I made him get rid of them when he went to university.'

'Have you any idea where he might be? We need to find him, before he attempts further murders.'

He grimaced. 'None. Although … There's one place he could be. He used to spend a lot of time with one of my farm workers who's now retired. They had a close relationship while Piers was growing up. They had a love of snakes in common.'

'We'll need his details,' Whitney said.

'Yes, of course.'

'What was he like with animals other than snakes?' George asked.

'We had cats and dogs on the estate and many other

animals. We did seem to find a considerable number of them had been killed. We blamed it on foxes, but there was always a niggle at the back of my mind that Piers might have been responsible. Especially as the number of deaths decreased while he was away at school.'

'Did you speak to him about it?' Whitney asked.

'No. I didn't want to cause further friction between us, as I wasn't sure. I put it to the back of my mind.'

'What about your wife? Did she think the same?'

'She didn't have much to do with the upbringing of the older boys. My second wife isn't their mother. Their mother and I divorced when the boys were young. I remarried twelve years ago.'

Whitney was anxious to see the farm worker he'd mentioned, and there was nothing further the earl could tell them at this point.

'I'm sorry this has been so hard for you. Please could I have the name and address of the farm worker who might know where Piers is?'

'He lives on the estate. Although he's retired, he's allowed to stay in the cottage. His name is Neil Meads. The cottage is beside some old barns and can be accessed via Windermere Drive.'

She showed the earl out of the station and they returned to the incident room.

'Attention, everyone. There's a possibility Piers Bagshawe could be holed up with an old retired farm worker on the estate. We'll take a team there now. He's dangerous, and we have no idea what frame of mind he's in or whether he has any weapons. We need to plan our approach carefully. We'll go in three cars and keep them out of the way. The good thing with the estate is that people are often coming and going and we shouldn't be spotted.'

'What about me?' George asked.

'Sorry, you know the rules. You can either go to work or wait for us to return and be part of the interviewing process.'

'I'll go to work, but if you call me on your way back, I'll come straight over.'

'Good. Matt, you can come with me. Doug, you and Sue go together. Ellie, stay here as our link to the station in case we require further help, or for you to look into something for us.'

'What shall I do, guv?' Frank said.

'You arrange for six uniformed officers to be standing by, close to the estate, ready to intercept the killer if necessary, and then drive over. Radio in when you're close.'

Chapter Thirty-Four

They drove to the estate and parked behind the old barns. Frank arrived ten minutes later and came running around to where they had congregated beside the cars.

'You'll want to see this, guv,' Frank said as he got close, puffing from the exertion.

'What is it?'

'Follow me.' She glanced at Matt and shrugged.

'Whatever it is, be quick.'

They walked around the barns to where one of the doors was now open. She was sure it hadn't been before.

'I thought I'd poke my head in here, on my way to meet you,' Frank said. 'Everything is here. The whole kit and caboodle.'

They entered the barn and her jaw dropped. On the ground by the door was a spool of nylon rope and next to it two handbags and a pair of men's shoes. She pulled on some disposable gloves and picked up one of the bags. Inside was a purse containing credit cards belonging to Davina Hill.

'Gotcha,' she said, to no one in particular.

'Guv, over here,' Matt called out from where he was standing, beside a metal container.

She hurried to him. 'What's this?'

'A cow trough. Large enough for drowning our first victim, Rita Selwyn.'

She looked inside and grimaced. There were human hairs stuck to the sides.

'Well spotted, Matt. All we need now is to find the place he used to drag Owen Baxter around.'

'It's bound to be somewhere on the estate,' Matt said.

'Agreed. Okay everyone,' she called to the rest of the team. 'Let's get out of here. Matt and I will speak to Meads. Doug, you and Sue go over there, so you're out of sight of his cottage.' She pointed outside to twenty yards away. 'Frank, stay behind the barns. We'll keep in radio contact.'

She walked with Matt up to the small, thatched cottage and knocked on the door. After a few minutes, an old man with white hair and a slight stoop, answered.

'Who are you?' he said.

'I'm Detective Chief Inspector Walker, and this is Detective Sergeant Price. We're looking for Piers Bagshawe.'

'He's not here.' He started to close the door, but Matt put his foot in the way, stopping him.

'We've been to see the earl, and he seems to think there's a possibility you've seen him recently,' she said.

'Why's that?' he said, jutting out his chin.

'Because you and Piers have a good relationship from when he was younger. Can we come in to talk?'

'If you must.' He opened the door and they walked into his small cottage.

'Do you mind if we look around to see if he's here?' Whitney asked.

'Do what you like. You won't find him.'

She nodded to Matt and he left the room to search the house.

'Let's sit down and chat?' she said.

'Why are you after him? People should leave him alone. He's a good boy,' he said, remaining standing.

Did he really believe that? Was he Piers' accomplice?

'We suspect he may be involved in a recent series of murders.'

'No. Absolutely not. He wouldn't do that.' He thumped the wall.

'We have sufficient evidence linking him to them, and we've been speaking to his father.'

'His father doesn't care about him. Unlike his eldest son, who can do no wrong in his eyes. The earl's always treated Piers badly. That's why the boy used to spend so much time with me.'

'Are you saying you don't think highly of the earl?'

'Not in all respects. He's been very good to me, but he has a blind spot when it comes to Piers.'

'Why do you think that is?'

'How do I know? Maybe because he reminds him of his first wife.' He shrugged.

'Is that a bad thing?'

'Yes. The woman took the earl for a ride. She ran off with a salesman, taking some of the family jewels with her.'

'Surely the earl could get them back.'

'He didn't want to bring attention to the family.'

'How is Piers similar?'

'He looks like his mother and isn't prepared to conform to the earl's expectations.'

'What about Piers' older brother, is he like his mother, too?'

'No. He's definitely like the earl, in many ways.'

He walked over to one of the chairs and sat down. Whitney did the same.

'We really need to speak to Piers. The latest murder involved someone being bitten by a venomous snake. We know he has an obsession with snakes, and that you like them, too. Do you keep any?'

He eyed her for several seconds before finally answering. 'Yes. I do have several.'

'Are any of them venomous?'

'Yes.' He nodded.

'Isn't that illegal?'

'Don't start on that now. My snakes are perfectly harmless if you know how to handle them. Which I do.' He folded his arms tightly across his chest, stony-faced.

'Where are they?'

'Out the back in glass tanks.' He gave a sharp nod towards the rear of the cottage.

'I'd like to see them.'

He let out a long sigh and got up from his chair. They walked through the kitchen and into an outhouse. The snakes were in several glass tanks. They slid along the bottom and she shuddered. She'd never understand the fascination with them.

'Here they are,' he said.

'Could Piers have taken one of your snakes without you realising?'

'No.'

'Where is he?' she asked, trusting her gut. He definitely knew.

'I've told you, I don't know.' He couldn't meet her eyes.

'You're not doing him any favours by hiding him.'

'Who said I am?'

'Has he taken any of your snakes, or are any of them missing?' Whitney pushed.

'No. But …'

'But what?' Whitney said.

'He did borrow one, recently.'

'What do you mean *borrow*?'

'He said he wanted to show it to someone.'

Now they were getting somewhere.

'A venomous one?'

He nodded. 'Yes.'

'And you trusted him.'

'Yes. He's handled snakes his entire life. He's always helped look after mine.'

'Where is he now? Do you know?' He averted his eyes. 'Tell me. Before this gets even worse. If not for you, for him.'

'Are you sure it's him who's committed the murders? I can't believe he'd do it.' His body tensed. Was she finally getting through to him?

'If it isn't, he'll be able to provide alibis. We need to speak to him, even if it's to eliminate him from our enquiries.'

'He's been staying with me for the last few days.'

'Did he say why?'

'To get out of the way of his father.'

'Where is he now?'

'In the fields collecting rats for the snakes to eat.'

'Does he do that often?'

'Yes, as I can't manage as well as I used to. There are lots of rats around the farm if you know where to look.'

'What does he use to catch them? Does he have a weapon?'

'He has an air rifle. It's quiet, unlike a shotgun, and won't scare the rats away.'

A weapon. They needed to be on their guard. All they had were their tasers.

'We'll wait here for him to return. If he's innocent, we'll soon find out.'

'Okay, I suppose so.'

They returned to the cottage where Matt was waiting. She signalled for him to come outside with her, where she radioed the team. 'We're going to wait for Piers to come back from his rat hunt. He's carrying an air rifle. We don't know how long he's going to be. Frank, I want you to wait around the back of the cottage.'

'Yes, guv.'

'Matt and I will stay inside. Doug and Sue, I want you out of sight, but somewhere close. We can't risk him scarpering, if he sees us.'

Chapter Thirty-Five

Whitney stood behind the curtain peering out through the dirty window. They'd been waiting for half an hour. She tapped her foot and was about to suggest they begin searching the fields when a dark figure stepped into the clearing two hundred yards from the cottage.

The dark curls were visible even from a distance. It was him. Piers.

'He's coming back,' she said to the team. 'Get ready. I'm going to wait behind the door.' She turned to the old man. 'Act normal when he arrives.'

After five minutes the door handle turned. She swallowed hard and placed her hand on her taser. The door opened slightly.

'Run. The police are here,' the old man shouted.

Whitney swore as the door crashed shut and footsteps pounded out back across the yard.

'He's escaping,' Whitney radioed. 'Across the field.'

Matt ran from the house and Doug followed. Whitney turned to the old man. 'Neil Meads, I'm arresting you on suspicion of being an accessory to the murders of Rita

Selwyn, Josie Potts, Owen Baxter, and Davina Hill. You do not have to say anything, but it may harm your defence if you do not mention something which you later rely on in court. Anything you do say may be given in evidence. Do you understand?'

'Yes,' he muttered.

She took out a pair of handcuffs and cuffed him. He didn't resist.

'I can't believe what you did,' she said.

'I was only helping him. He's had his whole life fucked up and this was just one more thing.'

She pulled out her radio. 'Frank, come inside and guard Meads.'

Once Frank had arrived, she ran across the open fields in the direction of Matt and Doug who were in pursuit of their suspect. Doug was the faster of the two and was a few yards in front of Matt, who was a little slower than he used to be, following a gunshot wound he'd received a year ago. He'd recovered but had an awkward gait which was accentuated whenever he ran.

Doug gained on Piers and once close enough he rugby tackled him to the ground. Their suspect's screams of pain as he fell face first echoed across the field.

'Get off me,' Piers shouted, writhing around to escape from Doug's clutches.

'No chance, mate,' Doug replied, not budging an inch.

When Matt reached them, he pulled out a pair of handcuffs from his pocket and cuffed the suspect.

Whitney caught up with them just as Doug had dragged the man to his feet.

'Piers Bagshawe, I'm arresting you on suspicion of the murders of Rita Selwyn, Josie Potts, Owen Baxter, and Davina Hill. You do not have to say anything, but it may harm your defence if you do not mention something which you later rely on in court. Anything you do say may be given in evidence. Do you understand?'

Piers glared at her. His shirt was ripped, and blood dripped from his nose. Was it broken? They'd have to get him checked out by the police surgeon.

'Answer the chief inspector,' Doug said.

Piers grunted a response and they escorted him back across the field towards the cottage.

Striding towards them from the opposite direction was the earl. When he reached them he stood beside his son.

'Father,' Piers pleaded. 'I didn't do it. I promise. They've got it all wrong.'

'I want to believe you, but how can I, having heard the evidence against you?'

'Typical of you to take their side,' Piers spat. 'How stupid of me to think you might actually stick by me.'

'It isn't like that, Piers. You're my son, and I'll provide you with the best legal representation there is. But don't ask me to be fooled into believing you're innocent.'

'You won't get me for this,' Piers said, turning to face Whitney. 'The lawyers will find a way. They'll use my past. I'll tell them everything. Did he tell you how many psychiatrists he's sat me in front of over the years? I'll bet he didn't. It's not good for the family reputation.'

Whitney scowled at the earl. 'What?'

'It didn't seem relevant.' He lowered his head.

'That's for us to decide. We're going back to the station.'

'I'll arrange for a solicitor, and meet you there,' the earl said.

'You won't be allowed in with Piers, and this will take many hours, so I suggest you keep in touch by phone. He won't be released from custody until we have a bail hearing, and we will challenge it being granted.'

Chapter Thirty-Six

On the way back to the station, Whitney had called George, and she was already there when they arrived. The two prisoners were taken to the custody sergeant to be logged into the system.

'We'll interview the old man first, as he's declined legal representation, and Bagshawe is waiting for his solicitor to arrive,' she said.

Whitney and Matt went in to conduct the interview and George observed from the adjacent room. Meads was sitting upright in the chair staring ahead. He made no acknowledgement of their presence when they entered the room. They sat opposite him and pressed the recording equipment.

'Interview on July the eighth. Those present Detective Chief Inspector Walker, Detective Sergeant Price. Please state your full name for the tape,' she said.

'Neil Meads,' he muttered.

'Mr Meads, please confirm that you understand you're under caution and you have waived your right to a solicitor being present.'

'Yes,' he said.

'Mr Meads, why did you alert Piers Bagshawe to us being in your house, despite being told not to?'

'You don't understand. He was like a son to me. I was more of a father to him than his real father ever was.'

'But you knew he had an obsession with snakes and that one of the victims had died from snakebites. I'm assuming you also knew he harmed many animals when he was younger.'

He couldn't meet her eyes. 'Yes, I knew.'

'And you accepted his behaviour?'

'He can't help it. It's because of what happened to him as a child.'

'You've already explained that the earl didn't treat him well because of his likeness to his mother. Was there anything else?'

'The earl's second wife, mother to the younger two children, treated him badly.'

'How?'

'In the ways that count when you're young. She ignored him. Gave him no love. Forgot his birthday. Somebody had to look out for the boy. His father sure as hell didn't.'

'Not if he's murdering people. Did he tell you what he'd been doing?'

'No. But I did suspect there was something going on. He seemed more preoccupied than usual. I swear him murdering people hadn't entered my head.'

'The fact that you tried to help him escape from us means you'll be prosecuted for being an accessory.'

He shrugged. 'Do what you have to. I haven't got much time left, anyway.'

'Would you care to explain?'

'I've been diagnosed with bowel cancer.'

SALLY RIGBY

'I'm sorry,' she said. 'We're awaiting confirmation, but believe Piers used your snake for one of the murders. He also poisoned one of his victims. Do you have any that he could have used? Potassium cyanide, in particular?'

'We live on a farm. There are all sorts of things left lying around.'

'Did he ask you for some?'

'No. But he's spent enough time on the estate to know where everything's kept. I've changed my mind about wanting a lawyer.' He sat back in his seat and closed his eyes.

'That's entirely up to you. I'll arrange for one.'

He was taken back to his cell and Whitney went next door to the observation room.

'Are you going to charge him as an accessory?' George asked.

'Possibly. I'll discuss it with the Crown Prosecution Service. It's pointless if he's likely to die before the trial. I've just had a text from the front desk, Bagshawe's solicitor is here.'

She waited until the prisoner was in the interview room and then returned. George remained observing.

Piers sat at the table; his blank gaze fixed on the wall. Purple and blue bruising was already showing under his eyes from the broken nose which had been treated by the police surgeon,

He didn't appear to even flinch when she and Matt entered the room.

'I can already tell he's going to put on an act,' George said in her ear. 'The vacant expression in his eyes vanished for a moment when you entered the room. You probably wouldn't have even noticed it.'

'Interview on July the eighth. Those present, Detective Chief Inspector Walker and Detective Sergeant Price.

Please state your names,' she said to Bagshawe and his solicitor.

'Samuel Driscoll, solicitor for the accused.'

She stared at the prisoner. 'Please state your name.'

'Piers Bagshawe,' he muttered.

'You're still under caution. Do you understand?'

He nodded.

'Please state your answer for the recording.'

'Yes,' he said.

'We'd like to talk to you about the murders of Rita Selwyn, Josie Potts, Owen Baxter, and Davina Hill.'

'No comment,' he said.

'Do you admit to carrying out these murders?'

'I was told to,' he said, staring defiantly at her.

'By whom?' Whitney asked.

'Here. Up here,' he said, stabbing his finger on his head. '*They* told me.'

'Perhaps you could explain further,' Whitney replied.

'My client is not able to comment on his own mental capacity,' the solicitor said, interrupting.

'I'm not sure whether it's for real or not,' George said. 'But strange it's only now that he's talking about *voices* after previously being perfectly lucid. I suspect he might be trying it on, but I can't tell. Keep going.'

'These voices you claim to have heard, what exactly did they say to you?' Whitney asked.

'They told me I was destined for greatness. That I was to do something no one had ever done before. They said I'd be remembered for centuries.' His bloodshot eyes flashed defiance.

'Did they tell you how to go about the murders? To use Shakespeare and heraldry?'

'No. I thought of that all by myself.'

The solicitor leant in and whispered in his ear. Whitney

couldn't hear but assumed it was to stop him from incriminating himself further.

'I'll say what I like,' Piers said. 'I won't be convicted.'

The solicitor shrugged and sat back in his chair.

'What about framing Professor Hamilton? Was that your own idea, too?' Whitney asked.

'The whole thing was down to me. How many times do I have to tell you?' He rolled his eyes.

'John Hawkins was our original suspect for Rita Selwyn's murder. Did you orchestrate that?'

'No. But it added to the fun.'

'He's getting cocky,' George said in her ear. 'Question his ability, and let's see his response. It will help if there's to be a psychiatric evaluation.'

'Mr Bagshawe, we understand you had to leave university after failing your course. Did you find academic work a struggle?'

'Of course I didn't,' he snapped.

'Yet you were unable to pass your coursework. That implies you weren't clever enough.'

'You're just a thick copper, I doubt you even know what the word *implies* means. I was late with my work. I didn't deserve to be kicked out.'

'According to Professor Hamilton, you weren't as able as you believed yourself to be,' Whitney lied, determined not to show any response to his remark.

'Excellent,' George said in her ear. 'You've hit a nerve. He didn't like that one bit.'

'What would you know, you halfwit?' He clenched and unclenched his fists, his face set hard.

'How did your father react to you failing your course?'

'How do you think? He's always thought I was useless and couldn't do anything. But he's wrong. I'm smarter than the whole of my family put together. As I've now proved.' A self-satisfied smile crossed his face.

'Ask him about the victims,' George said.

'Let's talk about Rita Selwyn, your first victim. Why was she chosen?'

'You think you're so clever, why don't you work it out?'

Whitney had to force herself to remain seated and not wipe the smug grin off his face. Had he no compassion for the people he'd killed?

'No, you tell me. Was it all part of some elaborate genius plan?' she goaded.

'It was a game of chance,' he said.

'What the hell does that mean?'

'I used a random number generator to choose my victims. For the first murder the number was six. Rita Selwyn was the sixth person to speak to me that day. Simple, but effective. And having the decision made for me saved unnecessary time.'

She exhaled a harsh breath. 'So, there was nothing about the victims themselves?'

'No. They were just lucky.'

'Lucky? Is that what you call it?' Whitney barked.

'Leave that for now and ask him about the cushion and the coat of arms,' George said. 'He's enjoying riling you.'

She gave a tiny nod, to acknowledge.

'You left your victims resting on a red heraldic cushion, what was that all about? To make them comfortable?'

'Nothing so mundane. It was done to add to the intrigue. It was unique and different. I've done my research. No killer had done that before.'

'We know you designed your coat of arms by inversing the one belonging to your family. That was very clever.'

'Observe how his chest is puffed out. He thrives on praise,' George said.

'Yes, very clever,' Whitney repeated.

'I only did what I was told.'

'Don't start with that again. Admit it. All this hearing voices is a load of nonsense.'

'You can believe what you like, I know the truth,' he replied, his mocking eyes staring directly at her.

'Let's talk about Josie Potts. What was her number?'

'I've had enough. You'll get nothing more from me.' He clamped his lips shut.

'It will be to your advantage if you cooperate. Remaining silent won't help,' Whitney said.

'He's not going to engage in further conversation,' George said. 'I wouldn't continue, if I were you. He's getting a kick out of ignoring you.'

Whitney ended the interview and arranged for him to be taken back to his cell.

She went into the observation room to speak to George. 'The CPS will want a psychiatric evaluation. Is he genuinely mentally disturbed?'

'It's the traditional *hearing voices* thing. But whether or not it's genuine, we don't know as he's never been diagnosed. Certainly, from what we know of his past, he's had serial killer tendencies.'

'I'm going to update Jamieson and sort out the press conference with him. Meet me for a drink later.'

Chapter Thirty-Seven

George walked into the pub and headed over to Whitney who was sitting with a pint and a glass of wine on the table.

'Hi,' she said.

'You're late,' Whitney said.

'Sorry, I got caught up on the phone. What's going on with Bagshawe?'

'It's all in the hands of the CPS. They're going to appoint a psychiatrist to assess him. Nothing can be done until that's happened. It could take months.'

'It's what you expected,' George said, taking a sip of her beer.

'Yes. But it's frustrating. He knew what he was doing. I'd stake my badge on it. Anyway, let's forget about it for now. How are you doing? What's happening with your dad?'

'That was the phone call I had to take. It was my brother, wanting to update me. My father is being prose-cuted, hardly surprising. Whether he manages to get out of it remains to be seen. But he's got the best lawyer. Maybe he can blame it all on his accountant, although I don't know if that will be accepted. He's managed it all without me being there, so that's fine. It appears that the media interview he gave when I was there worked, as his private practice is picking up again.'

'I'm sure you're pleased about that.'

George shrugged. 'What about you and Martin?' she asked, changing the subject.

Whitney blushed. 'I'm going out with him tomorrow night before he goes back to London at the weekend.'

'Are you looking forward to it?' Judging by her friend's response she imagined she was.

'I think so. I've got to work out how and when to tell Tiffany, but I've got plenty of time to do that.'

'You think that, but time has a habit of getting away from us. She'll be home before you know it,' George said.

'Thanks.'

'For what?' She frowned.

'I'd decided to put it to the back of my mind, but now I'm going to spend time worrying about what to say.'

'No need to worry. Tiffany will understand.'

'Yeah. Let's hope you're right.'

'Hello, you two.'

George glanced up. It was Claire holding a glass of wine in her hand. 'What are you doing here?'

'I invited her. You don't mind, do you?' Whitney asked, an anxious expression on her face.

'No. It just surprised me.'

She enjoyed Claire's company, so why would she object?

'I'd rather you didn't discuss my presence in front of me, if it's all the same to you.' Claire said.

'Sorry, Claire. Please take a seat,' George said, gesturing to the empty chair beside her.

The pathologist sat and took a sip of wine. 'I've just seen that obnoxious boss of yours,' she said, resting her glass on the table.

'Jamieson? Where?' Whitney asked.

'He was at the bar. He ordered his drinks and went into the restaurant. He was too preoccupied to notice me.'

'Who was he with?' Whitney asked, as she exchanged a glance with George.

'A woman.'

'Describe her,' Whitney demanded.

'Dark hair. In her forties. I think he called her Coralie.'

'Coralie? Are you sure it wasn't Caroline?' Whitney asked.

'It could have been,' Claire said.

'Ha. I knew it.' Whitney gave a self-satisfied smile.

'Knew what?' Claire said.

'He's having a fling with one of our family liaison officers.'

'Does it matter?' George asked.

'No. But it's good to know I was right. Anyway, back to us. I thought a joint celebration was called for. Police. Pathology. Forensic Psychology. A triple threat,' Whitney said, holding up her glass.

'I'll drink to that,' Claire said, as they all clinked glasses together.

'We're like the three musketeers. All for one…and one for all,' Whitney said.

'I wouldn't go that far,' Claire said.

'That's your opinion. Not mine. I'm incredibly grateful you decided to stay and not take the job you were offered,' Whitney said, laughing.

'Which one,' Claire said.

'You mean there's more?' Whitney stared at her open-mouthed.

'I'm always being offered something. But don't worry. I'm not going anywhere.'

'Thank goodness,' Whitney said, exchanging a relieved glance with George.

'At least, not for now.'

Book 8 - Whitney and George return in ***Mortal Remains***. A serial arsonist is on the loose at the same time as Whitney is in danger of losing her job. She has to find the killer before that happens. Before any more lives are lost.

GET ANOTHER BOOK FOR FREE!

To instantly receive the free novella, ***The Night Shift***, featuring Whitney when she was a Detective Sergeant, ten years ago, sign up for Sally Rigby's free author newsletter at www.sallyrigby.com

Read more about Cavendish & Walker

DEADLY GAMES - Cavendish & Walker Book 1

A killer is playing cat and mouse……. and winning.

DCI Whitney Walker wants to save her career. Forensic psychologist, Dr Georgina Cavendish, wants to avenge the death of her student.

Sparks fly when real world policing meets academic theory, and it's not a pretty sight.

When two more bodies are discovered, Walker and Cavendish form an uneasy alliance. But are they in time to save the next victim?

Deadly Games is the first book in the Cavendish and Walker crime fiction series. If you like serial killer thrillers and psychological intrigue, then you'll love Sally Rigby's page-turning book.

Pick up *Deadly Games* today to read Cavendish & Walker's first case.

FATAL JUSTICE - Cavendish & Walker Book 2

A vigilante's on the loose, dishing out their kind of justice...

A string of mutilated bodies sees Detective Chief Inspector Whitney Walker back in action. But when she discovers the victims have all been grooming young girls, she fears a vigilante is on the loose. And while she understands the motive, no one is above the law.

Once again, she turns to forensic psychologist, Dr Georgina Cavendish, to unravel the cryptic clues. But will they be able to save the next victim from a gruesome death?

Fatal Justice is the second book in the Cavendish & Walker crime fiction series. If you like your mysteries dark, and with a twist, pick up a copy of Sally Rigby's book today.

DEATH TRACK - Cavendish & Walker Book 3

Catch the train if you dare…

After a teenage boy is found dead on a Lenchester train, Detective Chief Inspector Whitney Walker believes they're being targeted by the notorious Carriage Killer, who chooses a local rail network, commits four murders, and moves on.

Against her wishes, Walker's boss brings in officers from another force to help the investigation and prevent more deaths, but she's forced to defend her team against this outside interference.

Forensic psychologist, Dr Georgina Cavendish, is by her side in an attempt to bring to an end this killing spree. But how can they get into the mind of a killer who has already killed twelve times in two years without leaving a single clue behind?

For fans of Rachel Abbott, L J Ross and Angela Marsons, *Death Track* is the third in the Cavendish & Walker series. A gripping serial killer thriller that will have you hooked.

LETHAL SECRET - Cavendish & Walker Book 4

Someone has a secret. A secret worth killing for….

When a series of suicides, linked to the Wellness Spirit Centre, turn out to be murder, it brings together DCI Whitney Walker and forensic psychologist Dr Georgina Cavendish for another investigation. But as they delve deeper, they come across a tangle of secrets and the very real risk that the killer will strike again.

As the clock ticks down, the only way forward is to infiltrate the centre. But the outcome is disastrous, in more ways than one.

For fans of Angela Marsons, Rachel Abbott and M A Comley, *Lethal Secret* is the fourth book in the Cavendish & Walker crime fiction series.

LAST BREATH - Cavendish & Walker Book 5

Has the Lenchester Strangler returned?

When a murderer leaves a familiar pink scarf as his calling card, Detective Chief Inspector Whitney Walker is forced to dig into a cold case, not sure if she's looking for a killer or a copycat.

With a growing pile of bodies, and no clues, she turns to forensic psychologist, Dr Georgina Cavendish, despite their relationship being at an all-time low.

Can they overcome the bad blood between them to solve the

unsolvable?

For fans of Rachel Abbott, Angela Marsons and M A Comley, *Last Breath* is the fifth book in the Cavendish & Walker crime fiction series.

FINAL VERDICT - Cavendish & Walker Book 6

The judge has spoken......everyone must die.

When a killer starts murdering lawyers in a prestigious law firm, and every lead takes them to a dead end, DCI Whitney Walker finds herself grappling for a motive.

What links these deaths, and why use a lethal injection?

Alongside forensic psychologist, Dr Georgina Cavendish, they close in on the killer, while all the time trying to not let their personal lives get in the way of the investigation.

For fans of Rachel Abbott, Mark Dawson and M A Comley, Final Verdict is the sixth in the Cavendish & Walker series. A fast paced murder mystery which will keep you guessing.

RITUAL DEMISE - Cavendish & Walker Book 7

Someone is watching.... No one is safe

The once tranquil woods in a picturesque part of Lenchester have become the bloody stage to a series of ritualistic murders. With no suspects, Detective Chief Inspector Whitney Walker is once again forced to call on the services of forensic psychologist Dr Georgina Cavendish.

But this murderer isn't like any they've faced before. The murders are highly elaborate, but different in their own way and, with the clock ticking, they need to get inside the killer's head before it's too late.

For fans of Angela Marsons, Rachel Abbott and L J Ross. Ritual Demise is the seventh book in the Cavendish & Walker crime fiction series.

∾

MORTAL REMAINS - Cavendish & Walker Book 8

Someone's playing with fire…. There's no escape.

A serial arsonist is on the loose and as the death toll continues to mount DCI Whitney Walker calls on forensic psychologist Dr Georgina Cavendish for help.

But Lenchester isn't the only thing burning. There are monumental changes taking place within the police force and there's a chance Whitney might lose the job she loves. She has to find the killer before that happens. Before any more lives are lost.

Mortal Remains is the eighth book in the acclaimed Cavendish & Walker series. Perfect for fans of Angela Marsons, Rachel Abbot and L J Ross.

Acknowledgments

This book wouldn't exist without the patience and support of my friends and critique partners, Amanda Ashby and Christina Phillips. Thanks so much to you both.

Emma Mitchell, I can't thank you enough for your continued support and editing genius.

Thanks also to Kate Noble and my Advanced Reader Team for everything you've done in helping me turn out the best book I can.

I'd also like to mention my daughter Alicia, who's always at the end of the phone when I have plot points to sort out. Your input has been invaluable.

My thanks, as always, to Stuart Bache for continuing to produce such amazing covers.

Finally, thanks to my family: Garry, Alicia, and Marcus for always being so supportive.

About the Author

Sally Rigby was born in Northampton, in the UK. She has always had the travel bug, and after living in both Manchester and London, eventually moved overseas. From 2001 she has lived with her family in New Zealand, which she considers to be the most beautiful place in the world. During this time she also lived for five years in Australia.

Sally has always loved crime fiction books, films and TV programmes, and has a particular fascination with the psychology of serial killers.

Sally loves to hear from her readers, so do feel free to get in touch via her website www.sallyrigby.com